Beeston Sp. Church

please return

THE PATH

Arthur F. Freer 16.5.04.

by
ARTHUR F FREER

CON-PSY PUBLICATIONS MIDDLESEX

First Edition
2003

© Arthur F Freer

Published by

CON-PSY PUBLICATIONS
P.O. BOX 14,
GREENFORD,
MIDDLESEX, UB6 0UF.

ISBN 1 898680 35 3

CONTENTS

To
my wife
Carole (Corney)
with all my thanks
for the many facts that she
has shown me during
the years that we
have spent
together

I am only just beginning to realise the immensity of the unknown

CHAPTER ONE
5mBC

The Development Committee was not required to meet frequently but the members had become very aware of the need for an early decision on the Earth Project. They had a growing sense of anxiety, a hunch, which they instinctively knew to be brought to their minds by the usually reliable method of telepathy, and they also knew that it must not be ignored. Such normal methods of communication were considered unsuitable for handling the various possibilities so they assembled in Alpha committee room and awaited the arrival of the Chairman.

When Ywancontin appeared on the dais, each of the other six members saw his penetrating eyes looking into their own. He then described the status quo verbally, despite knowing that they would be aware of the problem as soon as he formed the words in his mind.

" My Brothers of the Light, we are required to consider the facts of the situation on the Earth and make a decision regarding the requirements of the Project and the methods to be used to introduce the necessary amendments to these creatures. There is a growing recognition of our seeing an established species which meets all the necessary survival criteria but which requires some adjustment in order to help it move in the right direction. Let us examine the beasts as they exert their ability to survive. We can move into their vicinity for, perhaps, a year and record their strengths and their weaknesses. Let us consider the effect of their steadily enlarging brains, the growing strength of their instinct for self survival and also their ability to follow their reproductive urges at any time of the day or the year. We must take a long-term view of all the aspects and project where we estimate that they will be in each of the next long periods. Let us move as an invisible group to be with them".

As the dawn eased into a new day and the night noises had changed smoothly into those of the daylight, the first creatures to be seen were the hominids.

They had spent the time of darkness up amongst the growth

in the mighty trees. They felt safe there, in small clusters of bodies. The babies and infants had been kept warm amongst the adults who were lying along the large branches, intertwined with the sinuous creepers, which were also closely knitted into the forest canopy. Yes, the worst dangers came from the large carnivores that hunted throughout the day and night for these small creatures.

In the first short period of time, immediately after the dawn, the bearded males were the first of the group to venture down to the ground. They could see and smell some of the even smaller animals that were seeking food on the forest floor. The hunt was on. Those early forerunners of mankind had learned to take advantage of changing conditions, which might have improved only temporarily. They hunted in a group. They used their limited vocabulary of only about one hundred sounds, or grunts, in order to shout brief orders to the other members of the group. The waved arm of the leader sent the others into a rapidly created circle around the few rodent-like foragers seeking their own nourishment. The end was swift.

Each of the hominids held a rounded stone in his hand and used it to kill the quarry. Previous, but now defunct, members of the group had collected the stones when they had been hunting many years ago near the big water. They had been unaware that the tidal action of the water had ground the stones into their present shapes. They had merely applied their growing intelligence to the new-found toys. Experiment had shown them the amazing fact that they could be thrown accurately at any creature that they wished to harm, whether a food animal or another hominid. Practice improved their aim but they lost a large part of their stock of stones over a period of time. Some of this loss was replaced with new stones found during their journeys but these were rarely of the favoured smooth rounded shape. As the stock dwindled there was a sensible tendency to avoid throwing them but to retain a favoured stone in the hand, up to the point of striking a decisive blow. The possibility of fixing one in a split piece of tree branch, and making a hammer-like weapon, would not be thought of until the brain had evolved a little more, perhaps in a few thousand years time.

There were nearly one hundred of the creatures in this group under surveillance. Some thirty of them were the mature males, the hunters. The fact that they had the benefit of the invention of a crude but effective weapon gave them a growing confidence whenever they came up against any of the larger animals. Today, they were fully in control and the slaughter of the rodents was soon completed.

The excited winners immediately squatted on their haunches to eat the warm flesh in their hands. The furry skins were torn from the bodies with their teeth and the meat was swallowed after a minimum of chewing.

The remainder of the group had stayed near the trees, ready to climb to safety if danger was seen. A quarter of them were fully grown females and the rest were youngsters of various ages. There were no old ones amongst them. All were naked with hides that were darkened from exposure to the hot sun and the contact with the earth and plant growth. Many of them were scarred from damage received during hunting, or from fighting amongst themselves. They had appeared to be excited as they watched the slaughter of the small creatures, which they named as Carn, a word that they applied to any animal that could be considered as food.

"Carn, carn", the females called to their menfolk, hoping for some nourishment for themselves, but the plea was ignored. The males had had their fill and were already starting to move across the open space to look for more prey. One of them had eaten well and he was still holding a small body in right hand. He nodded to the leader, held up the meat and then nodded in the direction of the group of females standing near the big tree where they had all slept the night. The leader shrugged and turned to move away from him. Another hunter grunted "uhuh" and pointed to where the leaves of a small tree were moving unnaturally. They were not going to be distracted. An intense look came to all their faces and they moved very quietly and very carefully in the hunt for more food. They were soon hidden in the undergrowth, seeking the creature that had caused the movement.

The hunter with the meat had returned to the group of women and children. "Nga", he called as he approached. "Nga", he said, pointing to one of the females. The one that he had indicated was only just reaching maturity, with her bare breasts pushing strongly between the long matted hair hanging from her head. "Nga?" she asked, with widening eyes. She had not been asked

3

before now and she knew that she was only just ready for a male. There were no secrets or privacy about the mating habits of these primitives. It occurred at any time, whenever a creature of either sex was so inclined, in full view of the children and others that happened to be there. If the female showed a lack of interest or any resistance to the male's advances, she might be encouraged to be more co-operative by the simple persuasion of a blow from his fist, with or without the heavy stone.

Here was an offer of fresh food, which she had seen killed a few minutes earlier, and now it was offered to her. All she had to do was to let ming enter her until he was satisfied.

She took the meat from him, with a smile, and turned on to her hands and knees, holding the food in front of her. Her hindquarters were then raised ready for the ming, and she started to eat. It was nothing new. She had seen it happen so many times throughout her childhood. "Ming nga, ming nga", she thought to herself as she became aware of the penetration. The best part of it was the food, which she enjoyed as the hunger pains from the long night began to fade. Perhaps this ming will hunt for her again? Perhaps, she should show her appreciation in some other way. She moved her body and gave a few squeals of excitement, hoping that ming would remember her for another time. He rolled her over and ran his hands over her body before taking her again, but this time from the front. He was chuckling and grunting with satisfaction. Then, it was all over. He stood up. "Da", he said, and then ran off into the undergrowth to try to catch up with the other hunters. She liked the sound of "Da", but she was not sure whether it was meant to be a word of thanks or whether the ming was giving her a name, a grunt that would be recognised as and when he thought of her. It sometimes happened that individuals were named in this way.

The other females looked at her, some with envy, and one with hate. This last one was the pregnant one that her ming had been mating with regularly all through the year. The ming had given her the sound of Ud. Why was she angry? She had a big belly and she would soon be bringing a new life into the tribe. Perhaps it was because she knew that her baby would be arriving in the middle of the cold spell. That was a bad time to have a baby. It was a time of little food, a time when the older members and babies were all at risk. In the long cold nights of the winter it was often necessary to put the weaker members out in the cold, whilst the younger, livelier ones huddled under a fresh covering of leaves and bark. In the light of the next day the survivors would share the cold meat and maintain their strength. Nothing was wasted and the group would continue to survive for another year.

When the hunters returned to the rest of their group there was an awareness of anxiety amongst them. They had been successful in killing a horse-like animal, a forerunner of the quagga, and had brought it back for the benefit of their mates. They had also noticed that many of the smaller creatures had been moving quickly towards the direction where the warm sun spent most of its time. They must follow them in that direction or, perhaps, there would not be enough food for them in the immediate future. They were very aware of the regular cycles of the year. The warm period would make life a little easier for them but the cold period would bring serious problems.

There was a constant worry about the possible shortage of food, which could lead to the death to some of the children and reductions in the number of hunters, especially the more mature ones who had acquired a cough or damage to one of their limbs. It was a short hard life but the will to survive was strong in every one of them.

They had returned with the complete body of the quagga and proceeded to dismember it, using brute force helped by a flattened stone with a sharp edge. One of the females had found the flintstone recently and given it to her ming as a token of her desire to remain his nga. He used it later to kill a small carn and had been surprised to find that it had cut into the head rather than smashing it. It had also been useful in helping to remove the skin and to give access to the flesh. This stone was now used by the owner to help in the removal of the quagga's pelt, in one piece. This had never before been done.

All the famished group members gathered around the carcass, using their hands, teeth and favoured stones to pulverise the bones and sever pieces of flesh, which they swallowed or shared with their offspring. Their unwashed bodies were covered in more scratches and blood, but they were satisfied. The feast was over and most of the mature creatures then lay down where they were and slept. Some of the males mated with the nearest females before relaxing. They all stank, but none of them were repelled by the odour. In fact, it was the smell, or scent, that gave them a sense of unity in the group. They had no hesitation in knowing whether another creature was one of their group or whether it was an enemy, to be attacked and destroyed before being eaten.

A little time later, the leader roused the complete group and they obeyed his pointed instructions to climb to safety up their favourite tree. Two of the ngas carried the bloodied pelt up with them.

The next morning saw the two ngas take the pelt to the nearby stream and wash it thoroughly, in the clear fresh water, and scrape it with the sharp stone until there was no sign of any flesh or blood attached. They then took it up into their tree and fixed it in the branches, spread out to let it dry, using splintered bones as pins. They looked pleased with their efforts. They also looked much cleaner after the personal contact with the fresh water. Just before the sunset they examined the pelt. They screamed with frustration. The furry side of the skin was clean, smooth and pleasing to the touch, but the complete pelt was hard and rigid. Their mings looked up at the noise and examined the skin. One of them then picked up his smooth killer stone and beat the skin with it against the bark of the tree. This had the effect of breaking some of the stiff fibres and, eventually, softening the pelt until it could be wrapped around the body. The strongest nga of the two then grabbed it, as if it were her own property. After kicking her friend off the branch, down to the ground, she retained the prize, wrapping herself and her baby in it for the night.

Her late friend lay on the ground, with a broken back, moaning in pain, until a night predator found her and carried her away to be consumed.

The Watchers decided that some of the observations could be usefully discussed and mental notes made of possible ways of helping to lead these potential forerunners of mankind in the direction of advancement.

The medical member, Lucus, commented on high mortality rate. "It is rare for a creature to survive for long, after the age of twenty. In fact, older ones are usually looked upon as a source of food in times of shortage. They might be very effective hunters, using their experience to guide the younger ones to good sources of prey, but they can be surprised by a sudden blow to the head from the stone of a youngster, even from one of their own sons. Dismemberment, butchery and consumption quickly follow this activity. If the group can be helped to survive each winter they might realise the benefit of retaining the wisdom of the older ones".

"No", said Marcus, the enterprising one. "I doubt whether you will be able to encourage that reaction from the young ones. In their ignorance, they are not likely to recognise that time can be a teacher. They will make their own mistakes and they will have to learn from them. That is, perhaps, the basis of future progress for them all".

Surtyn, the member with the assured manner, the decision-maker, indicated that he had strong opinions that he wished to express.

"It is easy to make a prognosis. We need to keep in mind the fact that this is only one of a number of similar groups that are receiving such help, along their own paths, in order to make progress. With some of them, like this one, the survival instinct is so very strong that they could easily eliminate enough members of their own group so that it becomes weakened to the point of extinction. That could defeat the object of the exercise. No. I feel that it is essential that we retain the strong instincts for both survival and reproduction until such time that we can guide them to reduce the excess power of those instincts using their own willpower.

That will be long after the planet appears to be overpopulated, when survival appears to be assured, long after some of the spiritual paths are being followed successfully. There are so many other possible sources of danger and elimination that we must encourage their physical survival. The other carnivores are a constant danger and will remain so for many thousands of years. I believe that the time appears to be ripe now for a slight modification to be made. I suggest that the trait of compassion be introduced here, so that its *effects might be seen by all the group members, whilst it develops within the recipient. It will then be passed on to the future generations, subject to their survival and the pressures of the other members. It is possible that it might counter the worst effects of the two survival instincts mentioned. Depending on the fertility of the human chain involved, the trait might appear in a growing number of the future families within the group. Also, it can be passed from this group to one or more of the other groups with which contact will be made into the future.*

The result will be that we will see that the strong reproductive instinct will be an asset in encouraging these creatures to seek out other groups, not only for the food that will become available to them, but, also, for the pleasures of the sexual contacts and conquests. The survival genes and the compassion trait will then be passed on to the members of the other groups. The mated female conquests will also be likely to be retained within the winning group, therefore strengthening it numerically".

The other members of the Committee pondered the suggestion before they made their comments.

They heard Chairman Ywancontin encourage them to check, and recheck, their reactions to the proposal from Surtyn, before they expressed their thoughts.

The first reply came from the quiet member, Solem.

"There is a great deal of sound logic in the proposal from Surtyn and I recommend that it is considered before being implemented. We need to look forward in time when all these instincts will be so ingrained into the creatures' minds and bodies that they will not wish to relinquish them. They are already showing extreme pleasure when asserting their abilities to conquer other beings with force, whether it is to kill them for food, or to satisfy their lust for the females. As already mentioned, we could be creating a future situation where the gentler traits, such as compassion and some others that we might decide to introduce, are suppressed by the already forceful instincts. We need to monitor the progress at regular intervals"

Ywancontin looked at the seventh member of the Committee who had not yet made any contribution to the debate. "Bevak, we

8

have not yet had the benefit of your own thoughts? You have always been regarded as the Active One. You have tended to examine the possible results of any action before it is permitted. What aspects do you feel should be considered before we move? Your input is required".

"Oh, yes, I agree with the general trend of opinion, but I am aware of another aspect to bear in mind. The creatures, which we intend to encourage both physically and mentally, are already developing a strong instinct, which had not yet been mentioned here, that is the ability to use psychic powers. Consider their lack of language. They rarely use any words. They rarely give each other a recognisable grunt that could become a name by which they are recognised within the group. Also, when they are being hunted by other predators, animals that are expert in the art of concealment, one or more of the group is aware of a feeling of anxiety, or nervous tension, even when the threat is not to be seen with their eyes. The complete group is instantly aware of the need to move quickly to safety, either up a tree or by running away from the source of the danger. Neither of the communications is oral. They are both mental awareness and bring instant reaction, which saves the group from massacre. They can only be psychic, as we know, and are an indication that they are moving steadily towards an extremely sophisticated social structure. We can easily test this ability, if it is wished. We can permit one or more of them to have a fleeting glimpse of us during a period of close observation. We can then hear and note their reactions. They might be frightened, aggressive, or even comforted at the realisation that they have spiritual support. That is my proposal". Ywancontin nodded approval, as the others all indicated their agreement. "We will move on those lines, but we will also encourage the group to move to the north east, as the approaching cold period tends to make life more difficult for them in the present location. They will find better protection amongst the mountains".

And so it was.

When the seven members of the Committee moved around the sleeping group that night, noting the pairing of the adults and the comforting, interlocking positions on the wide branches, the eyes of one female, wrapped in the animal skin, were opening.

9

The full moon lit the group. The female with the opened eyes was the one named Da by her food provider and she simply could not absorb or comprehend what she saw. There were a number of tall strangers standing around them and looking at them seriously, but without any sign of being hungry or being ready to attack them. Although she was unable to count up to seven, it was obvious to the watchers that she had, in fact, seen them.

She trembled and screamed at the top of her voice. "Ga Ga Gaaaaaa!". Immediately, every member of the group was awake and starting to climb down the trunk, or falling from their branch, down to a lower level and, eventually, down to the ground. Some of the weaker members had broken limbs and all of them were shaken and bruised. They moved as a group to the next tree trunk and, after only a short hesitation, the fit ones started to climb up in the hope of finding security. The damaged members huddled in a small cluster at the base of the trunk where they remained until the break of dawn.

Da radiated fear and anxiety, which she could not express verbally. She continued to say "Ga, ga, ga", but that was the limit of her vocabulary for indicating fear. She knew what she had seen. The seven "tall ones" were all more than twice the height of the males that she lived with, but they were usually bent almost double as they searched the ground for grubs and scraps of food dropped by the others. She had never seen anything like it in her short life. What she had not realised was the fact that the telepathic abilities, used successfully by each member of the group in their normal survival activities, had evolved within her into an embryonic introduction to the art of psychical awareness. She had seen seven spiritual entities. She felt lost, terrified, and weakened to the point of being at risk, by not taking all the usual precautions when moving about during the approaching day. As it happened she was fortunate. The group leaders had also been frightened by her screams. They started the day by collecting all the stones that had been dropped during the flight down the tree and making it obvious that they were starting their trek towards the sun. All their instincts now told them that it was not in their interests to stay in that vicinity, the screams, the awareness that the smaller animals had already started to move towards the sun, and the growing chill during the past few nights up their tree.

10

CHAPTER TWO
THE TREK

The Watchers had instantly realised what had happened. The knowledge that one of these hominids had evolved to the point of having a rudimentary psychic ability had surprised them. They were not used to having such surprises. They looked at each other and questioned why the ignorance of the possibility had had that effect. Ywancontin indicated that they should not seek to put the blame on any one of them but that they should use the knowledge to move forward in the assessment of this group.

"We all are aware that this effect was in the original programme and we are pleased to find that it is moving forward for at least one of them. The ability will be passed, in some form or other, to the progeny of this female. What we need to do now is to decide whether to introduce compassion to the same creature. There will be some reactive results, between one trait and the other, but we can monitor them as and when they occur. It is possible that the strength of the psychic ability will fluctuate from one creature to the next. It is also possible that it will appear to lapse, from one generation to the next, but it will be retained in the genes and carried forward into the future." He paused a moment, looking intently into their faces. "Yes, I agree with you all. We will insert the awareness of compassion into the one named Da during the next sleep period." There was a grave nodding of heads to confirm the decision.

The stronger ones, the leaders and mature females, busied themselves as the sun was starting to clear the horizon, picking up their valued stones and babies. It was a time of anxiety for the damaged ones. Those with broken legs knew that they would be left behind to fend for themselves. They wailed with a sickening moan of resignation and flopped down on the ground where they had spent the last night. It might have been better for them to have been killed and eaten by the group. The roar of approaching carnivores could be heard some distance away.

The reduced group of a few more than sixty live hominids

looked to the north, where the sun would spend its time, and started to move slowly but surely in that direction. They were soon no longer able to hear the moans from those left behind. These unfortunates could hear the hunting cries of the giant catlike horrors that could now scent them. All went quiet for a brief time. They noticed that the other noises around them, the rustling of little bodies digging in the ground, the squeaking of other frightened prey, the chattering of small four-legged tree-climbers, all were suddenly hushed. These damaged hominids were unable to do anything to save themselves.

The roar and crash of a giant, long-toothed cat landed amongst them, tearing at the already-weakened bodies. It was an easy kill. Two other similar cats bounded up to their mother who was starting to satisfy her hunger of two days. None of the cats felt any need to follow the scent of the other food, which had walked away. They stayed there for the remainder of that day, gorging of the tender flesh, purring and burping with real contentment.

In the meantime, the main party had made good progress, eating as they travelled due north. They continued to walk through a heavy downpour of rain and this was of real benefit to them. Their tracks and scent on the ground were obliterated. It was unlikely that any hunter, that might have been following them, would be able to trace their path, unless it had been able to see them or scent them through the air. They were well concealed as they walked through the lush jungle growth. The rain had even helped to remove most of their body odours with the simple process of washing their bodies. New and old wounds had been thoroughly cleansed, and the exercise involved in the long walk gave them all a healthy appetite.

The surprise killing of another horse-like creature soon satisfied the hunger, and confidence began to return to the whole group.

As the light started to fade, they were able to find and climb a large tree in the more open valley through which they were walking. This routine of daily walking, interrupted by a short period of hunting, continued for many days. The cooling winds seemed to have been left behind and the warmer breezes and hotter sun reduced most of the anxieties that they had been aware of before the start of the trek. They could see that the land ahead of them was starting to rise. First, brown hills appeared and, behind those, they could see ever-higher land, in the form of blue mountains. There was still plenty of cover, if it should be needed, but the way forward looked promising.

They had met only one large carnivore. It was an old cat that had lost many of its teeth. When it threatened them, it quickly lost interest as it was pounded with a shower of accurately thrown stones. These were soon recovered when everyone in the group made a close search of the ground. Whilst doing this, some of them picked up more stones than they had thrown, in this way increasing the stock of weapons and their confidence even more.

On one of these days, the leaders led them into the foothills, which were still covered with useful trees and plenty of small, easily caught prey. Some large rocks were lying in the open and they soon found that the rising ground showed where the rocks had come from. Cliffs and crevices came into sight and in one of the cliffs they spotted a large hole. It was black and it smelled of the big cat that had threatened to attack them a few days earlier. The scent of the animal caused the hairs on the nape of their necks to rise, an easily recognisable sign of tension.

There was no sound from them as they moved to either side of the cave entrance. The leader threw his stone directly into the cave and expected to hear a challenging roar. Each adult held a stone ready for instant use against a possible attacker, but it was not necessary. The cave was empty.

Without any noisy excitement, they started to collect the larger stones and boulders from nearby and place them across the entrance, building a wall that would make it difficult for any outsider to gain entrance to the cave. All the members of the group were able to get inside and enjoy the safety of the protective wall. They shared the remainder of their recent kill and settled down in the unusual lodgings. This was another first for the group. They had never before used any building material, such as the loose rocks, to erect a protection. They had become builders! A strange feeling of security came over them and they huddled together ready for the night's sleep. The new feeling of contentment and the warmth of the bodies started a movement amongst the adults that soon became a frenzy. The babies and smaller children were ignored, or pushed aside, whilst all the vigorous males mated with the willing females. This went on for much of the night. After satisfaction with one female, her partner would turn aside to the next nearest available offer of sex, until there was complete satiation for all.

The security and contentment of the group resulted in all the females becoming pregnant and they stayed in that area for many years. The one known as Da had been pregnant before they had arrived and she became very protective of the new she-baby. She would sit nursing her for much longer periods than was usual. When other mothers would callously knock a squealing child out of their path, Da had become closely attached to her baby and never struck her. She thought of her as Ba and called her by that name, much to the annoyance of the other females. Jealousy started to create petty quarrels amongst them and it came to a head at a time of temporary hunger.

The baby Ba had just started to walk upright, and Da was justifiably proud of this achievement, when one of the males indicated that he was very hungry and moved towards Ba with the obvious intention of taking her for food. Previously, this would have been accepted by one of the other mothers, as a sad necessity, but it was not going to be accepted by Da.

All the creatures were quite used to seeing each other change instantly into a defensive, or aggressive, stance, when threatened by danger from outside their circle, or even during internal squabbling over food. This was the first time that they had seen one of them apparently being prepared to fight to defend another. The "mother instinct" had been seen in action.

The "Tall ones" noted the fact, but commented that it would be necessary to observe a number of similar expressions before they could be sure that compassion had been successfully introduced to this group. It would need to be observed in a large number of the creatures before they could record a partial success.

Da crouched, grabbing her stone in the right hand, and jumped at the male. The right arm swung round with increasing speed and struck him on the left temple. If it had been one of the more common rounded stones, it is possible that he would have been merely knocked unconscious, but it was a flat, sharp stone that Da had found some months before. The pointed edge penetrated the side of the skull, then the brain, and the male was dead.

For a moment, the whole group was in the defensive stance. Da stayed crouched with the blooded stone in her hand, ready to defend herself and her baby again. First one then another of the group returned to the task that had been occupying them before the incident. The point had been made. Ba was not to be taken for food by any of them. Some of the other females had noted the fact and felt a warm sense of approval. They had learned from the experience and could possibly feel inclined to copy the action, if it should happen to them and their babies. The hungry ones calmly started to dismember and eat the body.

"Yes", thought the Committee, "this has started a learning process that will help the unused brain cells to react to observation, and also gain benefit from practical experience. They require to adapt to the changing pattern of thoughts. This will stimulate a desire to communicate audibly and will take many aeons to develop into language. We must recognise that growth of speech will tend to reduce their skill with telepathic communication. It might even stunt an embryonic psychic ability. Such beneficial skills can always be adjusted artificially in the future, if deemed necessary."

The Chairman addressed the Committee.

"The major requirement, at this stage of progress, is to ensure the survival of some of the groups which have been developing in many parts of this planet. That gives priority to the instincts of self defence, firstly, and then reproduction.

The group under observation, let us refer to them as Group A, is already maintaining a reasonable numerical strength and they will soon be ready to divide their numbers in order to form two separate groups. An alternative method for growth will be for them to meet and blend with another group before such a division. That will, of course, require a reasonably peaceful amalgamation. An aggressive meeting would be counterproductive. We will extend the period of observation from one year to one hundred years. By that method we will be able to monitor four or five generations and assess the progress of the introduced trait of compassion".

Ywancontin then gave specific instructions to his team.

"Lucus, you will apply most of your time to the study of the group's medical conditions. As the newer bacteria develop you should be fully aware of the creatures' abilities to produce their own reactive strains. You will need to monitor the rate of the evolution of such micro-organisms.

Marcus, your interest in enterprise will help you to study the development of their brains, particularly in the ways in which they apply knowledge gained from experience in order to improve their skills, their environment and living standards. You might discover ways in which they can be encouraged to stimulate each other into action that will further develop the usage of their brains.

From you, Mellak, we will need to be advised of the progress of the trait of compassion. You should be aware of whether it develops from inherited inclination, or from their acceptance of learning from the examples of others.

If it becomes necessary to take any new action in order to correct a wrong trend, you, Surtyn, will gather all the relevant facts and present them to us, before taking any such action.

Solem will prepare an overall view of their development and apply his mental skills to reporting on the likely result of any changes that the others might put forward.

Bevak will have the interesting task of being with the members of the group at all times of day or night, living with them, experiencing their thoughts and actions, understanding their reasons for their actions. He will not show himself to them. The only exception to that instruction will be on the possible occasion of their applying psychic ability and opening their minds in that field. He has permission, at such a time, to give instant reassurance of there being no risk of danger for that observer. He should not take any action that would encourage the creature to try to develop the ability any further.

Do you all understand and accept these instructions?" Ywancontin accepted the mental agreement.

THE PATH

A period of stability followed the arrival into the area. The huge cave, with the small entrance, provided a security that they had not experienced before. On the few occasions that they were scented by their main predator, the huge cat, they were usually able to retire to the cave, and close the entrance, before they had lost more than one of their slower moving, smaller members.

There was plenty of food for their increasing numbers and they were able to spend some of the time contemplating their good fortune. Cannibalism stopped. The females were either pregnant or suckling the plump offspring. When a few of the males were examining their stones and comparing the shapes and weights, they began to question why some of the stones were more effective than others. The questions were entirely mental, but there was some acceptance of the fact that the sharper ones could penetrate the flesh, and the bones, more easily than the other rounded stones. Nods and grunts showed that something had been learned. They had noted and remembered that Da had used her sharpened stone so effectively, when defending her Ba. She was beckoned forward into the circle of males.

Da picked up her baby, and her stone, and moved hesitatingly into the circle of males. One of them pointed to her stone and held out his hand.

Da grunted defiance and held her stone to her side, ready for action. The ming was not disturbed in any way. He gave a low grunt of reassurance, putting his own, round stone, on the ground. "Carn", he said, indicating that she should treat it as if it were food, "carn", he repeated, striking his right fist into his left. Da understood. She brought her right hand, holding her sharp stone, round and down in one sweeping blow.

It struck the other stone and she screamed in anger. Her own flint-stone broke into two pieces. The larger piece was still in her hand but a shard lay on the ground for them all to see. It appeared to be almost as long as her piece, but one side of it was shining, and very sharp. The ming and Da both grabbed for it at the same time. The ming won. Then, he screamed. He had picked it up with his fingers across the razor-sharp edge and cut through to the bone. When he threw it down on to the ground, Da grabbed it carefully by

17

the safe side. She held it close to her face and studied it in wonder. Here was a wonderful new possession. A stone that could cut through flesh and bone. She stood up holding the two parts of her original stone, one in each hand. She was a formidable sight. A well-formed she hominid, nearly four feet high, with long black hair, matted at either side of her round face. She was naked. Her black skin showed scars and scabs where she had been damaged in the normal routine of the rough life. Some of the mings gave a grunted approval of her stance and of her appearance. They admired a fighter, and she had shown that she was prepared to fight anything or anybody that threatened her or her baby. She was again ready for mating, and had been from long before Ba had been able to walk. They would be after her that night. She now had a special advantage that gave her a sort of prestige in the group. She had the new tool that could be used to kill or cut anything that she chose. There was a lot to learn from the experiences of today.

The improved conditions helped the group to grow numerically and in general health. Soon, the increasing number of babies put pressure on the available living space and the elders realised that they would need to move some of them out of the cave permanently.

A start was made when some of the mothers were pushed out of the cave by the other, stronger females. There was some bloodshed. A few skulls were damaged. But the end result was that a small number of mothers started to build a shelter, just outside the cave entrance. Branches and large leaves were woven together to make some sort of roofing to deflect the worst of the rain, if any fell. That night they enjoyed the pleasure of having a shared home but without the snags of the overcrowded cave. Those retaining their claim to the old shelter were also delighted with more available space.

Everyone appeared to benefit. The 'outsiders' were quite aware that there could be problems from any passing cat, but they knew that they were within only a few paces from the cave entrance. If threatened, they were sure that they could run to safety. Those thoughts were based on the fact that the big cats had previously always attacked them in the daytime. They soon had a surprise. In the middle of third night one of them awoke to feel the foetid breath of a cat on her face. Her scream saved her, but the carnivore snatched her baby and ran off into the night. The rest of the party in the shelter grabbed their own offspring and all ran to the cave entrance. The 'insiders' had closed it with large boulders, and there was no possibility of reaching safety there. The screams of panic attracted two more of the big cats and they wreaked havoc on the wretched mothers and their children.

The cave was not opened until daylight. Da was the first to go outside. She had her Ba on one hip and she held her razor-sharp flint in the other. There was little she or anyone could do. Three of the babies and one adult had been carried away. She put out one hand to comfort a distraught young mother who had lost her baby. Tears were in her eyes and they held each other and simply sobbed. Such comfort and expressions of compassion were unusual, but they did not go unnoticed by the other females. There was some nodding of approval. The giving and receiving of comfort at such times was now considered to be good, but touch and mental attitude were the only methods of expressing those feelings.

The growing need for language had never been more obvious.

The leaders were also aware that they had a problem that required thought and agreement before the group could resolve the matter of over-population in the cave. The answer came from the action of the ming who had first taken Da. He beckoned her to join him with her baby and then pointed outside, indicating that he was prepared to leave the cave and seek a new home base. Da nodded and moved outside with him. They both looked back into the cave and implied to some of the other group members that they should go with them. Two mings and five young mothers soon made up their minds and carried their babies with them. They were all well used to travelling and hunting, sleeping rough wherever they found themselves at dusk. They were pleased to have a change in their routine and eager to continue the journey north towards the sun.

They walked steadily all day. The small babies were suckled on the move and the more independent members were scavenging for easy pickings, grubs, and small rodents and, for the first time, a bee's nest. It was curiosity that made one of the mings go near the round nest that was hanging from the branch of a tree.

The contented humming sound became louder as he approached. It should have been accepted as a warning to him but he wanted to know what made the noise. He soon found out. A few of the bees objected to his presence when he put his nose close to the nest and they stung him on the face and arms.

His reaction, of screaming and running away, alerted all the others and they followed suit. They were scattered in all directions, some of them also carrying stinging bees with them. It took some time before they were all able to be reunited and to continue their travels. Those who had suffered the stings were never able to go near another bee's nest. The stings continued to hurt them through the night but they were soon able to concentrate on more normal activity.

This was the first experience of the new sub-group where an outside threat had scattered them and they were all suitably frightened. Each of the adults called out when they saw Da's ming looking for them. Their cries had a hint of relief at finding him again, respect for his maturity, his experience and leadership. He did not query their attitudes and he accepted the appointment willingly. They had made a good choice.

His first decision was that each member of his group should have a name. He did not know, at that point in time, that the process would not only give the individual a strong sense of belonging, an identity, but it would enhance his own control of the group. He would be able to assert himself by naming and ordering each one of them to do as he dictated. He was not really aware of what he was doing but he heard an 'inner voice' guiding him, and he took that advice. It just seemed to be the right step to take.

After gathering the entire group around him, he pointed to himself and said, "Ingda", three times. He then paused and pointed to one of the two other mings. There was no reaction, at first, then, after a repeat of the pointing to himself saying, "Ingda", followed by pointing to the ming, there came the required answer, a hesitant, "Ngur". Ingda repeated the new name, pointing to the ming, "Ngur", he said, laughing, "Ngur, Ngur, Ngur". They each called the other's name, pointing and laughing. The rest of the group continued the game, pointing to both Ingda and Ngur, calling each by the given name. They then started to point to themselves but Ingda resumed control of the naming session. He hushed them and pointed to the second ming who immediately grunted the sound that he had chosen for himself, "Har", he said.

This was followed by the now expected routine of shouting the new name to the ming. The procedure was repeated for each of the five gnas, until all the eight adults had been named and those names engraved in the developing memories of each of them. They were all smiling with the new-found sense of belonging. Ingda was a good ming, and a respected leader. They had fed well during the day, so they followed Ingda when he pointed and moved towards a large tree where the small group would spend the night. The contentment continued. During the night each of the gnas was satisfied, more than once, with the shared pleasuring given by the three mings. There had been no attempt to extend the group naming to the youngsters or the babies, but each of the gnas had it in her mind to start working on the idea. It would develop in the normal process of trial and error. Of the fifteen children with them, four of them were approaching maturity, being about twelve years of age. A naming ceremony might be a good way of recognising their progress and the need to leave the control of their mothers. In the short time that they had been independent from the original group they had made noticeable progress, both physically in the northerly direction and mentally in the development and use of their growing brainpower.

The main anxiety in the minds of the watchers was whether this small group would be able to increase its numerical strength quickly enough to face and deal with all the trials that might appear in its path. It was certainly indicating a potential for rapid development.

CHAPTER THREE
VOLCANO

The elders of Group A had shown little regret when the smaller group had decided to leave the shelter of the cave and make their own decisions elsewhere. Their departure had certainly reduced the pressure on the limited amount of accommodation. With the passing of a few days they rarely gave a thought to them. Other, more frightening, activities began to affect the cave dwellers.

It was in the early part of one night, when the usual social activities were still causing some disturbance to those who wanted to sleep, that a strange rumbling sound was heard. None of them had heard anything like it before in their short lives. Each one of them became frightened and still. The sound seemed to come from underneath them, deep in the ground. Some of them moved to be near the cave entrance, but they hesitated before deciding whether to go out into the darkness, into the danger area of the night, where the cats could be waiting for them. Then, it became quiet. The group did not sleep.

Just before the dawn, they all heard the noise start again. This time it continued until long after the daybreak. Hunger pangs made them go about their daily routine of finding, hunting and eating. The rumbling certainly was coming from the very ground on which they stood. The young ones and the gnas kept looking towards the elder mings for some sort of explanation or guidance, but it was not there for them. All the mings were looking as scared as the others. It went on like this for the whole of that day and the next. Then it happened.

The louder and louder rumbling became a roar, then an explosion. They all rushed out of the cave, just before the dawn arrived, and they were horrified to see that the sky was red around the top of their mountain. None of them had ever seen a live volcano before and they stood in amazement, and terror, to see that the mountain was spurting flame and red rocks into the air. They all turned and ran downhill as fast as their legs could take them. Most of their few possessions were lost, and they did not stop to look for them. Hot ash and rocks started to fall around and ahead of them but they could not run any faster. As they ran, they hardly noticed that some

22

large cats and deer were passing them, all running away from the terror. None of them were interfering with the others. It was not a time for hunting but for saving themselves.

One of the group paused a moment and looked back. He could see that a mass of liquid fire had left the peak of the mountain and was making its way down towards them. He had seen water flowing before now but here was a huge mass of hot liquid chasing after them. He screamed and pointed to the danger. The others took up the screaming, until they were too short of breath to continue. They carried on running down the slopes but the lava was too quick for some of them. It had burst out of the mountainside, much nearer to their cave, and was soon overtaking them and curling round ahead of them. The hot gases choked those who breathed them in. The fortunate ones were those who ran the fastest and got ahead of the lava flow. They managed to keep running until they realised that the hot lava had turned away, down a strange valley, which took it in a different direction.

The exhausted creatures collected together but they continued to move steadily away from the danger. Soon, they collapsed on the ground, gasping for breath. After a time, some of the elders stood upright and looked around for the others of their group. Their numbers had been halved. Many of the missing ones were gnas and their babies. This was a disaster. The babies were their future. The loss of most the gnas would result in there being fewer babies. Most of their stones had gone. At least, they could start looking for some new ones, but where could they find some more gnas? None of them had eaten since running from the cave. Hunting was the first need. To do that they must find some stones. The leaders started to move more downhill towards the river. During that day they found sufficient new stones to feel well armed, they hunted successfully and fed all the remaining members of the group. They also found a clump of trees where they slept in comparative safety for the first night. A check of the survivors showed that there were only as many gnas as fingers on one hand. The thirty mings would be queuing for them until they could find another group, if that were possible. There would be a test of leadership in resolving this problem.

Ywancontin was aware of the question from Bevak at the moment of his thought. "No", he answered, "we shall not take any steps to help them to increase their numbers, other than those that have already been taken. This is a testing period for this group and they will survive if they apply what they have learned from past experience. They have strong urges for both survival and reproduction. Both Groups A and B will need to apply their inherent mental logic to realise what action they are required to take in order to remove the problem. They will have to discover for themselves that they really have two problems. The second one is the lack of language. Telepathy has proved to be extremely useful for normal communication, on the hunt, or when doing the usual chores of family life, but when they need to discuss their present situation, it would be enhanced by verbal debate, if that were possible. They are already well aware of the need to increase their numbers and they know that that takes a few years, if they only have the normal method of procreation. They require a few decades of security from similar disasters. We will help them only by encouraging them to create a greater awareness of potential danger. They must begin to think ahead automatically. They must start to ask themselves, 'What will happen if we do this, or take that action?' If they should find themselves near another similar group, they might be tempted to try to take some of the females from that source. If they do so, they could learn that it was an unwise move. Both groups could be numerically reduced even further. We must wait and see if the difficulties help them to advance mentally and verbally.

There are plenty of other groups developing in different parts of the planet. They will require to be monitored before we can give a full appraisal of progress. Continue with your brief, Bevak, I suggest that your report, at the end of the hundred years, will be very informative and will complement those of your colleagues".

The leaders of group A had been testing their brainpower to the limit in order to try to find an answer to the problem of the losses sustained from the volcanic explosions. They could find no answer. They realised that they were beaten and simply stopped thinking

Da's hair, which intrigued everyone. Some of them tried to pluck tufts from her head, but Pi reacted to her screams and physical violence against them, and he shouted and growled in a very aggressive way. This had the desired effect. Da was soon left alone, free from the unpleasant attention.

She found that her new companions had a confidence that she envied. Did it arise from that fact that they never appeared to be very hungry? They certainly had the benefit of regular supplies, gathered by the hunters from an area within no more than half a day's travel from the sleeping area. Drinking water was available in abundance from the river, which ran through the valley. All the gnas were either pregnant or nursing a newborn baby. Da hoped that she would soon be in the same condition. She had decided that there was a future for her with these people and they seemed to be hoping that she would come to that conclusion. Her feelings of compassion, when expressed to the other young mothers and their babies brought nods and smiles from them. Yes, the message was there despite the lack of language. The prospects were good.

The climate did not vary very much throughout the year and they all seemed to prosper with very little effort. The steady increase in the size of the group followed the regular arrival of more and more babies each year. Da continued to give birth to a new baby each year. She learned the few words and grunts that provided them all with a simple method of communication. Sometimes she uttered such words that she remembered from group B and these were used, repeated and tested until they became part of the accepted way of life.

Another point that helped her to appreciate the new security was the fact that the larger predators did not trouble the group very often. She saw only a few of the big cats and they kept well away from each other. The cats had learned that the two-legged creatures were much too dangerous to become an easy meal. The well-aimed stones had put fear into them. There were many other easier victims to be found.

The years rolled past without any serious anxieties for this group of hominids. Their numbers had continued to grow with the new babies far exceeding the losses from old age. They appeared to be aware of numbers up to around five but there was no desire to count accurately above one hand. The nature of their mental processes simply did not demand or even imagine that possibility. They were mainly carnivorous and there was an ample supply of replaceable meat in the small creatures that lived in the lush growth of grassland and forest. Da died in her mid 30's from the effects of a difficult pregnancy. No one complained. She had produced a useful number of sturdy offspring who were of a variety of shades of brown. Some of them had long hair similar to hers but others had short curly mops ranging from brown to black. Her cause of death was a common one. The members of this successful group disposed of her body in one of the usual ways. It was thrown into the big river and carried away. In the event of a death any distance from the river they would make some attempt to bury the remains before leaving that immediate area. They had never felt the need to consume the body for food. If they had ever been cannibals, the memory of the experience had long been suppressed, and, possibly, erased from the group memory.

CHAPTER FOUR
THE REPORT

The reports from the members of the Development Committee held few surprises but they were presented and recorded in the usual manner.

Ywancontin signalled to Lucus to start the presentation. Without any hesitation he spoke clearly and confidently. "This first report on the one hundred years of study of the three groups has raised some interesting facts and possibilities. We are already seeing a marked difference between all three. Since the time of the earlier study of their predecessors some half a million years ago, attitudes and abilities have been affected by the differences of diet and variations in security. Occasional cannibalism has continued with group A, and also with group B, which was recently formed from A. This negative habit had started during one of the periods of having ice covering the ground for most of the year. The creatures had seen such behaviour as a simple answer to the need for filling their bellies in the extended winters. They had used the very young, and the older members of their group, so that the fittest hunters and their fertile females could survive until their usual food became available again. We found that group C had suppressed or apparently eliminated the practice from their routines, if not from their memories. It will be interesting to watch for any sign of a latent desire to restart the habit, should conditions become more difficult for them in the future.

They have certainly shown development that has not yet been seen in the other two groups. They have willingly accepted a new member from another group and absorbed her and her traits, to the benefit of them all. Da was the first recipient of compassion, as part of our adjustments to the mental attitudes that were being developed. She carried it within her genes and also expressed it to others in both groups using mental and facial means of communication. The females certainly understood what she meant and enthusiastically agreed with the idea of developing mother-love for their babies. In the long term it will prove to be very beneficial to all the males as well as to the females, because a steady growth in numbers of surviving babies will build up the strength of the group and increase its power and ability to face the occasional disaster. The gentleness of compassionate attitudes will, of course, be countered by the aggressive nature required to succeed in battle and in hunting. This can become a possible deterrent to progress in the development of what we might call 'mankind', some time in the future. The creatures will certainly need their strong forceful traits well into their future. It is likely that the reduction in numbers of the groups A and B will stimulate their members to apply more thought to their own needs, if they are to survive. They have the latent abilities and it will help them to develop more quickly once they accept the fact that they are in a critical situation.

Medically, they are being exposed continually to the widening range of bacteria, which are simultaneously fighting for their own survival. The creation of antibodies will continue to be the natural method of countering any threat to the creatures. It is my opinion that we are seeing the progress of a developing creature, which will become the potential human, at the foot of a very tall ladder leading to the heights. Each one of them is unaware of any spiritual knowledge. They do not recognise that they have an inner self or even a conscience. Any new idea or thought that is given to them is accepted, without question, as the idea of the thinker. It will be a very long time before they will begin to realise that the 'inner voice' originates from another spirit. They are totally unaware of their own spark of spiritual life.

They do not wonder where they come from or ask where they might be going. These questions will not be raised until they have grown their brains to, at least, double the present size. Their limited telepathic abilities will tend to fade, as they develop any sort of verbal language, but the potential will be retained as a trace in their structure. These three groups are all in a favourable part of the planet. The temperate climate of what will become the continent of Africa will help them to grow in numbers without increasing any need for warlike aggression. That can possibly develop from their hunting skills, but we should continue to monitor the effect of this trait over a long period. The difference between self-defence and offensive action can be extremely small, and it will be necessary for them to learn where one stops and the other begins."

THE PATH

Ywancontin smiled his thanks to Lucus. "You have gone a little into the field to be covered by Solem, but do not be upset by that. He will add to the points that you have raised, no doubt, later in this meeting. Now, Marcus, what are your opinions and suggestions for our consideration?"

Marcus quickly looked around the committee room, knowing very well that his doubts were already the reason for some of the smiles of good humour.

"The question is as old as the one about the chicken and the egg. Which comes first? Is it the creation of a larger brain in these creatures, so that they can think more deeply, and make progress? Or should they continue with their existing capabilities, working through a long learning curve, until they have all developed and increased the size of their brains? It is possible that, by then, they will have a wide enough range of experiences to give them the confidence to act correctly in any situation? I am well aware of the fact that we are not restricted by any matter of time. Time will become of greater importance to these creatures after they have advanced much more. They are simply not interested or even aware of it at this point in their development. Their only sense of urgency is created by self survival, when threatened by a larger adversary; by hunger for food, over a long period; or the sexual urge to mate, which arises with little thought on their behalf.

In my opinion, they require a very long period of reacting to their present conditions and learning from their own experiences. It could be looked upon as the 'survival of the fittest'. I believe that that is the only way in which they can safely grow their brain size to be of real benefit to themselves. If we manipulate their brain growth in any other way, there is the possible disadvantage of their making apparent progress without the consolidation grown from experience.

Looking much further ahead, I can envisage these hominids becoming just the type of creature that will be needed to make continual progress in the aeons to come. The only real dangers, of which we are aware, are that they will place greater importance on the traits which will then have outlived their requirement but which are so necessary at this point in time. I am thinking mainly of the more aggressive aspects, the ability to fight and destroy other creatures, the need for sexual relief so frequently each day. Will those urges be retained over too long a period? Will they have the effect of suppressing the development of the gentler attitudes, which would help them on to the right path and in the right direction? Should we be helping them to grow a conscience?

I am sure that we all recognise that there is a great need to grow their brains surely and steadily. Then, the opportunities will be endless and are likely to grow in geometric proportions."

"Thank you, Marcus," murmured the Chairman, "let us now hear your thoughts, Mellak."

"The present, short and brutal lives of these creatures gives me some concern," said Mellak. "We must remember that they spend the first few years fighting for existence, all the time absorbing knowledge forced upon them by the environment, including the other members of their group. Their only real pleasures are a full belly and, after maturity, the frequent act of mating. They have no time for pondering on the basic facts of life, where they come from, why they are here or what happens to them after death, sudden and cruel as that often is.

I think that we should consider the method that we currently employ in order to guide the individual into the way of enlightenment. It does not appear to be strong enough to be having any noticeable effect. As I understand it, the spark of spiritual life, which is given to each one of them, at the time of conception, is in reality a separate, perpetual entity. We can call it the 'soul' to indicate that it is in that particular body only from its entry into the foetus until the death of that creature. At the birth it carries no memory whatsoever of its earlier history, but at the death it retains most of the knowledge of the experiences of that life, when it returns to the 'home plane' of the spirit world.

It has been noticed, on occasions, that a few of these returned spirits have retained an interest in, and even some almost affectionate thoughts for, those livings creatures that they have left behind. That has been considered to be progress, a positive attitude, which could lead to improvement in the outlook of all the spirits concerned. Spiritual Law has permitted them to revisit the part of the planet where they had spent most of their lives, but only on the *condition that they remain invisible to the living. I believe that this link between the two sides of the divide gives an opportunity for creating a growing awareness of the purpose of their existence. The crude, undeveloped telepathy, experienced between the creatures when on the planet, could grow into a gentle and effective form of communication between the two worlds. This in turn could lead to hints of guidance, which are created from the memories of the returned spirits. It can be very reassuring for a frightened earth creature to be given confidence, when in a dangerous or difficult position, even if it is unaware of the source of that good feeling. I can understand that a frightened baby or a growing child would be pleased to be aware of another child of similar age who was speaking directly into the mind.*

If proper safeguards are installed at the time of approval of these suggestions, this possible change in the procedures of the waiting and learning channels of our world can offer new possibilities for those spirits who are waiting and undecided on their next step forward. I offer these thoughts for your consideration."

The full committee signalled their approval of the suggestion with a simple thought and a smile. One of them immediately wished for it to be presented to the earth spirits of any age, not merely for the youngsters, and this was approved.

Ywancontin pointed out that the acceptance of this help, and its possible benefits to the creatures, would depend to a large extent upon their ability to grasp the facts and to recognise the inherent wisdom, and also to use their brains and memories into the future. The limitations of their skills to do so would tend to hinder any progress until they had evolved further. Some of the new abilities would help in the process of mental development and be passed on through their genes. Yes. The process should commence immediately.

Surtyn knew that it was his turn to give his thoughts and confirmed his full agreement, but the deep thinking Solem wished to add something.

"Let us extend these proposals before we put them into effect. If the introduction of opportunities for spiritual knowledge and awareness is given to every one of this type of creature, we know that it will help to develop the size and usage of their brains. We must

realise and accept the fact that the rate of development will vary in different individuals. Some of them will race ahead of the others. Some will possibly go down the wrong path, seeking more power and ability, but for the wrong reasons. Some strong groups will have the capability to seek out and destroy the weaker, gentler groups, which we might prefer to help to advance. Bearing this in mind, do we give the creatures the opportunities to make their own mistakes, and to learn from them, to choose whatever path that they might wish to follow?"

Bevak had no hesitation when he gave his opinion. "They should certainly be allowed to make their own mistakes, and learn from them! How can any of them hope to make progress without making mistakes? We are all here now, hoping to make progress for the world that we know. Are we all to be hindered by the fear of making our own mistakes? Any anxieties in that field can be reduced by the installation of a self-monitoring system of observation and awareness. Our activities are monitored, as we know. Let us apply a similar system to our present objectives."

There were approving nods from the others in the room.

Ywancontin decided to close the meeting with a programme for their continuing activity. "We will establish the proposed pattern of help for these three groups in the knowledge that we will be alerted if there is any major deviation from the World Plan. Time must be allowed to pass, giving the creatures the scope to make or lose the direction of their movement on their various paths. We will see what lessons they are capable of learning, how their brains develop, and how they adapt to changing circumstances. We will give them one long period of a million years without any interference, only our routine observation.

In the meantime, there are two other regions of this planet where similar types of creatures are becoming established. Both are to the north of the equator. We will firstly observe some of those on the eastern continental shelf. This is being affected by the collision of the southern landmass, which has been moving northwards for a number of long periods. The creation of the newer mountain ranges, added to the volcanic activity, will have a greater affect on the animal population than we have seen in the African area, where there has been a movement of a continental mass away from it, in a westerly direction."

CHAPTER FIVE
5mBC ASIA

The northern and eastern side of the landmass on the planet spent three quarters of each year under a layer of snow and ice. It was only in the summer quarter that there was growth of vegetation, and it was in that brief period that the warm blooded animals were able to nourish themselves. It was then that the wide variety of flying animals could be seen, but rarely touched, amongst the forest.

With the melting of the snow, all these creatures were very active from dawn to dusk, finding and consuming whatever food was available, fattening themselves for the next cold spell, and mating in order to continue the species. Many of them failed. Many potentially viable species disappeared from that part of the world. Amongst the survivors there were two varieties of bipeds, an early type of mammoth, some very aggressive large cats and a number of small mammals that survived by burrowing into the earth below the frost level. The mammoths were such hardy creatures that they moved to the north during each warm period. They were able to graze the grasslands in the north as the ice and snow melted ahead of them, building up stores of fat before returning to the shelter of the hills and valleys when the weather deteriorated each winter. Their thick skins and matted coats protected them from not only the bitter cold winds but also from the rare attacks of the long-toothed cats. They had developed their own telepathic form of communication and, when threatened, they quickly formed a ring around any cat attempting to pull down a member of the group. Their tusks and stamping forefeet had a final message for the intruder. The two-legged creatures, that were becoming more noticeable, had not yet thought of a method of using the flesh of the mighty mammoth for food. That was still to come.

The two species of hominids had grown differently during the previous few million years and now had little in common. They were both able to walk on their hind legs, and they usually did so. None of them were able to make verbal communication, other than a few grunts of pleasure, growls of warning, and screams of anger or pain. They were both able to warn their close ones of approaching danger by means of a thought, a sixth sense, which could usually put the others on the alert in time to avoid a trap. The members of the other species did not usually receive these telepathic messages.

Of the two, the smaller creatures appeared to be the most progressive, as they moved more quickly, they were possibly the first to establish the use of new ideas, new inventions, which were very rare but which became well established after a period of trial. They thought of themselves as the Utee, when they gave any thought to themselves as a group. Their name for the other group was the Yutee. The Utee did not like the Yutee and took every opportunity to kill them or drive them away from their own grazing areas. They were foreign to them in many ways. The smooth-haired Utee were only about one and a half metres tall, when they stood upright, whereas the Yutee all exceeded two metres and they were covered in long matted brown hair, from head to foot. This helped them to survive during the cold periods but it tended to make them feel lethargic when the summer sun raised the temperature.

The warmer days seemed to encourage the small group of Utee, which was grubbing amongst the fallen rocks on the side of the valley. They were enjoying a measure of success. Each member had filled its belly with a variety of nourishment, small wriggling larvae, furry creatures that could not run fast enough to escape the quick-eyed bipeds. The leader of the Utee, a mature male of about twenty years, had been the first to satisfy his hunger. He shook his head of black hair, hanging down to his shoulders, and studied the nearby females who were still looking on the ground for more food. Some of them were carrying a baby in one arm whilst using the other to disturb the vegetation and the soil. All of them were filthy and well scented in the familiar odours of the group. He grunted with contentment. His life was good. There was plenty of sex available and it was all for him, if he so wished. His was the first appetite that was to be satisfied.

The process was simple. He walked over the nearest female and grunted his demand. She responded by continuing to search the ground for food, but she acknowledged his instruction by raising her bottom a little higher and putting her legs slightly wider apart. He grabbed her by her long hair and entered her from the rear, grunting in time with his movements. He was soon relieved, but not satisfied. He kicked her on the thigh, making her fall down, and then went to the next female within sight.

She had been fully aware of what had happened. She knew that she would not benefit from antagonising the leader and she showed her interest when he grunted his demand. Her baby was put down on some dried grasses and she turned to face the sturdy male, lying down with her legs apart, arms raised in a gesture of welcome. His grunt was of promised pleasure as he almost ran the last two steps and knelt down between her legs. His hands went to grab her milk-laden breasts, squeezing them, whilst he bit her shoulder, and then he entered her. The grunts of delight came from both of them as they enjoyed the exercise. It required much longer before the male had decided that he had no more interest in this female. After he had stood up again he walked slowly round the group whilst she resumed her feeding. The leader tried to unite with one more occupied female before he decided to wait until later, perhaps after it became dark, before he put his manhood to the test again. As he sat down, some of the other males made their own progress with the rest of the females, who were by that time full of food and ready for them. They were all having a good day.

When they were about to move away from the scene of relaxation, they were startled by a scream, which came from higher up the slope, behind a cliff face. They moved as one. The males led the way, running easily up towards the noise, picking up handy stones as they ran. The females followed closely behind them, carrying their youngsters.

The scene that faced the front runners caused them to increase their speed without any hesitation. One of their younger females was screaming whilst being raped by a huge, hairy monster. The thought "Yutee" went through every mind in the group of Utee as they charged at the struggling couple on the ground. Snarling, shouting, small males of the Utee closed with the stranger and raised their arms, with stones held in their fists, when they quickly beat the animal's head into a pulp. It had started to move away from its victim but had no chance of escape, or even of defending itself against so many.

It was pulled in all directions as the stone weapons were applied to every part of the grotesque body. The leader of the Utee group noticed the long, thick hair, which covered the complete body and the putrid, rank stench of the creature. These added to his hate. One of the sharp stones was used to break open the ribcage and to tear out the still-pulsating heart. Holding the bloody organ above his head, the leader shouted, "Yutee," and started to bite the flesh and drink the blood. "Yutee", shouted the others in their excitement. None of them bothered to attend to the young victim of the rape and she moved to the fringe of the group, sobbing quietly. She knew that she had received the seed of the nightmare horror. It had been almost twice her height and covered with that stinking thick matt of hair.

When the excited grunting had died down the leader indicated that they should search around that place to look for any more of the enemy. This went on until it was almost dark. A wave of the arm then told them all to return to the nearest resting-place for the night. The hatred for the Yutee was impressed in the minds of all the members of that group of Utee. They were not likely to accept any possibility of co-operation with them in the future.

During the few summer months the group of Utee wandered at will over a large area of hills and plains enjoying the plentiful food, threatened only by occasional attention from the large cats. These, in their turn, had ample easier prey and they often avoided contact with the growing number of groups of these bipeds.

When accident brought any of these groups near to each other the procedure that was followed had become stereotyped. The first reaction was that both groups would stand very still. Their telepathy gave them instant orders from their leaders, but all members of the two groups could possibly understand these messages. The degree of understanding would depend mainly upon whether there were any family relations in the two groups. This might have happened during previous contacts over, perhaps, many decades. Distant cousins would be mentally aware of each other's existence and this would produce friendly grunts and smiles which spread very quickly and all the creatures would move closer together. The welcome would be confirmed if the individuals started to give small scraps of food to the young ones. If either group had been carrying any quantity of food this could lead to them all sitting down to share what was available.

These friendships could soon blossom into a happy party and a sharing of sexual pleasures. In this simple way, new blood was introduced to each group, to the benefit of all concerned. After two or three days and nights of partying, the groups would separate and make their own way in different directions. It was a refreshing experience. More new cousins would be arriving during the next year. There seemed to be no desire amongst them to remain together in order to form one large group from the two.

None of them was able to count, but there was an awareness of quantity. When any group grew to the point of having more than sixty or seventy adults, there was a tendency for internal bickering to break out and this would be resolved by approximately one third of them taking their youngsters and setting off alone to form a new group. In this way it was possible for a number of related groups to meet each other whilst hunting or grazing the fruit and nuts that were available in abundance during the summer period. After that beneficial quarter of the year all the Utee used to make their way to the south, towards the great bitter water. The Yutee stayed in the cold valleys and hills, where they led their own secret lives.

It was during the movement to the warmer south coast that the female, which had been raped by the Yutee, dropped her firstborn. The group were all in attendance and they showed their feelings when they saw the baby. It was a large male but it appeared to be a small version of its father, hairy and grotesque. The elders immediately picked up stones and hammered both the mother and her new born into oblivion. The accompanying cries of "Yutee" were filled with hate, leaving the group in no doubt about the feelings of the majority. Any Yutee that they might meet in the future were likely to be attacked on sight. The hate for them was retained in the group memory until the opportunity arose to vent it on a small group of the strange monsters.

The time spent in the southern, warmer area was passed in the usual ways, hunting and grazing without any sense of urgency. Numbers increased steadily over the years. Sturdy babies soon became independent young adults that wanted to challenge the authority of the elders. The decline in the strength of the older ones started soon after reaching their twenties, sometimes hastened by broken limbs resulting from falls out of trees or down cliffs. It could result from the efforts of a developing young male that wanted to take the equally young females from an elder. Then it would happen quickly, without the telepathic warning that was usual when fighting broke out within the group. A stone would be picked up and swung to the head of the elder, with fatal results, just when he was about to take his normal rights of copulation with one of the young females. It was over very quickly. The precocious youngster would be accepted as a substitute for the dead elder, at least for the sexual encounter of the moment. It was always possible that he would have to fight others of a similar age before the new leader was fully accepted.

It was only within recent centuries that these hominids appeared to have started to develop any long-term memory of unpleasant experiences. One such experience was the rape of the young female, and the subsequent killing of the Yutee involved, and, later, of both the female and her baby.

Two years after the event, and after two annual travels to the north and back, this group came unexpectedly upon a small number of the detested creatures who were grazing in a valley which had steep cliffs on both sides. The telepathic surge of hate welled up in the minds of the Utee and they rushed quietly forward to surround the hairy monsters without any hesitation. Some stones were flung accurately at their heads and legs before they closed with them holding their hand stones. These were either rounded or sharp-edged, according to the preference of the owner. They created havoc amongst the twenty Yutee who were very quickly killed and dismembered. This was followed by the larger number of Utee repeating the victory procedure of tearing out the hearts of their victims and consuming the organs to screams of "Yutee! Yutee!" coming firstly from the watching females and then from the successful fighters. All members of that group were excited and happy at the outcome. They flashed these thoughts to each other many times during the remainder of that year. It was in their minds whenever they moved into new areas where they might possibly meet their enemy.

THE PATH

When the Committee met for the usual review of their observations in the Eastern land area over the past century, the dominant point in their comments was the strong growth of the creatures' tendency to develop but with a more aggressive attitude.

Solem was selected to make the first report. "We are all aware of the signs of the growing use of force by these Utee and it is now obvious that it does not depend on their need for self defence or for the protection of essential sources of food. It arose from their natural wish for revenge, after the unpleasant sexual attack on one of their more vulnerable young females. Their previous history records many occasions where they have suffered the loss of one or more of their members, but not one where they held a grudge, as they have done this time. Their first reaction had usually been sorrow, quickly followed by a return to whatever had been occupying them before the accident. We now have a completely new and possibly lasting change of attitude. We must ask ourselves if this change indicates a new step forward in their mental processes? Is this a sign of the progress that we have been planning and expecting? If it is so, then we should record the achievement. We should also make some assessment of the possible side effects and decide whether they are to be welcomed and developed, or disliked and deterred.

Let us project this trait forward for a long time and decide whether it could be of benefit to all creatures, or whether it will grow out of proportion to the size of those benefits and move towards a position of becoming uncontrollable. We can imagine the dangers of one strong species multiplying in numbers until it controlled the complete planet; it could develop absolute power over all other creatures, all nature and, even its own species. We should also consider whether the Yutee have any possible future if they continue to live in proximity with the Utee. The fact that they were able to interbreed with each other indicates that there is a history of common ancestors. The rarity of such a happening is proved by the apparently strong differences in their appearance and habits. Should we not encourage the two species to live in areas that are widely separated? This might enable the Yutee to survive longer, in case the Utee should meet some unexpected disaster and be eliminated."

Ywancontin smiled his acknowledgement of Solem's report

and opinion. *"Bevak, please?"* The 'active one' jumped to his feet, eagerly.

"Why should we explore the possibility of helping such an unlikely species even to survive to the point of being considered a possible 'leading species'? If they are not able to survive the contacts with the Utee, then we should simply let nature take its course. From what we have all seen, they are lacking in attractiveness, perhaps they are too large for the hard world where they have found themselves, some of their own genes are obviously well established in their enemies, so it will be possible to resurrect the species, if it became necessary. I propose that they are permitted to continue living their lives as they choose, wandering around the snowline, and, if they dwindle to the point of extinction, then they will disappear from the planet. The Utee seem to be much more promising as a viable species." Lucus received the signal to say what was in his mind.

"There is another aspect in the favour of the Utee that we should note. Their diet has been of great interest to me, especially when we are aware of the growing developments in the variety of plant life. They are usually willing to try tasting any new vegetation that they discover and they are beginning to receive the benefits of consuming a wide range of herbs, as those plants adapt to the soil and climate where they find themselves. This knowledge and appreciation of feeling better in health and strength is also helping to make their brains grow in size and scope. We know that they only use a small part of their available brain capacity but they must surely make progress when a larger brain develops. I believe that we only really need to monitor their progress over a long period, whilst keeping our records of these discussions, in case of there being a need for us to impose a change."

Marcus had a different aspect that he thought should be raised for consideration. *"Should we not encourage some of these creatures to travel to new areas where they will meet other groups? There is always the possibility such meeting will be of benefit to all concerned. Some small groups are becoming rather inward looking, and losing resistance to disease, because of too much inbreeding. They may already have some desirably strong points that should be developed, so that the entire species will benefit in the future. It is important to ensure that these bipeds are capable of successfully breeding with the other groups that are developing in all parts of this planet.*

Our recent study in the western side of the land showed that there are serious risks of such groups being eliminated by a number of means. We know that they can suffer from accidents and disease, and that they will grow in determination when they feel that they are being threatened. We need to know if they will accept the arrival of complete strangers in their midst, or whether such a surprise will increase their aggressive attitudes. This could be tested without any serious risk by letting a group from one area move into another area.

These Utee appear to be quite suitable for such an experiment. We could help them to find a way through the developing mountain ranges to the west. I would propose that we do so, sometime during the next long period. We could also do the same for one of the newer groups in the west area, encouraging them to move further to the north where they would have contact with some of those that survive in the central area of the land. They might find that there are distant cousins who will make them welcome. Whatever happens, something will be learned from the contacts."

Mellak had been studying the Utee from an entirely different aspect. He had always been inclined to look for the good points, the positive side of his subject. He looked at Ywancontin and quietly stated his experience.

"When I was considering their spiritual side, I made myself appear to the them at different times and under different circumstances. There was only one occasion, and that was at dusk, when I heard any indication from them that I had been seen. They had been settling down for sleep, after the usual false alarms and changing of partners, when I moved closer in order to read their mind patterns. The young female that I was near suddenly opened her eyes after she had been seeing my image in her mind. She realised that her dream was a reality. The tall, smooth skinned Yutee(?) was really standing there in front of her. Her screams and mental turmoil aroused the complete group and, of course, I had immediately disappeared from sight. She was the only one that reacted in that way, when it was possible for any one of them to have been

aware of my being with them. I assume therefore that only a few of them are likely to develop any strong psychic abilities in the near future.

There appear to be some good reasons for us to extend our studies of these bipeds in their full spiritual condition, both before being introduced to the Earth plane and after their return to Spirit, at the end of their short experience in the body. There are signs that they are accumulating spiritual experience of a deeper nature than that of the other creatures. Some of them are recognising a desire to continue their contact with, and knowledge of, those that they have left behind. Some even show a wish to return to the body in order to gain more experience. These are all positive signs of spiritual progress. A comparison of this situation, with that at the end of the next long period, will be a means of measuring their progress."

Surtyn then came into the discussion with his usual decisive approach.

"I agree with all that has been said so far. There seems to be no doubt that the Utee are very likely to survive, in the long term. The Yutee are likely to be so reduced, numerically, that they will lose any possibility of dominating the other species. It is even possible that their tendency to remain in the snow covered areas, where their food is not easily found, will have them locked permanently into the minds and memories of the Utee as the 'awful snowmen'. After they have dwindled and faded out, their only memorial might be as that of a nightmare, with a similar name.

But first, the creatures will need to create a desire for a spoken form of communication. Again, that is going to require time and an improvement in their brainpower. The two needs can develop side by side, using the same long period of time. We are aware that such progress could lead to a reduced ability to use telepathy. This could have the disadvantage of retarding the development of spiritual progress, so we should monitor that area of their paths.

Regarding the proposed contact between groups from the distant areas of the west, the east and the northwest, I think that this is likely to occur naturally with the natural, continual, movement of each group. Curiosity will surely cause the creatures to move into 'new territories' when they find them ahead of them. There will also be pressures created by increasing numbers of individuals and groups over along period, pushing some of them to look forward and acquire the need to find out for themselves what is ahead of them. It will all be part of their learning process. Perhaps, it is a little too soon to make decisions on these points until we have made similar studies of the small number of groups in the northwestern area."

Once again, Ywancontin signalled his thanks for the contributions made by each member. "You are all being very helpful. I agree that we should make a similar close study of the third area, which we have not recently visited as a committee, before we make any final recommendations. But before we commence, I must inform you that a natural situation has arisen which requires our attention in that area.

A large number of groups of hominids are periodically to be found in the long rift valley which separates the landmass, that will be known as 'Africa', from the north eastern area, that will one day be called 'Europe'. In time to come, this valley will be given a name meaning 'the centre of the world'. We know that it is very productive and it is sheltered from the extremes of the colder spells of weather. For much of each year it provides a large surplus of food for the many creatures that use it. Unfortunately, the valley is separated from the saltwater ocean by the narrowest range of mountains at the western end. There is an imminent possibility of the huge mass of ocean breaking through these mountains and pouring into the valley.

It is an area of volcanic activity and eruptions could easily occur without warning. All that is required is a slight raising of the sea level, possibly from the melting of ice from the poles, at the same time that the strong westerly winds might build up the height of the usual high tides. Once the water is able to break through between the high points of the land, it will steadily erode a path for ever-increasing volumes to drown the entire valley. There will be little warning, or opportunity, for all the *creatures that occupy the valley to escape. It is important that we are aware of the possible disaster and that we encourage as many creatures as possible to have representative groups on the higher ground to the north and on the south of the endangered valley. There are various methods that we might use for this purpose. The most important fact is that we should be applying our awareness to that end.*

Thank you all for your contribution to the discussion. Let us move into that area now."

CHAPTER SIX
MEDITERRANEAN

The most successful of all the groups of hominids, that had been the subject of a report to the Committee, had given themselves the name of Gyps. They had continued to wander around the northern part of the landmass that would be called Africa. Food was plentiful in the warm climate and they felt no sense of urgency about any of their activities. They had long forgotten about Da, and her being captured and absorbed into the group, but her introduction of the unusual trait of compassion had been noted and remembered. Her offspring had passed it on to their succeeding generations. It was steadily being distributed throughout the group following the continuing promiscuity of the mature adults. It was sometimes the subject and cause of criticism amongst the male warriors, who prided themselves on their own strength and ability to defend the group by killing any possible aggressors. Compassion was considered to be an indication of the female outlook on life, suitable for the females only, not for the males.

Within the two centuries after the short life of Da, some of the group had started to develop their mental abilities. Each individual was then given a grunt for a name at birth. New words had been introduced into their very small vocabulary and these were used more and more by each new generation. The younger ones had then discovered that they could hold limited communication with each other without the elders reading their words telepathically. It had created a more independent attitude amongst the youngsters, and the reactions from the older ones were very mixed. The observer members of the Committee watched this with great interest. The deliberate change in the method of communication indicated both a growing awareness of 'cause and effect' and an ability to apply mental reasoning during their decision-making.

The Gyps went about their usual daily life, completely unaware of the observation being carried out by the Tall Ones, and they enjoyed being the occupants of the productive valley where they had spent the past few years. The open valley was full of lush growth of vegetation nourishing many different species of animals. The wide river flowed from a freshwater lake, which was many moons walking to the south of them. It then turned to the direction of the rising sun and eventually poured into the saltwater sea.

The successful and confident Gyps had often needed to protect their valley from invaders from other groups, and they had done this with determination and the strength of numbers. Their reactions had been automatic. Under strong leaders, who were growing in intelligence, their telepathic messages of alarm spread almost instantly, from those who first saw any strangers, to every single member of their large group. Reaction was immediate. Weapons were collected and every adult fighting member rushed to the scene of any such invasion.

Usually, it was a case of another itinerant group accidentally wandering into the Gyp territory. The sight of the organised defendants rushing forward, with their stone weapons held high, was usually sufficient to cause the strangers to turn round and move quickly and steadily away from the danger. Any hesitation would result in the killing of many male adults, and the capture of any females who were too slow to escape.

Roh had been the selected leader of the Gyps for almost ten years. His ability to learn from experience had helped him to develop his skills to the point where there had been no attempt to depose him for most of that period. He had identified and promoted a few potential leaders, giving them training for the responsibility of jobs that would help them to enjoy that promotion.

One such job was the exploration of the large rift valley to the north.

A lively twenty-year-old called Hsu was told to take a small group of six males, of similar age, to explore the valley. They were to travel north for four days and then turn to the setting sun and go in that direction for two moons. The purpose of the journey was to discover what the valley contained that could be of benefit for the Gyps. They were to avoid being seen or captured by any of the local inhabitants. Whilst they had permission to capture any isolated females that came their way these must be used quickly and disposed of before their males might react. Whatever happened, Hsu and his group were expected back within five moons. All these instructions were given to them telepathically so that each one was fully aware of the details. Any attempt to give them verbally would have resulted in doubts, mainly because of the inadequate vocabulary.

The group of explorers set off after a night of farewells with their mates. They were soon out of sight but they and the remaining group were mentally aware of each other's interests.

Hsu led them, in line, at the casual pace used when hunting, although they were carrying sufficient supplies of meat for two days and had no need to hunt for a kill. He felt no sense of urgency, only a strange awareness of being promoted. He was now the leader. Even the fact that he had received instructions was rather odd. Usually they relaxed when hunting, up to the point where a quarry was sighted and the message was instantly received by them all, 'stand still'! The first four days passed very quickly.

The weather had been mild, as usual, and the terrain had hardly changed. The ground had been sloping downwards very slightly up to that point when they reached a wide river flowing towards the setting sun. Hsu decided to camp near the water for the night and they started to eat the meat from the previous day's hunt. No other bipeds had been seen but there had been frequent sightings of herds of the medium sized food animals. These were in quickly moving groups that survived for that reason. The hominids knew very well that only the careful setting of a planned ambush would catch perhaps one or two of them.

The night was spent sheltering in some large trees, which were established near the edge of the freshwater river. Heavy rain fell throughout the dark hours giving the travellers little sleep and a surprise when the dawn broke. The rain had also been falling further upstream and it had built the level of the river to the point where the water was now swirling around their trees. Hsu looked down into the torrent and he could see a dead animal being eaten by a scaly monster with its large jaws full of sharp teeth. The others saw it also. They looked at Hsu and he knew that this was his first test of leading the group. The water did not appear to be very deep but he had no intention of risking any lives by trying to wade to the edge of the water, many hands of paces to the south. He climbed to nearer the top of the tree and assessed the chances of moving through them. Yes! There was a possible way through the branches. He signalled to the other six to start moving along the larger branches, towards the south.

Hsu indicated that he was going to lead them through the branches, back to the dry ground. It was second nature to him. His ancestors had spent most of their time living in the security of the trees. He edged his way along a large branch until his weight caused the thinning wood to bend downwards, towards a similar branch on the nearest neighbouring tree. Letting go of his grip, he grasped the new branch, which sagged with his weight, and he was soon moving along it until he was near the trunk of the new tree. He looked back and saw that the others were now following his path and copying his methods.

Continuing to move through the trees, Hsu was very soon at the edge of the wooded area and looking across a few paces of open water to the firm ground. He waited until the others of the group were near before he climbed down the tree and stood in the murky water, which reached up to his chest. Remembering the nightmare creature with the huge jaws he waded, as quickly as possible, to the edge of the water, and he was soon standing there, on firm land. The other six followed suit. One by one they dropped into the water and splashed their way towards Hsu. Aig was the last one to leave the tree, and he was the unlucky one. He was halfway across the stretch of water when he screamed and disappeared. The water was in turmoil. The scaly tail of the monster and the body and limbs of Aig were occasionally seen in the upheaval, but it was over very quickly. Hsu looked at the other survivors who were all shocked. They had suffered their first casualty. They all moved away from the edge of the water and Hsu started to lead them in the direction of where the sun would set that night. Whilst they were all used to seeing the death of their group members, this was the first time they had suffered from an attack of the water creature. They would not forget it.

Moving forward at the leisurely pace of casual hunting, the reduced group of six Gyps settled into the routine of the day. They had saved their stones, and this fact helped them to accumulate the surplus meat that would last them for another three days. The valley was well stocked with easily killed animals. Hsu had registered in his memory that this part of the main valley would be an ideal area for the main group of Gyps to be established, if they ever needed to move from their present valley. Hunting was even easier here. Possibly this was because there were no other hominids to be seen nearby.

The journey along the south bank of the river continued for half a moon, until there was a change in the smell of the air. They all stopped and sniffed. It was a new and puzzling odour. Looking well ahead, they could see that the skyline was changing from being flat, with some slight undulations, to a blue range of hills well ahead of them. As they moved nearer to those hills, the colour changed slowly from blue to green and a faint skyline of mountains was appearing behind those hills. And they were blue. The river continued to flow in the same direction but it was wider and slower. Gradually the river appeared to stop flowing. It became the start of a wide lake, which went ahead of the travellers to reach the hills in front of them. The strange smell became stronger and more irritating to their nostrils at the same time that the ground became softer from being waterlogged.

Hsu applied his leadership experience. Water could be dangerous. The ground would be safer if they were moving at a higher level. He changed direction to lead his group to the south, until he knew that they were well away from the lake. He then turned towards the setting sun again. They continued until nearly dusk before they had their last food for the day. The failing light gave them a new surprise. The dark clouds that they had seen on the high land ahead of them were now glowing red and orange. The colours flickered amongst the cloud and each male looked at the others, mentally asking if they were as frightened as he was. They were all trembling with fear.

Roh was receiving the awareness of this situation, back in the home territory, but he was unable to give any return message, other than sympathy. They were alone with their problem. This was another test for Hsu.

The six of them huddled together in a large tree, well away

from the water, supporting each other throughout the long night. Dawn came and their confidence started to return. The dark clouds remained on the mountains but they were no longer showing the flashing lights that had puzzled them. Climbing to the top of their tree, they could see some new items of interest. Firstly, there was a new river flowing into the lake and this came from the west, the direction in which they should be moving. It seemed that the lake was being fed from all directions. It must be the lowest point in the valley. Also, they could see large numbers of hominids, at the other side of this river, all moving away from the high land with the demon clouds of the night. They appeared to be agitated, looking to the rear at frequent intervals. Hsu wondered about the cause of their fear, was it the lights in the cloud on the mountains? Strangely, he was able to detect some of the stress running through the minds of these new creatures. He, and the other five with him, received pictures of the hillside opening up and burning rocks pouring out in abundance. They had never seen a volcano erupting before and they were as frightened as the strangers obviously were. Masses of red-hot rocks and ashes had been seen to be spouting out of the ground to a great height, then the strong wind had taken control and blown the waste matter towards the rising sun before falling back, down to the ground. The trees and bushes in the undergrowth had immediately burst into flame and the fires had spread rapidly in all directions. This was the start of the building of a mountainous mass that would be known Sicily some millions of years ahead.

Hsu had only one thought in his small mind. He must take his group as far from this place of terror as possible, and as quickly as possible. They all followed him as he ran towards the south where he could see some slight rise in the level of the land. They ran at varying speeds for most of that day. He decided that it was safe to stop in some woodland, when the sun was setting, and they ate the remainder of the meat that they had carried with them. One or two of them stayed awake at intervals throughout the dark hours but they each had some sleep and were more rested by the dawn.

Once again, they started to move to the west. Not one of them even thought of changing the plan. The usual routine of hunting and moving steadily in their chosen direction continued for another moon, until they realised that they were in the hunting grounds of a group of strangers.

Khi was the first one to see them. He was the darkest skinned of the six of them and he had the shortest black curling head-hair. Some of the others had their vision obstructed at times by their straighter, and longer, hair hanging over their faces. Their body hair never seemed to grow very long and it did not cause any such problems.

Khi grunted and pointed down a shallow valley ahead of them. "Gna, Gna," he said, mentally, and they all stood very still, looking firstly at the strange females and then at Hsu, wondering what his reaction would be. They had been without any sexual relief for too long and Hsu was well aware of this. He instantly agreed with the others. They all needed some Gna and he led the way forward, mentally giving them his immediate reactions to the possibilities.

"We all need some Gna. We have never been without easy relief being available for such a long time. Yes! We will take it. But let us make sure that we are successful and that we get away from here afterwards without any problems from their males. We cannot lose any more of this small group if we are going to complete the job that we were given." They were moving steadily, down the slope towards their targets, when Hsu gave them a sudden shock. "Let's remember how well we manage this part of our pleasure back with the main group of Gyps. We always seem to make better enjoyment for ourselves by preparing the females before we grab hold of them, don't we? They all seem to prefer to be pleasant with each other for most of the time, something to do with what they call compassion. Take the lead from me when we get nearer to them. Don't get hold of any of them until I give the word." The other mentally gave their agreement and wondered if the strange females would be receiving the same signals.

They must have received something if only an awareness of possible danger, whilst they were collecting useful stones and a few sparse nuts that were still on the branches of the trees and bushes. They were working in silence, spread over the open ground, when one of the small females saw the approaching Gyps. She gave a short squeal of alarm and pointed to them walking slowly down the hill slope towards them. Hsu raised his left arm, which was not carrying his stone, and showed the empty hand to the five females. At the same time he turned slightly in the direction that would take them past the targets, but still within a few paces of them, on the higher side of the slope.

The ploy appeared to work. The fact that the strange males had made a friendly gesture, instead of rushing straight at them, and had then shown that they were preparing to walk past them, all reassured them. They waited. Curiosity kept them there. They wondered if these new males were from one of the nearby groups with which they sometimes had meetings. Those occasions usually resulted in an orgy of mating and subsequent new babies, with new blood that helped to build stronger adults.

Their thoughts of mating were received by the Gyps, who immediately sent out all the usual mental return signals, without needing any encouragement from Hsu. He knew that they were going to succeed and he sat down where he was, signalling with his hand for the tallest of the females to come to him. She hesitated for a brief moment and then walked slowly towards him with a smile on her face. The other females followed her. They could see that the naked males were all becoming aroused and there was an overpowering urge to unite with these strangers.

There was a total of eight females and two of them were pushed aside by their stronger sisters to wait their turn. The laughing, excited Gyps shared their pleasure with all eight of the strangers, more than once, until they all found themselves resting and relaxing in the afternoon sun. They shared the remains of their food with their new mates, confirming the pleasure of the day. None of them seemed to want to move, but Hsu gave the signal that they must continue their journey. The females tried to pull them down the valley, towards where they knew they would find the remainder of their group, but he would not be led in that direction. He turned his men towards the setting sun and they were a long march away before they rested for that night.

The diversion of the sexual activity had a refreshing effect on the whole group. Each one of them had a feeling of well being, combined with the urge to make progress in the main task that they had been given. They hunted willingly and easily, whilst continuing to move in the westerly direction. Their diet was supplemented by eating any nuts that they found on the trees, also, they ate the contents of the occasional eggs that had been laid in nests in the branches of the same trees. It did not matter whether the eggs contained the formed chicks or the natural food that was put there at the time that the egg had been laid. The varied diet was good for them.

At no time did they suffer any real threat from the larger predators, mostly of the cat family, as they appeared to any creature that came near that they were a disciplined and determined force that expressed itself with a strong mental communications skill. Easier prey for the carnivores was almost always available nearby.

The daily routine of hunting and walking rapidly to the west continued, with the group arriving very near to the great saltwater sea at the end of the second moon of their journey. They had not been deflected from the route by any more diversions. In fact, they had seen only two more groups of strangers since the afternoon with the female pleasures. Both of them had been hunting parties who had warned them of their existence by the telepathic noises of the hunt. Hsu had taken no chances of losing any more of his team and had led them out of the way of any possible danger. His mental reports to Roh, back at their base, had been received and noted. When the group had filled their lungs with the salt-laden air from the big sea ahead of them, Roh had been curious enough about the strange new smell that he urged them to continue to the west for a few more days.

That short time was sufficient to allow the six Gyps to continue along the side of the mountains on their left until they reached a sight that none of them had ever experienced before. They arrived on the sandy beach facing the endless waves of the ocean. The salty smell of the western winds was blowing into their faces and they did not understand what was happening to them. They needed water to drink and here in front of them was an endless supply. Not just a stream, a river or a lake, but the whole world in front of them was water; a live moving mass of water which picked itself up into the air and then threw itself down on to the ground, for them to do what they wished with it. The noise of it alone was frightening.

But, they were thirsty. Hsu started to run down the slope of the beach until he was standing ankle deep in the shallow brine. The others followed suit and they all bent down to cup the water in their hands and drink it in gulps. The reaction was the same for them all. Their stomachs revolted and they vomited the foul tasting fluid on to the ground with cries of horror. With their minds in turmoil and feeling the urgent need for some fresh water, they turned to the north where they could see some hilly ground. Their hope of finding a small stream of fresh water was answered, and they washed away the last of the awful taste of the sea.

Hsu decided to spend the remainder of the day and that night resting and eating from their stock of meat. He also wanted time to think about the situation. They could not move any further in the westerly direction. They had reached the limit of their journey in time as well as in land. It was about time for them to start to move in the direction of their home hunting grounds. His curiosity was making him think about the situation.

What was to the north? What was to the south? Looking towards the north east, he could see the western end of the huge valley through which they had travelled, whether they had been actually down in the lower land or moving along the foothills of the mountains. The low ground reached to the point just below where they now found themselves. As he looked down into the valley, he was aware that the enormous mass of salt water behind him was at a level that was higher than the valley.

The night was spent with the group sheltering in some scrubland near the stream. They all had a sense of achievement at having reached the limits of their task, but they felt in no mood for turning round and rushing back to retrace their steps. They were content when Hsu informed them that he was going to look to the north for another day or two.

Keeping the salt sea on their left side, they walked steadily in the chosen direction. Khi grunted and pointed to his left. The sandy beach had changed in appearance. It was now covered with pebbles of a wide range of colours and sizes, ranging from very small to larger, hand-sized ones. The amazing thing about them was that they were all nicely rounded. The hominids did not understand that they had been rubbed together by the action of the waves over a period of millions of years. They were merely intrigued by the quantity and pleased to find so many weapons offered so freely.

Chuckling at the novelty, they started to pick up the smaller stones and throw them, one at a time, at a large boulder higher up the beach. They soon improved their aim and became able to hit the target with almost every one of the projectiles. The effort had the effect of tiring them and they stopped in order to have some of their food, squatting on the ground and handling the various sizes of stones. Ghea was sitting well away from the others, near the target boulder, when Khi picked up a small pebble and threw it casually at him. They were all surprised to see Ghea fall over and lie still. They instantly knew that he was no longer aware of them. Their mental knowledge recorded a blank and they all ran up to where he was lying on the stones. Yes. He was dead. The cut on his forehead, where the stone had hit him, was oozing blood. The rest of the group looked at Khi and he realised what he had done. A thought, meaning, "magic", went through the remaining five males. What had they found? Did a thrown stone become a new method of killing? They decided that it did exactly that!

Hsu indicated that they should each pick up only two hand-sized stones to carry away with them. They then made a small hollow in the stony beach and laid Ghea gently in it, before covering his body with a mound of the larger stones.

The saddened five then started to resume the planned journey to explore the way to the north. It proved to be very enlightening. They had only travelled for one day when their path was barred by an impassable water barrier.

They had been walking to the north, with the roar of the ocean on their left and the low lying land of the valley on their right, when they came up to the barrier. There was a fast moving flow of salt water coming from the left, through a fissure in the ground, and flowing to their right to form a waterfall into the valley. The water was moving so rapidly that it shot out into the space above the valley in a jet. The force of the water was having the effect of eroding the sides of the channel which were falling into it and being washed away at a high speed. The hominids moved back as soon as they realised what was happening. They did not understand anything about water levels or geography but they always reacted quickly to any frightening event. The noise and the speed of the water flow, added to the nasty experience of the taste of the useless water from the sea, gave panic signals to them all instantly. They rushed back to the south for a day until they were again on rising land in the foothills of the mountains. There was no indication from any one of them that they should do anything other than start the long return journey home. This they did.

During the first day they could hear that the noise of the seawater, spurting into the valley, was getting quieter as they moved away from it, towards the east, until there was a very loud, long rumble that became a roar. They did not understand what had happened. They could not realise that the erosion of the sides and bottom of the channel had allowed more and more water to flow from the sea, until the top of the ridge crumbled and fell into the valley.
With the high tide, enormous quantities of seawater broke over the ridge, taking more of it away and letting even larger amounts of water to flood into the valley. It was a major disaster for anything living in the previously sheltered valley.

The small group of Gyps had been wise to remain on the higher ground for their return journey. They had been aware that there were strange demons following behind them, creating awful noises, particularly on their left. They continued to run towards the east and the noises followed them closely. Four days later, they could sense that the demons were coming nearer to them when they saw some of the tumult of flowing seawater. It appeared to be boiling. Broken trees and branches were floating on the surface. Dead animals and a few hominids could be seen amongst the flotsam.

The Gyps kept moving on to even higher ground in order to get away from the noises and the sight of mayhem, and they kept running until they dropped from sheer exhaustion. After a short rest, they started the usual procedure of hunting whilst continuing their journey to the east. The water moved more quickly in the valley.

Rho had been alerted to the disaster by the telepathic messages from Hsu and the other four males. He immediately ordered the entire group of the Gyps, remaining in the home hunting grounds, to move upstream, on to higher ground. They had no accumulation of artefacts other than a few spare stones. Babies were picked up as the large group of more than one hundred souls moved as ordered. They were just in time. The foul salt waters had reached the other end of the huge valley, carrying all before them, and sweeping into the land that the Gyps had only just vacated. The debris that was deposited on the edge of the waters showed that there were many groups of creatures similar to themselves who had been eliminated. Each survivor felt the awareness of the loss of related beings. They, in turn, thanked Rho for being the leader who had sent the team with Hsu at the right time to warn of the approaching dangers.

CHAPTER SEVEN
COMMITTEE DECISION

Ywancontin called the meeting of the Development Committee.

"*You have been invited here in order to receive the observation reports from the individual members for the 5mBC period. We can then consider recommendations for any adjustment and come to a conclusion, ready for implementation after approval. Bearing in mind the reports from our previous meetings, we should refresh our minds with the main points that were raised. Will you please start, Bevak?*"

It pleased Bevak to be asked to be the first to speak. He smiled, remembering all the earthly activities that he had actually experienced, whilst occupying one of the small but lively hominoid bodies.

"*There is no doubt, in my mind, that the two strong traits of self defence and the reproductive urge are essential for the survival of this species. They can both become troublesome in times ahead, perhaps when the planet is covered by many millions of these creatures, but that would become apparent nearer that time. We should not to take any action at this time in order to suppress them. There is a continual need to encourage the different groups to move around the planet, to explore and learn from their experiences. This will help their brains to be developed by being used. They will react to the different situations that they find. Such stimulation will help in their survival and future progress.*

I have spent time, recently, with the few groups of hominids, that were to the north of the rift valley before it was flooded, and I would like to comment on their chances of survival. We know that they originated from stray small groups that had moved north from the forests of the African landmass. The majority of them were eliminated in the flooding. The few groups that were beyond the reach of the waters all show signs of promising progress. Some of them had been safely positioned for some hundreds of years and had been developing their own paths, unaware of what has been happening in the rest of the planet. They make the right cyclical movements to the north and back again to match the annual climatic changes. Their numbers are growing steadily each year and they are capable of meeting natural disasters, if and when they should occur. The more heavily populated areas are in the parts of Africa, which we have covered, and in the eastern land of the Utee.

In each of those areas there are a few thousand of the creatures, living in groups of up to a maximum of about one hundred souls. (Not exactly to be described as 'heavily populated'.) They have a growing awareness of psychic phenomena. The creatures' brains are simply not yet ready to absorb such knowledge and, I know, Mellak has more to say on that topic, so may I leave it for him to report more fully on that point?"

The Chairman nodded to Bevak and Mellak started.

"Thank you. I would like to record something of the shock experienced by all those who observed the flooding of the rift valley. The enormous volume of water, rushing from the ocean and filling the lower ground, destroyed approximately 20% of the hominoid population of the planet. Some of them had been on ground which is above the water level, but they were drowned by the huge wave that rushed towards the eastern end of the valley.

It was of interest to hear that Hsu was the only survivor of the six explorers who had seen the seawater breaking through the barrier. It appears that the remaining five of the group had been making steady progress to the east when they realised that they were again in the land of the willing Gnas. The thought, the desire and the agreement were in all their minds immediately. Unfortunately for them, the male hunting party nearby could read the lustful messages.

Hsu and the others quickly read the anger of the hunters and knew that they had become the quarry. They scattered and ran. Four of them were caught and despatched.

The interesting lesson to learn from this experience was that, when the males used the traits of warmth and compassion, they received the benefit of love from the stranger females. They had not locked it into their minds that, without applying those traits, they would not have enjoyed those pleasures. They paid the price. It remains to be seen whether Hsu will deduce the facts for himself. His brain was certainly stimulated by the experiences of the journey.

There was one benefit from their travels that will develop with the passage of time. Seed from the Gyps was sown in areas that they had not previously visited. This will continue to be scattered by the normal method of promiscuity. We will be able to recognise the effect of different climatic changes on groups of a similarly basic nature. There will continue to be the required result that all groups, from all parts of the planet, will be able to interbreed successfully, into the indefinite future. There will be an infinite range of colours, blends, of all possible types of hominoid creatures. They will all be put to the many tests for survival. The eventual survivors will inherit the earth.

The question arises, will they be anything like what is intended?" Another smile came from Ywancontin. *"Marcus?"*

"During the period under review, a number of milestones have been noted and their importance should be highlighted. These creatures are showing signs of the real mental progress being made under very mixed conditions. For example, we have seen forward planning, and execution of that plan. The leader of the Gyps decided to have the fertile rift valley explored, in a very basic way, and this decision had some beneficial results. He was able to give orders for his plan to be carried out, the orders were obeyed, almost to the letter, and communications were maintained over the full period of the exercise. All those who were aware of the activities recognised that they received warning of the floods in time to save themselves only because of Roh's control and discipline. His leadership and enterprise saved the group for the future. Locked into their subconscious is the memory of an appalling flood disaster, which eliminated a large percentage of the planet's biped population. This memory will be retained through the future generations, until the time of their acquiring the ability to speak fluently. Later still, it will be recorded in the written word, as a partial explanation of the development of mankind. In a similar way, the memory of the tall, hairy Yutee will be carried forward to the time of modern man.

The most obvious of current changes in the nature of these creatures is their ability to use the knowledge that they acquire and apply it to the decision making required for some entirely different project. This is proof of the fact that their brains are growing and that they are using the increased mental capacity. I am content with the choice of these hominids as the potential leaders amongst the mammals. We have the facility to monitor each of them indefinitely. That is my recommendation."

The Chairman inclined his head and asked Lucus for his views.

"The mental and physical development is most interesting," started Lucus. "Throughout the period of this study, we have seen indications that the biological and mental processes have been moving forward, in the desired direction. Trial and error, accident and recovery have all helped 'nature' to take its course. That is a procedure that we wished to see established. Actions, followed by reaction, have become the automatic process that has developed throughout the many millions of years prior to this date. All this now continues. Each new experience helps to educate and improve the brain of all those who are aware of it. Some of the genes of the more experienced creatures will pass the abilities forward to the offspring.

If it is desired, there is the possibility of introducing some skills, abilities or traits into the souls of the embryos prior to birth. We can keep this idea in reserve. I would recommend that it should be retained, but for use only where it becomes essential to avoid a major disaster. That could be considered part of the eternal spiritual law?

It appears likely that the hominids will continue to make progress, learning from experience. They can take as much time as may be required, to learn to accept instructions from their leaders, and that the application of discipline has benefits for all concerned. And the leaders will need to learn the dangers of the misuse of total power and the arrogance that may grow from it." Lucus inclined his head towards the Chairman.

"Will Solem now let us hear his thoughts". Ywancontin looked across to the fifth member, awaiting his words.

"We have touched upon the subject of the hominoid spirit prior to birth," he said, "and I feel that we should open this up a little more so that we are fully aware of the possibilities that face us.

The basic facts are that these creatures are, as yet, totally unaware that their bodies are merely containers for their eternal spirits. They are fully aware that their lives can be, and often are, *ended very abruptly after very few years of growth. Some of them still look upon the bodies of others as a source of nourishment, or for the satisfaction of their own carnal lusts. At times of food shortage, there are occasions when a group has survived because the members consumed the flesh of their own offspring, or that of the elders who were nearly past their peak of physical health. That tendency seems to have faded a little since compassion was first introduced, but the memory is still with them. Cannibalism may still recur, under certain circumstances. It has not yet occurred to them that death is anything other than the end for the particular individual. They may feel sorrow, or deprivation, when they lose the companionship of a group member. They do not ask Spirit why it has happened. They do not yet have any awareness of the existence of God.*

They are very much aware that there are happenings that they do not understand. The telepathic awareness of a visit from one of this Committee is apparent when they panic at the sight of a tall one. We have tried to avoid that sort of awareness of our presence, but mistakes are sometimes made, and we have left some of them with a fear of the 'unknown'. There are times when a few of them attempt to find an explanation for various happenings, disasters such as earthquakes, volcanic eruptions and stampedes of herds of large animals. They try to blame imaginary creatures such as 'bogeymen' and dragons, which have been absorbed into their group memories.

When they reach the end of mortal life, their spirits soon adjust to the 'return home' and they quickly show interest in the situation that they have very recently left on the planet. This begins to fade when they realise that they are unable to make any effective contact with those on the earth plane. Their mental processes and abilities are not changed by transition to the spiritual plane. Only a very few of them show any desire to return to live the harsh and dangerous way of life back on the Earth. Perhaps we can permit a limited number of them to be reborn and experience another life and it would be interesting to check on whether there is any memory transferred with them at the second birth. We know that spiritual law does not permit that. I believe the system should be tested at regular intervals and we would then be aware of any improvement in the development of those who have had the benefit of more than one

Earth life."

Solem bowed and looked across at Surtyn, the last member to speak. Ywancontin nodded and Surtyn gave his views.

"There is little for me to add to the debate other than congratulate my colleagues on covering the majority of the points that I had noted. I agree with them. I am sure that the traits that are established are vital to the survival of those under our study. I believe that it is necessary for us to continue to monitor the effect of experience on each creature. They must help in their own brain development. I recommend that they are encouraged to create language, because aural communication, later followed by the written word, will surely help to speed up the growth in the number of new brain cells in each head. Progress will advance geometrically, rather than arithmetically. That will also bring its own problems and it will enforce the need for the individual monitoring that I have already mentioned.

It is possible that the regular use of speech will have the side effect of reducing the use of telepathy for normal communication. There will still be a trace of the ability to speak mentally. It could even recede into a simple form of 'mind-reading', to the consternation of some of those who have lost the ability, but it will be possible to reintroduce some of the skill when the spiritual ones practise their clairvoyance. That, of course, is well into the future. Telepathy will still be available, for the purposes of study. It has been used for aeons, during the movement of the shoals of some fish, also with some flocks of birds. It will not be lost to the world as a skill.

We should also give some time and thought to the fact that the large continental plate is floating westwards, away from the main landmass, and that it will eventually find itself approaching the same landmass in the east. Contact will first be made in the north. The plate, which will be known in the distant future as the Americas, has its own range of creatures, which are developing and evolving in their own way. The bipeds do not yet show the same promise that we have seen in those included in this review and they might not be suitable for long term planning. They tend to grow so much larger than the subjects of our recent study and that size did not show any great promise with the Yutee of the east. Time will tell.

The point that I would like to make is that, during the next one or two million years, the two continents will meet in the north. It will then be possible for a few groups to be moved across, from the east, as we see it, on to the newly arrived continent. It appears that the Utee are sufficiently adaptable to suit our purpose. They are growing in numbers and skills. They are survivors. They would be able to continue to live naturally in a land that is full of fresh water and food supplies, awaiting the attention of the hunters. Some of them would be able to move steadily, over a long period, from the point of crossing in the north to the far south of the continental plate. The scattered groups would develop in their own way and become established over a long period. I ask that this suggestion be recorded and kept under consideration."

"You have made a valuable contribution to this meeting, Surtyn," said Ywancontin. "I thank you all for the points that you have made and which will be studied and given the fullest consideration. There are a few points that I would like to be added to the record.

The small numbers of hominid groups that were left to the north of the rift valley flooding will find themselves living under similar conditions of varying temperatures and climatic extremes to those of the Utee in the east. They will tend to become migratory and will experience similar testing during the cold spells. They will change and adapt in order to survive. Those that try to avoid so much movement might find that they develop new trends such as different colours of hair and skin. Their brains will develop in different ways. New skills, both physical and mental, will appear and be improved. The infinite range of human types will be to the advantage of all. Yet they will retain the ability to mate and produce offspring from the diverse range of mankind that we shall see throughout the planet. This, in turn, will create even more variations for further development.

On the more difficult subject of spiritual contact with these various developing types of hominids, I hear the points that you have raised. I agree that there will be the possibility of accelerating the rate of growth of the brain, if there is regular contact from free spirits. It could also happen that a 'wayward' creature could be nudged back on to the right path, if it was considered to be essential. We must always bear in mind that there should be no forced interference with the right of free will. I am inclined to recommend that the soul of each creature will have a spiritual guide (or helper) made available for support, when it is either required or requested. This can take the form of 'an inner voice' or conscience. Such a trial may commence immediately. The spirits taking part in the trial will monitor it automatically. This committee will next meet in the year designated 4mBC."

CHAPTER EIGHT
4mBC

The continual search for food and water was a way of life for the biped creatures that roamed the north coastline on the flooded rift valley. During the past few thousands of years they had settled into wandering groups, each of up to two or three hundred adults at the most. Hunting the small and medium sized animals usually produced sufficient nourishment for them to maintain their strength in numbers. That was important for survival. They were subject to suffering losses of the most productive adults for a variety of reasons. Hunting accidents and casualties from fighting other groups were the most serious causes of loss amongst the males. The females sometimes never recovered from giving birth to their offspring, and they were pregnant for most of their adult years. Few of them lived for thirty years. They all had a short, brutal life, and yet there was a serious side to their mental attitudes.

The strong instincts of, firstly, self-defence had enabled the strongest groups to survive. Secondly, the constant urge to mate and reproduce had ensured the growing numbers of births. Mother-love and compassion had continued to spread amongst these creatures and had helped to maximise the number of survivors. The males had continued to enjoy the thrill of battle with any strange creatures, whether they were food animals or bipeds of a similar appearance to themselves. They also enjoyed casual sex with any stranger females that they were able to catch during their hunting forays.

Communication within each group, or tribe, had become less and less dependent upon telepathy, as the use of verbal names had developed. Thought reading was still used at vital times during the hunt or when defending themselves against the attack from another group, but there was a deliberate attempt not to use it when there was a risk of the thoughts being read by an enemy. It appeared that, as the bipeds' brains were growing in size and efficiency, they were using the improved capacity in order to increase their opportunities for survival. That seemed to be the result.

THE PATH

The tribe of Gols had been well established in the mountainous region near the big salt sea for many generations. They had found the cave system by mistake and had quickly adapted it for their own use.

Two hands of them had been chasing a small furry animal, when the leading Gol, named Puit, and the quarry, had both disappeared from sight. The others soon came up to the place where they had last seen Puit and they stopped, just as they were about to follow him into a hole in the ground. They had discovered crevasses and caves in the mountainous areas before now, often using them for temporary shelter, but this was the first time that they found a hole that went straight down into the ground. The entrance was overgrown with grass and a small bush and Puit would not have noticed it when following his quarry. Maw called down to him and he heard a grunt of pain in reply.

He removed some of the cover and was able to peer down to see that the hole was wide enough for him to climb down to the injured friend. He was lying on a rocky ledge and the hole continued to go further into the ground, but at an angle, which would make it easier to climb further down. Most of the Gols remained on the surface. They did not feel very brave when in the dark, especially in a strange tunnel. Two of them had followed Maw into the hole and they tried to help Puit, who had only suffered a severe bruising, and shock from being 'eaten by the ground'.

Maw had a curious nature and he realised that his vision was quickly becoming adapted to the poor light. The clearing of the growth at the entrance to the hole had allowed more daylight to filter through to where he was sitting and he now could see that there was a much larger empty space ahead of him. He sniffed at the dank air and could find no trace of the smell of predators. The big cats had not found the hideout. His immediate reaction was the thought; 'here is a good place to hide, if we want to do so'.

None of them wanted to explore any more at that time but they placed three large stones around the opening in order to make sure that they would be able to find it again. They all looked around, in every direction, mentally marking all the possible landmarks. The tribe would be fully informed about the find and they would decide if there would be any value in visiting the site again.

On the short journey back to join the main party of their tribe there were murmurs of doubt about the recent experience.

Vaya, 'the one who could see things', said, "It is not good to be eaten by the ground. There are bad things down there, waiting for the food to walk into their mouth. Let us never go near that place again". Puit laughed at the comment. "The only food that walked into the hole was the long legged 'furry' that I was chasing. I would have killed it if I had not fallen. Anyway, you can often see things that none of the others can see. Go and tell your story to the females. They will listen to you."

This referred to the fact that Vaya had sometimes told stories of seeing things in the dark. He called them the 'tall ones' and told of seeing them just when he was about to go to sleep. The nervous members of the tribe, mainly the females, worried about these visions, but the more aggressive males criticised him for his weaknesses. Some of them told stories of two-headed, sabre-toothed cats that would wander about, during the night, looking for frightened bipeds to be used for food. Vaya ignored the criticism, knowing very well that he really had seen the tall ones more than once. He always felt comforted by their presence, never afraid. There were occasions when he believed that they had spoken to him and given good advice. He did not try to explain this to the doubters. A few days later, he was about to be surprised and to be proved wrong about his dislike for the underground hole that Puit had discovered.

Both the males were part of a hunting party when they realised that two giant cats were stalking them. They were instantly on the alert, looking for an escape, when Puit remembered that they were near the recently discovered 'hole in the ground'. With a quick "follow me", he led the way to the marked entrance and was the first to go down, out of sight. The others followed. Their doubts about going into the ground were overshadowed by the sight of the two big cats tearing towards them. They had only just built a pile of large rocks inside the entrance to the hole when the carnivores arrived and started to tear at the barrier with their long fangs.

Vaya immediately started to pile some more of the rocks in the narrowest section of the tunnel. The others understood his reasons and joined in strengthening the defences. There was still a small hole there when the first cat pushed its snout into the darkness, sniffing the smell of fear coming from within the dark passage. With another example of quick thinking, Puit hurled a well-aimed sharp stone and hit the cat on the nose. The immediate result was that the first cat disappeared, only to be replaced by the second one. The defenders simply gave it the same treatment, which not only broke off one of its sabre teeth, but also blinded it in the eye. It withdrew with a howl that could be heard fading as it ran away.

During this time in the hole, the hunters' sight had adjusted to the darkness and they were able to make out some of the limits of tunnel. Those who had penetrated the farthest found that they could stand upright without being able to touch the roof. They were in a large cave system, which penetrated into the utmost blackness. A new kind of fear overtook them. Were they going to be taken into the ground and dropped down an even bigger hole? Vaya came to the rescue. He had a feeling of safety and confidence.

He was aware of the presence of one of the 'tall ones'. He calmly told his companions, "Cave good, cats gone. Join others".

He was right. He had faith in those that he saw, but he knew that the others did not 'see' his helpers and he had the wisdom not to talk about his secret. It was possible that he lived longer for keeping it to himself.

When they rejoined the main group of Gols, those who had been saved from the cats all made a point of telling them about their experience. They were unable to use grammatical tenses, and they mostly spoke as if in the present tense, but they were able to pass the message that there was a real benefit for the tribe if they were shown the entrance to the cave for any future retreat from danger. That was done immediately.

Each member, infant and adult, was shown the three big marker-stones and made to enter the passage down into the earth. Without a portable light none of them would go far into the cave and they all showed pleasure when they emerged back into the daylight.

They felt an excitement after having been involved in a planning exercise for spreading some new knowledge that would benefit them all. It was a new experience for them and it helped to stimulate more mental activity.

Soon after the experience in the cave the leader of this tribe of Gols decided that they should make another annual journey to the northern coast in order to replenish their stocks of fighting stones. Many generations ago they had discovered a stock of rounded stones on the beach that could be aimed very accurately at any target they wished to damage. They were unaware of the fact that these stones had been ground into the useful rounded shape by their continual movement of the salt sea waves. Their origin did not really interest them. All they knew was that there were always sufficient for their needs whenever they sought them.

The usual procedure was to hunt on the journey to the big sea and have a feast on arrival at the top of the rocky cliff. This normally resulted in a night of mating activity, as a celebration of the end of the long journey. The next morning they would all climb down the cliff and gather more stones than they could possibly carry away. After some time spent sorting them, the rejects were used for target practice aiming at some of the shellfish to be found amongst the rocky cliffs. This would start another feast of the shellfish, added to the crabs and the other unusual foods that they had found. After that the group would begin their long trek back to the usual hunting grounds.

On this occasion, there was a different experience. They had arrived on the sandy beach as the tide was receding. The small bay had been filled with a shoal of fish that had not moved quickly enough away from the water's edge and Puit had seen them. He quickly signalled to the others who followed him, in a single line, into the water, between the fish and their chance of escape into the deeper water. Walking back towards the beach, splashing the water with their hands, they drove many of the fish into the shallows and they were then able to catch some of them and throw them on to the sand.

The excitement and laughter lasted throughout an orgy of killing. That was until there was a scream of fear from Puit, who was in the deepest water, the farthest from the beach. He had stumbled over a submerged rock and twisted his ankle, which made him lose his balance. The fast ebbing tide quickly took him out of his depth and away from the possibility of any help from the others.

It had happened before with the same result. The casualty disappeared under the water.

The other members of the group were subdued as they returned to the sandy beach. They each picked up a few of the fish and started to eat them. They knew that they had a long journey before they would be back with the main party and food was not always so easily available. It was better to start off with a full belly. Also, they each had an animal skin bundle of many of the selected stones that they would carry all the way to the home base.

The journey was uneventful and they soon accepted that the loss of one male on the expedition was usual for their way of life. The welcome back was as warm as they would normally have expected and little thought was given to the missing Puit. His female joined in the group mating each night. She was not punished in any way for her loss. That was until one moon later.

The hunting party had not been very successful during the day and the Gols had not had anything to celebrate. Because of this, they had all gone to sleep in the usual huddle of bodies in the thick undergrowth of the forest. Vaya was disturbed in the darkest hours of the early morning with a vivid dream in colour. He was walking towards the sanctuary cave of the three stones when Puit climbed out of the tunnel and came to him, with outstretched arms, smiling and looking straight into his eyes. "Vaya, good hunter. Puit safe. You know!" Vaya awoke, trembling, and Puit was still there, to be seen, in front of him. One of the 'Tall Ones' was standing at his side, with a hand on Puit's shoulder. Vaya was shaking like a tree top in the wind. He held out his hands towards Puit, who smiled, as he began to fade. Then, he had gone.

"Puit. Puit", shouted Vaya, wakening all the rest of the sleeping Gols. "He is here, he has come back", he insisted. "He was with the Tall One". That was his mistake. They could accept that he had dreamed about a lost friend. They often did that themselves. But for Vaya to say that a stranger had been there within their sleeping area was too serious.

"Mad", was the cry. "Stone him". The fear and anger spread like a panic attack through all the Gols. The nearest ones quickly picked up a few of the replenishment stones and Vaya was knocked

75

down and his head was pulped in an instant. None of them returned to sleep. The body was pulled away, to be left in the forest, and fear remained with the group for most of the next moon.

Interim Report to the Development Committee.

At the request of Solem, Ywancontin agreed to accept a preliminary report from him regarding the current situation to the north of the flooded rift valley.

Solem apologised to the Chairman for this breach in the usual procedure. "I feel that there is a possibility of a problem arising that we might avoid, given the awareness of the cause and the likely effect. I fully understand that the Gols would benefit greatly if they had the ability to create fire and, therefore, light, with which they would be able to explore their cave. Is it too early for them to be introduced to the taste of cooked food?

My main concern is the growing awareness, within some individuals, of spiritual communication. We have seen how they have reacted to the sudden disclosure that Vaya had seen the spirit of Puit. It is fortunate that Vaya had been very effective in his sexual activities and there are numerous offspring who will be carrying his genes into the future. I wish to recommend that the activities and future wishes of Vaya's spirit are monitored and considered by this committee. He might be suitable for a second life in the body. If this is agreed, may I suggest that he should start the second life with no memory of his first?"

Ywancontin had been following the words of Solem, as they formed in his mind, and he was ready with an answer.

"You are correct in giving a preliminary report with your suggestions". He smiled. "It is acceptable that we should arrange for the reintroduction of an experienced spirit into a new creature, prior to birth, but this change in the normal procedures must be viewed as a trial, and not as the start of a new routine. It is agreed that there may be up to one hundred such trials during the next century but they must be strictly controlled and monitored. You will be responsible for that part of the exercise. The rules that you apply will

76

include the fact that the new infant will have a completely blank memory, as if it was the first visit to the planet. On returning home at the end of its earth life, it may retain the memories of that life but it must not be considered for a third visit until we have accumulated and considered the data from all other approved reincarnations. We might well decide not to project the system further, for a much longer period.

Regarding the possibility of introducing the use of fire, and subsequently the pleasures of eating cooked food, that is a different matter. These creatures are already developing their brains from the experiences of the hazards of living on the planet. They are improving their thinking processes and learning from those experiences. Sooner or later, they will have closer contact with fire and a few of them will use their mental capacity to plan the controlling of it. They will learn to take a burning branch into a dark place, like the cave, and understand the benefits of having that light.

Much later, they will realise that friction can be used in order to create a spark, and, therefore, the simple fact that they can make light at will. That is the way that they will progress. Each small experience will be added to the knowledge gained from previous happenings. That is the path that has been planned for them. It is essential that they develop their brains as a direct result of experience. That is the way that they will take. We know that there is so much more knowledge that will become available to them in their future.

We will not move from that preordained future. Experience is the teacher. If they do not learn from experience then they will have to face the same problem again and ask why it is still there in front of them. When their brains have developed sufficiently then they will be able to understand and solve the problem. Do nothing to try to accelerate the learning process"

CHAPTER NINE
EXPLORATION

It was at about the same time that some of the North Eastern tribes of Utee were enjoying the experience of frequent meetings with each other. Sometimes there was the pleasure of intertribal mating after a feast of welcome. This was beneficial to all concerned. Rarely were any of the fertile females in a condition of childlessness.

Each group learned something from these contacts with the others. They realised that the standard of skills in the handling of the primitive tools tended to vary to a great degree. The successful hunters had become very adept at using their precious stones. These weapons were used in two ways. They were either thrown at the target or held in the hand for the purpose of striking and killing. The throwers knew that they had somehow to retain a striking stone on their person in case of the victim being only knocked off balance with the previously thrown projectile. It was usually folded into the animal skin that they had started to wind around the waist in a primitive type of skirt. There was no intention of hiding any part of the body. There was no modesty amongst these advancing creatures, only the need for the application of mental agility to the serious problem of efficient hunting.

By trial and error, some of the brighter males had learned from watching the others as they experimented with folding their pieces of animal skins, shaping them with the sharp, flatter, cutting stones, and fixing them around their waists by twisting and tucking the ends inside the tightest parts. The occasional production of a long thin strip of leather, which had been trimmed from the edge of the main piece of the skin in order to reduce its size, became the plaything of one of the younger males. He in turn learned that it could be used as a whip, to annoy his fellow trainees. Together, they found that they could make a semi-permanent knot around the end of a stick and create more fun by whipping each other. The elder males, who suffered the pain of flagellation, quickly smashed the new toy by using it on the tormentor, when it was then discarded. But the simple knot had been seen and noticed. It was never to be forgotten. The thin flint stones, with the sharp cutting edge, became treasured possessions, and they were not used as projectiles except in an extreme emergency.

These new items of knowledge, that had been gained by accident and retained by the growing brain cells of memory, were discussed and debated during many of the social meetings of the different groups or tribes of the Utee. Their brains continued to be developed by the stimulation of being used. They were aware of the fact that they were making progress but they were far from being ready even to understand how to make any move that would help to increase the rate of learning.

Continual movement in the search for food was the main fact that helped them to develop further. Their travels through a continually changing climate showed them a wide variety of different animals and plants. They developed their taste buds by sampling the different leaves and flowers that they came across. They were making progress and they were unknowingly using the methods that had been stated by the Committee.

It was during one of the annual migrations that one tribe of Utee went further to the north than they had ever been before. The reason was that their hunting party had seen what they thought to be a small group of the dreaded Yutee. None of them had ever seen any of the hairy monsters during their short lives, but they were fully aware of the descriptions that had been passed down to them from their parents and grandparents. The descriptions of the ogres had been used to frighten awkward youngsters into accepting some primitive forms of discipline.

A reinforced hunting party, closely followed by the main group of the tribe of Utee, moved steadily and swiftly away from the cold mountains, across the unexplored flat plain, until they arrived at a seemingly endless stretch of frozen water. The journey had taken nearly one full moon, hunting and eating on the move. The occasional glimpse of two hands of tall hairy bipeds, moving equally swiftly ahead of them, was sufficient incentive to keep running after them. That was the last that they saw of the Yutee.

The light was fading as the quarry disappeared across the ice in the direction of where the sun had risen that morning. It was now already setting behind the frustrated Utee. They camped and shivered together until the next morning.

As soon as the weak sun rose above the ice in the east they all stood up, as tall as possible, and studied the geography. Some of the tallest Utee claimed that they could see hills rising in the distance, at the other side of the sheet of ice. They indicated that they should all start to cross the ice and chase the Yutee, but there was an immediate problem. When they actually moved on to the ice they found that it was already broken into insecure floes. Two of them fell into the water and disappeared. The others rushed back on to the firm ground and refused to continue with the chase. They decided that the Yutee must all be drowned in the ice-cold water. They had travelled much further north than ever before and they wanted to get back to their own hunting grounds again.

The knowledge of that mysterious new land across the ice was logged into their memories. It would never be erased - just the same as the fact that the hideous snowmen were still in existence. Perhaps they had been able to cross the ice and reach the other side safely?

At a similar latitude, on the other side of the planet, a group of primitive bipeds was unknowingly under observation.

Gur, of the Hoon, a western tribe of Utee, was the leader of the hunting group that was following the party of Tarls in order to decide whether to attack them or not. There were only two hands of the big Hoon hunters and they remained hidden in the undergrowth of the wooded slopes of the hills. They had been quietly following the smaller Tarls, who outnumbered them by three to one, for four days. Gur had been puzzled by the fact that the quarry was apparently so well organised.

They were all males and they carried both throwing and cutting stones which they used at any time there was an opportunity to use them successfully. The stones were carried in a similar type of skirt or waistband to their own but these were supported by a leather strip over each shoulder, and which crossed on the individual's back and across the chest.

Up to that point in time, Gur, and all his tribe of Hoons, had despised the little Tarls for a number of reasons. They were only about two thirds the size of the big Hoons. They ran away whenever they saw the Hoons approaching them and they had never willingly joined in any mating sessions with them. There had been the occasional times when the Hoons had trapped a small number of the Tarls so that they could not escape. This invariably resulted in the males being slaughtered and the females being raped by each of the Hoons. They were then killed also.

This time, the Hoons were watching and learning. Gur told the watchers to continue to keep quiet. Their language was entirely vocal with a variety of guttural grunts and fingers used to point and to signal a closed mouth. They did not use any form of mental communication as this had faded from their natural skills and abilities.

The Tarls, on the other hand, had retained and used the skills of telepathy and, therefore, they appeared to be a much quieter race. They hunted very successfully, without any of the fuss and noise made by the Hoons. Each member of the group appeared to know his job and was able to carry it out without any noise that could warn the prey of its danger. This quiet confidence continued during the period of the butchery of the kill and even through the feast afterwards.

Gur did not like what he saw. The little, round-shouldered, hominids were too efficient, too successful. They needed to be killed, eliminated! He sent one of his party back to the main base of the tribe with the message that he needed another fighting group to join him in order to destroy this threat to their way of life. He knew that it would take at least two days before they would arrive, but he was prepared to wait and watch until help appeared.

The group of Tarls continued to follow their established routines of hunting and eating. They showed no sign of being aware of the observers, despite having learned of their presence by mentally reading the thoughts of the Hoons at the time of their sending for reinforcements. They were fully alerted to the risks that they were taking, but they had the quiet confidence of the knowledge that they would be alerted long before the watchers were ready to attack them.

The little Tarls were probably many thousand years more advanced than the big Hoons, but they knew that they were no match for them on a basis of one for one. At the moment, they were able to outnumber the big creatures, and the leader decided that this would be an opportunity to eliminate them.

The plan was thought through amongst the Tarls. They would start to move steadily toward the hills a little to the north of them. As soon as they had entered the narrow valley, and passed round the first bend in the trail, the leading first two thirds of the group would run ahead and hide on either side of the path. The smaller second group of them would continue to walk forward at the usual pace and lead the followers into the ambush. At the given mental signal the hidden Tarls would attack the Hoons, with all their stones being skilfully used to do as much damage as possible. At the same time, the first party of the Tarls would return on the path and join in the slaughter.

It was a good plan. It should have worked. The Hoons had no mental ability to read the messages from amongst their enemies and learn of the trap, but they had still retained some natural instinct. Gur was puzzled by the sudden move in the direction of the hills and, especially, by the choice of the narrow valley. He signalled to the other nine to change direction to the right and to climb the slopes, in order to be above the enemy. It was a wise move.

They found that they were looking down on to a similar number of Tarls, who were lying in ambush, with their backs to them. They quickly rushed down on to them and killed them all. Across the valley were the other ten Tarls who were unable to reach them with their stones. The first party of the other ten were now returning along the valley, in the hope of finishing the Hoons, when they, themselves, were ambushed and stoned to death.

The remaining ten Tarls quickly realised that they were at risk and started to run away. They simply were not quick enough to escape from the bigger, fleeter Hoons. Their end was very quick. Some of the victors were still drinking the blood of their victims when the reinforcements arrived later that day. The enlarged group of them celebrated by feasting off the meat that the Tarls had been carrying with them.

Gur was shown great respect by the others for being so astute and enabling ten of them to kill three times that number of Tarls. He boasted that he would wipe them all away, wherever they might hide. The message was spread throughout the land of the Hoons. The Tarls were to be destroyed.

THE PATH

Solem was the first to give his report to the Committee. He waited until Ywancontin smiled his approval before speaking.

"We have now seen two important steps taken in the development of the Plan. There is no doubt now that the Utee have made serious progress in their advancement and, at the same time, they have moved into a wider field, with some of the groups becoming diversified, almost to the point of their appearing to be very different types of hominids. We have seen some of the dark-haired, north eastern Utee, with their pale skins tending to be of a more yellow hue, showing the desire to explore that part of the planet merely to learn more about it. When they chased a small party of the taller Yutee to the sea, they were even prepared to follow them across the ice. They did not realise that they had merely ensured the survival of a small group of the doomed Yutee who had crossed the straits between the newly arrived continental plate of what will become the Americas. The large, big-footed hominids will be able to establish themselves in the new land before they are eventually followed by some future generations of the Utee. By that time, their original groups will have been eliminated and almost forgotten by the successful Utee.

It appears that the urge to survive enhances the desire to destroy any similar creature that could possibly be a threat to their own survival. There have been no reports of any productive mating between the Utee and the Yutee in the last million years. It is now possible that both races have now evolved to the position where it would be impossible to achieve fertilisation, even if there should be any basis of desire or agreement.

On the western side of the continent there is a growing tendency for the larger hominids, the Hoons, to assert their greater strength in order to eliminate the smaller, but more advanced, Tarls. This appears to have arisen from simple jealousy. They have recognised that the little creatures are superior to them in every aspect except size and speed when running. The Hoons have an arrogant trait, which helps them to win when in battle with others, but which causes them to be more aggressive than might be necessary for the survival of their race.

I would recommend that we should look for ways in which some of the strengths of the Tarls can be passed in their genes to their oppressors and continued into the future. That could be of benefit to all future generations of hominids. I am thinking particularly of their more advanced intelligence and survival skills, their telepathic communication and their quiet confidence in general activity."

Ywancontin nodded his appreciation and thanks to Solem. *"You have made some very useful suggestions and I understand your reasoning. It is possible that you have been influenced by the desire to encourage the development of the most pleasant type of creature that you have seen on the planet so far? We must not forget the original intention. We must ensure that a viable form of hominid is to be encouraged to develop within the guidelines and limitation of the controlling genes that are now in the creatures, and which will develop under the natural law. At any point in time, now, we could be stopped and turned to another project. Ask yourself. 'Is the plan moving in the right direction? Will these hominids grow and develop into the intelligent form of mankind that will be the best way of advancing the Knowledge?'*

Is it possible that you have gained some awareness of what the future holds for the current candidates for such advancement? You should not let a glimpse of future facts affect you judgement of the present. There will come a day when words and language will become corrupted by the passage of time. The name of the Tarls might become something like Neandertarl, or it could be distorted into Trolls, the little mischief makers of the northern countries. And the Yutee might become the Yeti. Race memories will be retained of both the intelligent little men who were full of fun, and, also, the horrors of the abominable snowmen in the eastern areas.

Our involvement, at this point in time, is to decide whether and when to make any small adjustments to the plan. Before we continue with this examination of the present situation we must be sure that we are reviewing all the main groups of bipeds on the planet. I am not aware that there has been a completed study made of those in the area that we are naming as Africa. I suggest that we pause until that report is available".

CHAPTER TEN
AFRICA

Three members of the Committee were immediately involved in planning their method of operating in the large Dark Continent. They were aware of the variety and the displacement of the main groups, which were developing independently, each within its own area.

To the north, where the continent met the flooded rift valley of the Mediterranean, some of the paler Gyps had grown their brains to the point of being able to have an understanding of their path ahead. They showed signs of a potential spirituality, which was advancing alongside their physical development. They continued to experiment with the eating of a wide variety of fruits and grains, when is season, whilst their main source of food came from the various animals that their hunters were able to find and kill.

In the extreme south, there were a large number of groups of itinerant hunters. Their physical similarities of black skin, rounded head, topped with black curly hair, showed that there had been frequent mating between members of different groups throughout their very existence. They continued to meet sporadically which resulted in either a massacre or a fruitful mating of all those who were willing.

The huge area between the north and the south was lightly populated with a wide range of changing groups of hominids. These varied between some of the tiny creatures, averaging three feet in height, which survived by eating the smallest animals and grubs that they could catch by hand, to some well-developed bipeds who were the tallest on the continent, often over five feet high. Living in a climate of heat and rain, over a period of aeons, had ensured that those with the blacker skins had been better able to hunt and survive under the heat of the sun. They had all learned something about their own varied terrain. This included mountainous areas, that were being reshaped by volcanic activity, a few large lakes of fresh water, some open grasslands that were being grazed by a wide variety of animals, but, most of the undulating land was covered by a dense forest.

The small groups tended to spend much of their time in this forest. Frequent, heavy rains watered it, and the rapid growth of vegetation provided all their needs, including a measure of security. Some of these hominids never emerged from the cover of the trees. They were completely unaware of what was to be found more than a day's walk from their hunting grounds. In a similar way, the active groups that preferred to develop outside the thickest wooded areas were equally unaware of the hidden forest dwellers.

The Committee members agreed that Marcus should be responsible for the investigation into the northern hominids, Bevak would cover the extreme south and Mellak would study the many small groups in the central forest and mountain area. The remaining members would support these three as and when such help was required.

If the spirit of Da had been watching the activities of her descendants she might just have recognised some of her own traits in the hunting group as it moved towards the west. The compassion, which had been introduced through her so many millennia ago, was affecting the attitudes of some of the muscular male hunters. Ga was one of them.

The hunting group, of four hands, had had only a little success during the past three days, but now they had arrived at a time for decision. Their leader, Bod, had given the mental signal to them all to stop in their tracks and remain silent. He pointed to the other side of the small trees ahead of them and held four fingers up. Four of them crawled forward.

The mental picture was immediately relayed back to the others. In a small hollow in the open space there was a small group of strangers who were eating raw meat from an animal that had obviously been killed quite recently. There were two males, four females and four or five youngsters. They were all of dark skin and hair and not likely to be closely related to any of the hunting Gyps.

"Kill them all and take their meat," signalled Bod. He was confident that the strangers would not be able to read his mind messages, because he had heard them chattering to each other during their meal. He did not expect to hear the message that he received from some of his males.

"No! Kill the two males and keep the others for use later!" This came from the mind of Ga, and it was immediately repeated by two more of the hunters. "We agree that we should keep the females and the little ones for later."

Bod was livid. It had never happened before. He had always expected and received instant obedience when on the hunt. Their lives depended upon it. He sent a blast of rage at the culprits that caused them to jump up and groan. The result was that their intended victims were alerted to imminent danger. They stood up and prepared to flee, leaving their food and some of their stone weapons on the ground.

Ga, and two other Gyps, rushed down to slope and were able to kill the two males. They then turned round to face the others of their own group, ready to defend the females and young from the threats of Bod. The strongly assertive attitudes of some of the males were to be seen quite easily. These traits might have been the major reason for the survival of many of the original groups of bipeds but they were now faced with the reactions of some of the gentler members of their group. Bod knew that he must use his brain rather that his weapons to resolve the dispute.

He walked down to where the bodies of the two males lay on the ground. The females and their young were whimpering together in a huddle nearby, expecting to be slain by these strong creatures. Bod, looked at Ga and his two fellow rebels, whilst keeping his protruding eyebrows squeezed together. He snarled, "You claim these for yourselves?"

Ga shrugged his shoulders calmly. "What use are they dead?" he said. "We can use the females, now, but why kill them afterwards? We can always use them again, later. They can carry our food, as we find it, and the young ones will be no trouble. Some of them will be ready for a male before the next hot period, so why not think about keeping them for the future? We can always kill them if they make trouble, or if we are short of food."

Bod was puzzled by the new approach of thinking before taking action. He was still angry with Ga for his disobedience and immediately challenged him. "I am leader. You do what I say, or we can all be killed. Now, you fight me if you want to make yourself leader." He threw his stone, but missed Ga, who had ducked. Ga had been expecting the challenge and he was ready for Bod's attack. He was already holding his cutting flint-stone in his hand as he whirled round, his straight arm took the sharp stone swiftly across the bare abdomen of Bod and disembowelled him. None of the others showed any desire to tackle Ga and he was accepted as the new leader. He merely pointed to the new captives and said, "They are mine. We take them with us when we return to the main group."

Hunting was resumed and the other males commented openly on the new points that they had noticed. Some of them were pleased with the novelty of slaves being taken and retained for the first time in their knowledge. Others were surprised that Ga had been able to think about the leader's order to kill the strangers, when there had always been a better alternative. Why had they not thought about it for themselves? The whole experience had benefited them all - except Bod! Ga's explanation of the changes was given the full attention of the seniors when they returned to the main group, some four days walk away. They listened to his reasoning for taking slaves, and accepted it. They were more interested in his reasoning before taking the action that he did when he decided to disobey Bod.

Up to that point in time, there had been two schools of thought amongst the natural leaders of the Gyps. The strongest ones had asserted themselves by sheer force of muscle power and their personal weapons. Any threat to their position was immediately removed by personal challenge and a fight to the death, as in the affair between Bod and Ga.

Some of them, who carried the compassionate genes inherited from the descendants of Da, had tended to give consideration to the question of benefits for others in their group. This had almost always been tempered with strong benefits for themselves. Ga had not only increased the size of his own family group, but he had also been promoted to a position where he had more power and was able to prove his own abilities. He had gained more respect than Bod had ever received from his hunters. He was a success. All the Gyps benefited from his advancement.

This did not have the effect of reducing any of the usual

respect given by the majority of the Gyps to the archetypal male hunter-killer. The regular production of meat food depended on the continuing success of that type of member in all groups. Mother-love might have helped to maximise the number of survivors amongst the youngsters, but it was not to be encouraged amongst the assertive males. They had physical superiority and they believed that they also had mental advantages over the females. When in doubt, they used their strength to make the point.

Within the limitations of the available vocabulary, there was sporadic conversation amongst the largest group of Gyps about the effect that Ga had introduced to the way of life. They were based near the northern coastline of the continent. The race memory retained the trauma of the great flood so there was a natural fear of the dangers from the salt waters. Any new or unusual situation was likely to create anxiety and the introduction of slaves gave many of the females a sense of foreboding. They were fully aware that the females and young ones were already a type of second class member of the group. Their lack of the physical strength of the males confirmed that. They were now seeing an even lower grade of Gyp - the slave that had been captured and brought into the family when the normal procedure would have been to kill them. Yes, they were mostly females, although some male infants had been retained. Within a very short period of time the 'slaves' were absorbed in one or other of the family groups. Relationships began to develop that blurred the lines between 'slaves' and the established mates. The males had always been promiscuous and polygamous. Any implied criticism from the females was quickly stopped by the simple process of a sharp knock on the head with whatever stone was at hand. The comments continued after that, but only amongst the females, and well out of earshot of their mates. Most of the questions were about the physical appearance of the new slaves. The height, skin colour and sexual attraction created the most stress amongst the questioners.

Gree was one of the females that Ga had brought back with him and she was considered to be very attractive by the other males. In fact, his hunting partner, Kia, asked to be given a share of her body, "Two nights each moon, or when you do not want her yourself?" Ga had more than enough females to give him pleasure, so he shrugged his shoulders and nodded. Later that month, they compared experiences and agreed that Gree was unusually satisfying. "She is strange in some way," said Kia and Ga agreed. "Sometimes she is not with me. Her mind is in the jungle or up in the mountains". They did not raise the matter with Gree but simply continued to use her whenever the desire took them.

On the other hand, Gree was well aware of the situation with the males. She enjoyed the sexual part of her new life. Both the two usual mates, Ga and Kia, were strong successful hunters and she was well fed. So far she had only borne one boychild and he had been killed and eaten by a big cat during the past year. Now she was hoping that her two mates would give her another one. She knew that they thought her strange in some way. Perhaps, it was because her skin was slightly darker than theirs was, and she was much shorter and only able to touch their chins with her head, when she was standing.

She knew that they could not hear the voices that she heard. That was her secret. Ever since she could remember, from her earliest days, she had known of her ngung. It was her own private friend, neither a male nor female, just her special secret. It was with her whenever she felt the need for comfort, when she was hungry, frightened or lonely. Her mother had usually been trying to find enough food for her large family and she had been left for long periods alone in whatever part of the land they had been at the time. She had never had enough words to be able to tell her mother about the ngung, in any case. The voices had started later. They were good for her. They were never hard or cruel, like those of some of the males. She only seemed to hear them when she asked herself a question. In a strange or frightening situation, she would think, "What shall I do?" or "Where can I go?" A helpful answer was usually given to her. "Run for you life," or "Climb that tree." She knew that she had a secret friend who could be trusted. As she matured she never even tried to tell anyone else of her secret. Her inner voice told her that it would be unwise.

The Gyps continued to increase in numbers. They spread along the southern coastline of the salt sea using their hunting skills to maintain a steady supply of meat food for their members. Fruit and nuts were added to the diet whenever they were available.

Another form of food was introduced occasionally.

The salt waters usually frightened all of the bipeds because so many of them were aware of the danger of being drowned by losing their step when walking in the surf and beyond. They also knew that small fish were sometimes stranded in the shallow pools, as the tide receded. These were easily caught and eaten. There were the odd times when a shoal of fish moved too far into the small bays along the coast. If these fish could be encouraged to move even further, nearer the sandy beach, then many of them would be trapped. The persuasion was created by the fish-hunters either throwing many stones into the water between the shoal and the path of escape, creating splashes, or by the bipeds rushing into the water and creating the splashes themselves. This was a dangerous method. Some of them could easily be drowned if they lost their balance, and they often were lost in this way.

When successful fishing sessions were completed there was great rejoicing as the spoils were carried back to the waiting family groups. The new food was welcomed and enjoyed. The change in diet, sporadic as it might well be, stimulated excitement, feasting and, as usual, much sexual activity. Their brains were also activated with questions about any other means of catching fish, more often and in larger quantities. They were not yet anywhere near the point of advancing their skills to improve safety, or of discovering more advanced methods of catching fish.

Marcus had observed some of the effects of the introduction of slaves to the Gyp economy, and he decided to make some notes prior to preparing his report for the Committee.

It appears that the idea of taking slaves, as an alternative to slaughtering all captives, was inevitable. The benefits, to both victim and victor, were not all obvious at first. The victims were naturally relieved to find that they were not put to death immediately, although they suspected that they would not live much longer, once the novelty of ownership had faded. They had real doubts about how they would be treated in the future.

The victors, on the other hand, would need to feel constantly reassured that they would continue to gain from the ownership of these creatures that would require to be constantly fed, and guarded to prevent escape. The novelty of the idea kept a momentum in the thinking amongst the owners. The whole concept stimulated thought and exercised their brains. This side effect was of benefit to the whole group of Gyps. It would help them to develop during the aeons ahead of them. It is important that the idea of retaining and developing the system of keeping slaves is encouraged at every opportunity. It is recommended that every thought or question on the subject is given a spiritual hint to retain the system. As the suggestions are proved, by experience, to be wise, there will be the added benefit that the thinker will make a habit of wondering which way to go, which path to take, what to do next? And he will be given the best possible advice from within his own conscience. He will be reassured. He will be aware that he has wisdom within his own mind. Then, it is entirely his own decision whether he acts upon that advice or whether he ignores it and recognises the result of taking that step. It will all be part of the plan for his progress.

Whilst Ga and Kia may be about to start receiving some effective spiritual guidance, they will not be told of the fact that Gree is already aware that there is more to her life than the physical side. She does not have sufficient words to raise the matter with them. Inwardly, she knows that she would almost certainly be put to death if she claimed to have anything like spiritual help. That concept simply does not exist in the hominoid mind. She will require some time before she is able to understand the Gyps' ability to use telepathy. She is also completely unaware of the fact that she lived a separate spiritual life prior to being borne on the planet. She is one of those selected to experience an earthly life and, thereby, have the opportunity to learn from that short time allotted to her. Her records will form part of the final review of this period.

CHAPTER ELEVEN
CENTRAL AFRICA

The southern part of the continent was very different from the remainder of the landmass. The extremes of heat and humidity were only felt for part of each year, and, for most of the time, the pleasant conditions helped to make life reasonably comfortable for the naked hominids. They were hunters, like all of the other groups on the planet, and they had learned from their contacts that they could use the usual weapons, both round and sharp stones, for this purpose.

They had also become used to wearing the soft leather pouch-belts in order to carry a supply of stones ready for a hunting kill of animal meat or for the slaughter of their enemies. These foes were identified as any biped that was not born into, or accepted by, their own group.

Jealousies had developed within each group during occasional times of food scarcity, when a successful hunter might have killed only enough meat to feed his own family. He would then refuse to share the meat with the other, less productive, hunters' families. This sometimes resulted in damaging, often fatal, fighting within the group. This tended to restrict the growth of any one group.

When the jealousies were applied from one group to another, the trend of reducing the numerical strength affected the number of groups in the whole of the southern part of the continent. Some groups attacked others on sight, without warning. It had become the normal, expected result of seeing each other. During any conflict, the intention was to kill every single member of the other group. If any of the females managed to survive the fighting, they were killed later, after being raped and tortured.

The net result was that whilst the size of the winning groups remained almost static, the total number of groups tended to be reduced.

Bevak realised that he did not need to make a long study of the southern hominids in order to prepare his report and recommendations.

93

Mellak knew that he had a much more complex task in assessing the central area and he had wisely asked for help from the other members of the Committee who were available.

The wide, impassable, river, which would one day be known as the Congo, split the dense central rainforest into the north and the south. Rising in the volcanic mountains of the central heights, it meandered towards the west, becoming wider as it moved. All the varied creatures that existed on either of its banks knew that they could not move to the other side. For many millions of years it had been a limitation to their movement. They had evolved naturally, in their own way, without any possibility of mixing their blood with similar looking creatures on the other bank of the river.

The only exceptions to this fact were the descendants of the amphibious dinosaurs, the forerunners of the crocodile. They had the ability to cross to either side of the river, but they showed no desire to mate with any other species. Their only obvious desire was to eat any meat that fell into their jaws.

A few small groups of hominids lived their precarious lives on the southern bank. They were able to move about through the trees, going from one more open area to another at a good speed. This method was much faster, and safer, than travelling on the ground. It gave them the opportunities to ambush their prey and jump down on to the selected meat for the day. It also helped them to go to the edge of the flowing water and still keep out of the reach of the waiting jaws below. They were all well aware of the dangers, and they often saw the horrible jaws disposing of the bodies of other creatures that had been floating downstream, after falling into the river further to the east.

They had adapted to survive in that particular part of the forest. They had no idea of what they would find more than one day's journey in any direction. They were simply not curious and used all their energies in finding their needs of food for one day at a time. The hazards of their life prevented them from growing into a large community and, occasionally, similar groups had perished after some disaster. It was rare for any two groups to meet.

Gan was the leader of the group under surveillance. He had found himself in that position after his predecessor had stepped on to a large log, floating at the water's edge. The 'log' turned out to be a sleepy amphibian that objected to being disturbed and immediately snapped at the tasty morsel and took it down into the depths.

Gan, and some of the others, had seen it happen. They had seen it happen before, a few times. One female gave out a wail, whilst the others gave a gasp of shock, and they then continued to search for the next meal. As Gan was the oldest male, having survived perhaps four hands of years, they all turned to him for guidance on direction through the trees towards the next hunting space.

The females came to him first when they were ready for service. This small pleasure was the incentive that made him accept the responsibility and the males of the group accepted his right. They knew that they could mate with the same females at any time, when he was not looking. Jealousy was not often seen, except on those rare occasions when the group met strangers.

It happened the day after the new leader was appointed. Gan was leading them along the middle tier of wide branches, away from the river, when he stopped with his right arm held up to warn them all of danger ahead. Without a sound, they froze in the position of the moment. Peering down, to a lower layer of branches, they could all see a smaller group of some three hands of bipeds moving in the opposite direction, towards the river. The strangers were of a similar build, colouring and size, to their own group, possibly related a long way back into the past. Gan had never seen them before and he hesitated.

A twig cracked and dropped from behind him on to the branch of the newcomers. They looked up and knew that they were in the worst position. Their leader was a quick thinker. He held up the carcass of a small furry creature and called, "For you?"

That made Gan, and his group, pause for long enough to realise that there was no need to attack these strangers below them. They came in peace. The previous leader might easily have used their strong position to attack, but their new leader was not so experienced in the ways of the jungle. He smiled and climbed down to accept the present of the newly killed meat. The others of his group followed and smiles were shared with them all. The greetings, which included some touching and more smiles, was followed by the ritual eating of the food that had been offered. That was quickly consumed. Gan then told the visitors that they were going a short distance to kill some easy meat food that was available, then they could have a feast! More smiles and agreement followed. The males of the two groups combined to hunt and kill a sufficient quantity of the little deer-like animals that they had seen previously. All the males had used their round stones to kill and their sharp flint-stones to skin and dismember the animals. They all then ate their fill and followed with the promised mating, with each female enjoying many males from both parties. Many of the offspring born during the next year would then have relatives in the other group. It augured well for the improvement in the genes and the strength of the new arrivals. It would also tend to prevent any future meetings of the two groups starting with friction or aggression.

Both the groups realised that they had learned very little from the others, despite the fact that they had not met at any time in the memories of them all. They faced the same problems as each other, used the same weapons and tools, and had the same pleasures, as and when they found sufficient food for a feast. They all assumed that any other groups in the same jungle-forest would have similar abilities and problems.

None of them had any idea of the size of their continent. They felt no inclination to travel continually in any one direction. There was no desire to seek out any other similar groups. It simply did not happen, except by accident. They had little ambition, except to find enough food for each day and to live long enough to enjoy it.

The hominids that lived to the east of the dense jungle had a different attitude to life. They were more mobile, very curious about anything new, and both aggressive and yet capable of defending themselves as and when this was needed.

The two general classifications were in the height of each individual. Those known as the Pugs were usually only about twelve hands high when mature. They had the benefit of a quick-thinking brain, as well as being very agile and capable of running long distances at speed, in order to evade contact with their enemies, the much taller Geti. Whilst the two types seemed to have their height as the most obvious difference, they had both known a hate for each other for many thousands of years. They reacted at the sight. The Pugs ran away and the Geti ran after them, usually without much success. Perhaps, the main difference between the two types of hominids was the fact that the smaller Pugs had developed a slightly more advanced intelligence. As they lacked the strength and height to fight the Geti, and succeed, they used their brains to find the most efficient way to avoid destruction by the larger type. They kept alert for danger and they ran when they recognised it.

Living in the very mixed area of Central Africa, they found that years could pass without the two types meeting each other. There were a number of large freshwater lakes, surrounded by mountain ranges, of volcanic origin, with larger areas of open grassland. Huge herds of grass eaters moved around and provided excellent hunting for the hominids. So much food was so easily available that the number of the bipeds should have been increasing rapidly. But, any increase appeared to be only temporary.

One group, of two hands of Geti, was hunting near one of the lakes. Ngaat was the leader, and he had never forgotten losing the track of a party of the little Pugs a few years ago, on his first hunt after becoming a leader. They had simply outrun him and his new group. Learning from that experience, he had developed a new technique for trapping quarry, not just the Pugs, but any quarry. He had encouraged his brother, Nguut, who was the leader of his own group, to hunt near him, within signalling distance.

In practice, both groups would watch from cover until some grass eaters approached the edge of the lake in order to drink the fresh water, usually near dusk. They would then creep towards the drinkers, one group at the north and the other at the south of them. Both groups of Geti would spread out until they formed a crescent shape, surrounding the quarry and closing in on them until they were noticed. The panicking creatures would become easy targets for the well-aimed stones of the hunters and large quantities of meat would be taken back to the main party.

On this occasion, both the brothers had seen the group of little Pugs approaching the edge of the water before they could have been seen. They waved to each other and immediately the two groups dropped to take cover in the grassy approach to the lakeside. The usual crescent was formed, it moved surely towards the little people and the trap was sealed. The surprise gave the advantage to the Geti who were in a killing frenzy. They received only a few cuts and bruises in the attack, whilst the four hands of Pugs, males, females and youngsters, were slaughtered very quickly. Four of them tried to escape by going into the water, but they were drowned, after being stoned from the shore.

The two brothers decided that they must make a quick kill of meat, take it back to the main group, so that all of them could celebrate such a successful day. It was a day that they would remember and always use as a reminder that they had developed such a winning strategy.

CHAPTER TWELVE
4mBC REPORT

The Committee met for the last time in the 4mBC period in order to complete their report on the hominoid progress to date. The Chairman called, firstly, for the verbal reports from Marcus, Bevak and Mellak, to cover the state of the creatures in the continent of Africa. They raised few surprises.

Bevak started with the matter-of-fact comment. "*The population of the southern area has the opportunity to take advantage of the enormous quantities of food available, in order to help them to grow rapidly, both in the strength of each individual, and also numerically. Their brains have developed since the last survey, but they are using this improvement only in order to survive and to maintain their existing numbers. Their traits of self-survival and reproduction are strongly imprinted in their genes but the aggressive urges appear to push them into the most destructive attitudes. Suspicion of all and any strangers stimulates their killer tendencies. The reactions are immediate and very effective. This had the obvious result of the smaller groups being eliminated. The larger groups also lose many of their members in the frequent fighting, and they fluctuate in size. There could be a logical case prepared for the recommendation of our introducing some form of pacification, but I do not propose that we should deal with the problem in that way at this point. There is still a good opportunity for the smaller weaker groups to move out of the reach of the offensive ones. The land area is very large and it includes attractive areas, further to the north, with plenty of food available for them. Imminent volcanic action should help to encourage them all to seek new hunting grounds*".

The Chairman nodded his thanks to Bevak and indicated to Mellak that he should give his report on the central area.

"*The central part of this continent has perhaps the widest range of geographic features,*" *started Mellak.* "*New mountains are being created by the frequent volcanic eruptions. The surface is covered with the densest of tropical jungle, in some parts, and large, fresh water lakes, in others. The lush plains support countless herds of grazing animals that can provide plenty of food for all the predatory* creatures, including the hominids. The last named are, themselves, hunted by some of the large cats, and they need to be both defensive and aggressive in their attitudes.

There are two main types of hominids that have developed since the last review. They are either the small, agile, quick-thinking Pugs, who survive by running away from the larger, taller Geti, who usually attack them on sight. Both these types appear to be capable of surviving and developing into the future. I believe that they will both continue to prosper in their own chosen way. They will surely learn that the size of the landmass is an advantage for both of them. If they avoid each other they can both grow steadily over the future years. None of them seem to give much time to thinking about what the future may hold for them. They are a long time away from the major step of learning to control fire and from benefiting from the pleasure of cooked food. There is still the need for growing their brains more in order to help with their progress and survival."

"Marcus", said Ywancontin, as he nodded his thanks to Mellak, "your northern population were showing more promise of early progress, were they not? Will you now please tell us of your thoughts for their future."

Marcus stood up, feeling that, perhaps, he had been able to identify the secret of the more noticeable advancement of many of the creatures that he had been studying. "There are a number of differences that have been noticed in the northern groups. Any one, or all, of these points could be the vital factor that gives them the advantage over the southern and central groups.

We have been aware that the most successful group of the Gyps are settled in the north eastern area, in the fertile valley where the river flows northwards into the flooded rift valley. They have a 'race-memory' of the disastrous flooding of that valley, but that includes the knowledge that they were saved from the worst excesses by the wise use of telepathy, to warn them of approaching danger. They have continued to use that means of communication but they have learned to control its use so that it does not leak to the enemy during any period of fighting.

They have started to develop a parallel method of communicating by the formation of a basic vocal language. It has a very limited *vocabulary, at present, but it will be the basis of fluent speech, as it develops with time. They have an awareness of numbers, up to five or ten, using one or two hands. The stimuli from these new thoughts have helped their brains to increase in size and usage.*

You will recall that we introduced the trait of compassion, in a very small way, in an earlier study, and that can still be identified. It is mostly to be found in the females, in the form of mother-love, but it is recognised and appreciated amongst the families. The main objections are to be found amongst the younger males, who are proud of their ability to hunt and fight. They quickly forget the benefits that they received from being reared by a doting mother. The trait is now so well established that it is unlikely to die out in the foreseeable future.

Their diet is also more varied than that of the other groups to the south. As well as the plentiful supplies of raw meats, the Gyps are aware of the pleasures of adding fruit and nuts to their meals, when is season, and they also delight in eating fish, when they can catch them without being drowned. The varieties of foods, in plentiful supply, are helping them to grow in size, both physically and mentally.

A recent change in their attitudes arose when they introduced slaves, captured during a battle, and retained them within the community, both as servants and as concubines. If they continue to use them in this way, they will find that the brains of the 'thinkers' will grow even more quickly. They will have the time to philosophise, and stimulate more and more thought processes.

To summarise, I would like to suggest that the Gyps have the most promising future ahead of them. That, of course, is subject to these new thinkers not taking control of their destiny and possibly leading them into some disastrous path or way of life. A limited number of them are showing signs of psychic awareness. We will need to know how this develops".

Ywancontin thanked Marcus. "Your assessment is appreciated. I agree that you appear to have studied a very promising group and there will be continuous contact with them through the usual spiritual lines of communication.

We must not forget that all the hominoid groups on the planet have some common ancestors, and that they are continuing to be able to interbreed. That will be essential if it is found that certain groups can benefit from the introduction of genes from members of other groups with different experiences.

Let us examine some of the comments that you have made to this Committee. You all show a commendable wish for these creatures to succeed and develop into the future. The suggestion that they should be helped to learn to control fire comes from your knowledge of the future. That must not be used as a reason for taking such action. They will learn how to handle and respect fire from the experience of close contact with it. That is the whole principle of their system of progress.

Without experience, they will not remember sufficient detail to help them advance further. That will apply to good, bad or indifferent experience. They will eventually remember seeing their first knot, tied in a leather strip, and use that memory in order to experiment with other strips of leather, and, later, other strong materials. This will lead to their experimenting with adding the weight of a stone to the haft of a fighting stick and creating a type of hammer or an axe. They will then learn to understand that the added weight will increase the kinetic energy in the swinging weapon and therefore increase the effect of blow. The knowledge will spread very quickly and the new weapons will be copied throughout the known world.

Those who are showing awareness of spiritual visions are already learning to keep that fact to themselves. They have seen the automatic reaction of the other, more aggressive, males to any suggestion that the Tall Ones are in their midst at any time. This psychic awareness is another stimulus to the thought process. Meditation helps their brains to improve their thought processes and stimulates even more growth. This ability is then passed on to their offspring and into the future.

You have all observed that there is a tendency for the bigger creatures to react aggressively when they are near some of their smaller neighbours, even to the point of attacking them on sight. I agree with you. It is not a welcome trait and not to be encouraged. But, we must take no steps to discourage it, either. It is an inseparable part of their survival need to defend themselves.

You have commented on the fact that the smaller hominids are tending to develop their brains and other skills at a slightly faster rate than the larger ones. This is a possible reason why the little ones have learned to think and run more quickly in order to survive. It is quite possible that they will be eliminated in some parts of the planet.

Where that does happen, they will probably be remembered as 'the little people', and, surprisingly, they will be recalled with some sort of affection. That will be the reaction to the way in which the bigger, aggressive types had destroyed them deliberately. We will continue to monitor the trials of those cases where the reintroduction of a limited number of spirits is permitted. Spiritual Law will continue to apply.

When we notice and record the slow rate of progress during the last million years, and when we project the probable rate for the next period, it would appear likely that there will be no dramatic changes that require much of our attention. Certain steps, that we have mentioned already, might well have been taken, but I believe that we will find that it is possible to move quickly through 3mBC, noting the changes, and then proceed to 2mBC for a fuller and more thorough report. We will act according to the situation at the time. Thank you all for your help so far."

CHAPTER THIRTEEN
3mBC CURIOSITY

This was a period during which the ice crept from both poles of the planet, spreading over one quarter of the surface. All warm-blooded creatures were very aware of the change in the climate. Even the hardy mammoths moved further to the south and found their way into lands that had been too warm for them before the Earth cooled. The slow movers became trapped in the nocturnal ice. Some species were lost forever.

The main survivors were those that had learned to become adaptable to change. The quick thinkers reacted smoothly, and they seemed to accept that life required them to behave in whichever way was obvious to them. The hominids had the advantage of growing to adulthood in ten years and not living long enough to acquire a memory of much more than twenty years. They accepted whatever life gave them, and they reacted in order to survive.

As the encroaching ice moved towards the equator at a rate of only a few miles in a hundred years they had no awareness of the insidious dangers. They merely noticed the fact that it was becoming cooler and then they moved towards the warmer land nearer the equator. Even some of the mammoths travelled south, as far as the African plains and also through the mountain ranges into the subcontinent of India. They would eventually shed their thick shaggy coats and adapt to a climate that was later to become warmer than any that they had experienced before the migration.

Amongst all creatures, the survivors were those with the mental abilities, or the ingrained instincts, to move and explore. The enquiring minds were aware of the question. Where are there some better conditions? The answer was usually - towards the sun. The hunters were well used to travelling long distances to find their quarry. They now took their families with them.

The various tribes of Utee began to move to the south, over a period of a few hundred years, and, from time to time, they came into contact with groups of the Gyps.

Atta had been the leader of his tribe of Utee for five years, after he had killed the previous leader during a dispute over his female. He had been successful throughout that time, mainly because he had an enquiring mind, and he had made a discovery that had revolutionised his own ability to fight. He had invented a new tool.

The Utee had long been using the broken-off horns and shed antlers from a variety of deer that they had killed and eaten. One single antler had always been recognised as an obvious weapon. It was easily swung in one hand so that the pointed end could strike a target and cause serious damage. The two major problems with using such a weapon were that, firstly, every self-respecting hunter carried one or more similar tools, and, secondly, they were not really heavy enough to give a fatal blow to an alerted adversary. Atta had given the matter as much thought as he could and he had eventually found a solution to both problems.

He had been trying to tie a reliable knot with a piece of leather thong and he had succeeded. Using this knowledge, he had selected a suitably shaped flat stone and he had fixed it into the shaped curve of a reindeer antler, tying it in place with a number of simple hitches on the thongs. This gave him a formidable heavy axe. Swung with his two hands, it was faster and more effective than anything any one of them had ever seen or experienced before.

Used within the group, it had ensured that he was never challenged for his position as leader. When used against outsiders, it had the effect of terrifying them with the awesome results. Heads and limbs were severed from their bodies with apparent ease. The few opponents who began to realise that this warrior had some special power, and who were near enough to see that the weapon had some secret extra weight, simply did not survive long enough to spread the news to the others of their own tribe.

Atta was a strong creature, made stronger, to the point of becoming invincible, by the invention of his own brain. Eventually, he helped some of his hunting team to make similar weapons for their own use. Those who had suitable horns and antlers already in their possession were shown how to select matching stones, and then how to tie them into position, so that they would not become loosened with use. After a trial period, Atta had a superior force of hunter-killers.

The migration to the warmer south had been a continuing

process for the past two years. The hunting group had led the way, followed by the remainder of the tribe, perhaps half a day behind them. Any strangers were killed on sight. No prisoners or slaves were taken. They all fed well and they had frequent periods of resting in pleasant valleys. Many babies were born and almost half of them managed to survive to the age where they could walk with the others when on the march to the south. This was the situation when they reached the southern sea at the point where they needed to turn either to the east or the west.

The Utee group was in an unoccupied area of rivers and fertile plains. Meat was there in quantity, and there was fruit on some of the trees. The temperature was very pleasant and many of them were willing to stay there for a longer period. Atta agreed with them. There was no urgency to move away. They would stay and hunt in that area.

The Gyps had controlled their main hunting area for such a long time that they had never doubted their right to be there. They had developed routines that had grown from the habits of many generations. Zil was their leader at the time, when two of their hunting parties had returned to the base with tales of seeing groups of complete strangers hunting near them. This was over a period of three moons.

It had happened before now, but the strangers had always been identified as belonging to fringe groups from their own descendants. They had usually exchanged greetings, when hunting had been successful they had enjoyed a feast with some degree of welcome, followed by the usually pleasant mating frenzy.

This time, Zil pondered over what might be the cause of the invasion. 'Were the strangers a threat to the Gyp way of life? Were they going to take their meat, or their females?' It was important that he knew the facts as soon as possible. The second report of seeing them had been given by Gib, the leader of one of the most successful of the hunting teams. He was a strong young male with an enquiring mind. He had sent a mental message, including a picture of the insurgents, adding his own anxieties after seeing them kill a meat animal for their own food.

Zil told Gib to leave two of his team to continue the observation of the strangers, whilst he and the others were called back to the main area. They then had as full a discussion as possible about the appearance of the weapons, which were such a surprise. Zil quickly realised that the situation was serious. If he waited for a large group of the strangers, armed with these new weapons, to find this ideal territory of the Gyps, it could be a disaster. He made a quick decision and took Gib to his own secret store of a possible new weapon.

"You must go back to join your two spies and make an attack in order to capture some of the new tools used by the strangers. It must be done in the dark, when they do not expect an attack. Your group must take these horns and use them to kill any of those who try to stop you". He uncovered a pile of rare deer horns that he had hidden under a large tree. They had all been broken off at the root, next to the skull of the animals that had been killed and used for meat. Each horn was very rigid and straight. It tapered to a hard point, which could easily penetrate a victim's eye or any soft part of the body, particularly the lower abdomen. The horn was heavy enough to have a damaging momentum when swung in two strong hands.

After picking up two of the horns, Zil passed one of them to Gib and pretended to fight. Gib quickly read from his mind, that they should practise attack and defence, but that it was important not to damage either of them. They turned, together, towards a tree and thrust the natural rapiers into the bark. After pulling them out, with difficulty, they laughed at their success. They had their own new weapon in their hands. The strangers would have a surprise. The first ever noted fencing lesson then followed. Each of the two Gyps in turn made a slow-motion attack on the other, who reacted instinctively with a defensive parry. They both surprised each other.

This exploratory session was soon followed by the introduction, and training, of the complete Gib group in the art of swordsmanship. The excitement and laughter, at the experience of using something so completely novel, was quickly stopped when the first casualty occurred. The lack of complete mental communication between the combatants allowed a careless thrust of a horn to end in the penetration of an unguarded belly. One of them collapsed with his entrails hanging out. The culprit was knocked down with a reversed horn in the hands of the leader, Zil. "Now, you all go to join your others and attack the strangers in that way!" He showed his anger at the waste of a strong life.

An outside observer could be excused for thinking that the Gyp hominids had an uninteresting lifestyle. For most of the time, they appeared to be sitting on their haunches and grooming themselves, or their offspring, whilst digesting the last meal. Few words or intelligible noises were heard. They had lived in this apparent state of bliss for many thousands of years, without making any progress, but they had been developing their thought processes. Their telepathic communication had developed to the point where each member was aware of the thoughts of all the others for most of the time. The only blanks were where a member wished to retain privacy.

The thoughts of the Gib group, on their journey to the eastern edge of the Gyp territory, were being received and understood by the entire tribe. The two members, who had been delegated to spy on the intruders, were also reading them. They were looking eagerly forward to receiving their own issue of the horn swords. They wanted to know if they could practise using them as a javelin, as all the hunters were expert at throwing stones to kill or maim the target with the first projectile. Whilst they had been observing the intruders, during their own hunting forays, they had seen them using their weighted antler weapons to kill their prey, and also, on one occasion, in an internal fight between two of their hunters. The big creatures, with the heaviest weapons, would not automatically win a battle between the Gyps and the Utee. The thinkers, amongst the defenders, were already working out possible situations and remedies for any apparent advantage held by the invaders. The vital fact was the security of their thoughts, whilst each of their own members was kept fully informed, instantly.

Gib held a council of war as soon as his group was reunited, about half a day's walk from the camp of the Utee. The spies gave an interesting piece of news. They had given the invaders the new name of Hoons, soon after they were left behind to start their work. They had noticed that the enemy had a habit of shouting, 'Hoon, hoon, hoon,' as a sort of battle cry, when attacking any animal, in order to kill it for food. They wondered if they would hear the shout, when they became locked in battle with themselves. The Gyps were usually very quiet whenever they were involved in such action.

Gib decided to spend another full day for his group to have more practice in using their horns as both swords and javelins. They moved away, to one day's distance, and exercised with the new weapons, until they were all convinced that they would soon eliminate the intruders. When Zil was informed that there were a similar number of the Hoons' male hunters to those of the Gyps, he agreed that Gib could select his own method of attack. He did not need to make it in a dark period, if he was sure of the outcome. They would have the benefit of more than one surprise.

They had learned, from the long period of observation, that the Hoons were totally unaware of their presence. They also knew that they would be shocked by the fact that the Gyps had more newly invented weapons than the weighted antlers, frightening as those could be if seen for the first time.

Gib made his decision. They would be in a strong position at dawn the next day, ready and waiting for the Hoon hunters to see them as they left their females and families in the sleep place. Each Gyp would be armed with his usual supply of throwing stones and a cutting stone, all carried in his waist bag. Added to them, he would carry two of the horn weapons, one to throw at the enemy before they were near enough to use their antlers, and the other to be retained for use as a sword for close combat. The intention was to disable all the hunters before they could come within reach of the Gyps, where they might be able to score a hit with their deadly antlers.

It was a normally bright dawn of a warming day when Atta led his hunters out of the tree-covered area where they spent each night. He had previously seen traces of a grazing herd of deer to the north of there and he was prepared to spend two or three days finding them.

The screams of fear from the females left behind him stopped him in his tracks. The hunters all spun round and saw unexpected disaster at the other side of their sleeping place, now occupied with only their mates and offspring. A large group of complete strangers, armed and aggressive, appeared to be advancing from the south towards their camp.

Without a moment of hesitation, Atta and his hunters rushed back to defend their families, back to attack this new enemy, before they could do any damage. The Hoons were all well rested, fully armed and ready for a fight that had been thrust upon them. They simply reacted to the circumstances without any thought for planning to tackle an armed group of similar numbers. They knew that they had their own secret weapon, the heavy club. They did not know that they were opposed to an intelligent enemy who had planned every move for their downfall.

The Hoons quickly ran past their sleep place and continued towards the waiting Gyps who were standing their ground, round throwing stones in each hand, the horn weapons placed beside each one of them, concealed in the short grass. "Hoon, hoon, hoon," bayed the attacking Hoons, waving their heavy antlers in the air. They had seen similar groups of strangers threatening them during their travels from the more northern regions. Their war cry had always been effective in frightening smaller groups, who had quickly succumbed to their novel weapons. This time it was very different. They were met with a barrage of well-aimed stones that put nearly half of them down on to the ground.

The survivors were still too far away to swing their clubs and do any damage, when each one of this enemy bent down and picked up a light stick. 'Too small and too light', thought Atta. 'We will be able to smash those before they can hurt us any more'. The Hoons were in for another surprise.

The enemy did not stand and wait for them to come within range to hit them with the sticks. They were within three lengths of each other when the 'sticks' were thrown very accurately, pointed end first, at the Hoons who were rushing forward. Each of the targets was hit. Most of them were hit in the lower body, some in the chest, and only one received his javelin in the arm. That one was Atta.

He pulled the strange weapon out of his left arm and attacked one of the Gyps using his heavy club. He was the only Hoon left standing. All the others had collapsed and most of them were writhing in agony, wrenching at the horns protruding from their bodies. Atta was unlucky. He was surrounded by four laughing Gyps, of whom each was pointing another 'stick' at his body, and they all lunged forward with their swords and penetrated his belly at the same time. His swinging club was released from his hand and it struck one of the other Gyps who were watching the amazing slaughter. He was the only casualty for Gib to report.

After a moment of hesitation, Gib led his hunters down the slope, towards the female Hoons, who were still watching them with horror at the sight of all their males being killed so easily. The message from Zil came through very clearly. "Kill all the males. Do what you want with the females, but do not bring back more than one for each of you, if you so wish. Do not let any escape to go and tell any other such Utee or Hoons in our area. Destroy any of them that you do not wish to keep".

This was done. Half of the females were made to carry all the Hoon weapons and spare food back to the Gyp home area.

CHAPTER FOURTEEN
3mBC COMPULSION

The steadily falling temperatures seriously affected all the groups of hominids living in the northern parts of the planet. Their first reaction was to try to find some way of keeping their bodies warmer. This resulted, eventually, in their testing various ways of softening the pelts of the animals that they killed for food. Failure followed failure.

Many of them tried to make some type of covering after scraping the flesh from the inside of the skin. They then found that the new pelt set hard, very quickly, and became useless as a garment. Washing many times in water gave little improvement, until one inventive male tried to beat the leather into a soft condition, using the branches taken from different trees that happened to grow nearby. The bark from only one of those trees acted as a tanning agent. His mates were astounded, as he was, when they noticed that some of his skins remained soft and pliable almost indefinitely. They were all very frustrated when they were unable to find the cause of his success.

Their growing brains helped them to realise that they must give the problem all their creative thoughts over a long period. Eventually, many years later, they had tested separate lots of skins being beaten in water, using different tree barks for each lot. Only one lot was successful. The skins retained the desired pliability. The tree was identified and remembered. Later still, they were able to find and recognise that variety of tree in the different parts of the forests in which they hunted.

The news spread from group to group and tanned leather garments became the normal apparel. During those years of trial and error, chilled and hungry hominids, particularly the young ones, succumbed to the cold. Many groups were decimated and lost, as the ice and snow moved further towards the south.

The survivors succeeded, partly by accident, rather than by their own planning. They followed the herds of grazing animals to the south and found a warmer part of the planet. They also continued to enjoy the nourishment from the meat that their hunters brought back for the weaker members of their group.

The news of improved weaponry spread very slowly, but surely, through the various types of hominids. Sooner or later, each group came up against strangers who were adept with such things as weighted clubs, animal horns used as swords and javelins, tactical planning and the use of spies for intelligence purposes. Some of the more aggressive types used the knowledge, gained from these advances in ability, in order to attack the stronger creatures, such as the mammoths, and for defence against the big cats. Later on, the shortage of suitable animal horns gave the inventive minds the opportunity to create similar spears, using selected straight wooden shoots from some of the hard wood trees in the forests.

Further experimenting with flint splinters led to sharp stone chips being fixed into the ends of the wooden spears. These enabled the strongest hominids to throw their spears and penetrate the thick skins of larger animals, such as the mammoth. These giants became very aggressive, when attacked in this way. They had always been able to use their weight, in order to deter carnivores such as the sabre-toothed cat, but they now found that they were being attacked by a smaller creature, that used its brain to its own advantage.

The groups of hominids began to follow the large herds of mammoths in their migrations. They went to the south in the cold winters, and tended to try to return to the northern grazing grounds in the warmer summer periods. Even during this ice age, the seasonal changes in weather encouraged a regular, annual migration, in order to use the best grazing possible. The hunters followed the prey - and survived.

"We have seen a definite improvement in mental activity and achievement since our last meeting", started Ywancontin. "This proves that the general standard of brain development, amongst the subject of our study, is moving forward. The rate of progress is not important, at this time. It is the direction in which they move that is the vital factor. It would be useful to hear the opinions of a few members of this Committee who have been involved in the recent observations. Will you please start with the Gyps, Marcus?"

"It is a pleasure to give my report," Marcus began, *"particularly as this group is showing signs of being the only one, under observation, that has retained the original ability to communicate mentally. They are already aware that they have advantages over the other groups with which they have come in contact. They are living in a productive area that is rarely affected by the climatic changes. We have seen how they used their skills in order to eliminate a threat from the invading Hoons. The instant form of communication gave them such a benefit, both before and during the battle with a formidable enemy, who were armed with an awesome new weapon. They used their intelligence in every sense of the word. They knew the strengths of the enemy. They planned to counter the dangers by inventing their own new weapons, and they were able to use them with confidence and tactical success. We should note that there is a possibility of the group being affected by some form of arrogance, after such a successful battle.*

They have proved to themselves that their varied diet of meat, fruit, nuts and some roots, really does help them to maintain their strength and increase the usage of their mental capacity. We need to monitor their thoughts on the subject of self-advancement. They are already so far advanced, ahead of the majority of the other groups in Africa, that there is a danger of their confidence giving them the idea of becoming the masters of all other groups with which they come in contact. That is my caveat for the Gyps.

I would like to record the fact that the Gyps also show promise for future improvement in the desired direction. They will be a suitable group for consideration in the field of spiritual development. Their retained skills in telepathy will be of help in that area. I have been able to find signs of the retention of the trait of compassion, which we introduced such a long time ago. That might help to counter any offensive tendency".

Ywancontin inclined his head and showed his appreciation. *"Thank you, Marcus, you understand that their future depends, as always, on their ability to react to the various stimuli with which they come in contact. The climatic changes are likely to have less effect on them than on those who are active at distances much further from the equator. They certainly are going to be affected by the trends of the northern tribes to move to the south, and to stay there until the cold period ends. Such invasions might well create more defensive fighting, and casualties, for the Gyps, than they can absorb, without the loss of some of their land area. Strong as they are at the present time, they need to increase their population and train more warriors ready for their own defence. They have proved that they have the mental skills to plan in this way. Their very survival will depend on their doing so.*

Now, Lucus, your report on the changes in the north, and the effect on the hominids from that area, will help us to complete this brief review".

"The most surprising fact about the northern tribes is the dramatic change in the numbers", started Lucus. "There have been times when I felt confident that the more numerous Tarls would grow even stronger and assert authority over the larger, but slower thinking, Utee. Their more advanced intelligence indicated that they would continue to be more effective in all their enterprises. Their smaller stature seemed to be an advantage.

When they used their initiative and planned to destroy a group of Hoons, there were all the signs of imminent success. But, it did not happen. The Hoons had retained just a trace of telepathic power that gave them sufficient sense of mistrust to make them take precautions against a surprise attack. From that time onwards, the little people, the Tarls, were the target for destruction by the groups of larger hominids in their area.

A similar type of bullying has been reported in other, widespread, parts of the planet, in different continents, where the trait is not likely to have been transferred by word of mouth or by observation. The small people of the mid-African deserts have suffered in the same way. It seems to have grown out of the strongly entrenched hunting instinct. A male arrogance tends to encourage the most successful hunters to try to impress the females, and the weaker males, with their physical strength, and their ability to force their own wishes on the others.

There is no doubt in my mind that, when we apply time to experience, all these creatures, under observation, will continue to make progress. Some negativity does creep into the equation, but there are signs that this is recognised by many of the more enlightened creatures. The seeds of philosophy have already been sown, and we can look forward to the time when this positive trait can be monitored and appreciated to the full. May I suggest that we will be able to prepare a confirmation of my comment after our review in a further one million years?"

There was a gentle drumming of fingertips on the table. Ywancontin nodded, "Yes. Unless there are any more views that require expression, I will close this meeting until it is reconvened. Thank you all".

CHAPTER FIFTEEN
2mBC PROGRESS

During the previous million years, the ice had retreated and advanced a number of times. Volcanic eruptions, together with the movements the continental plates, had tortured the land and disturbed the development of all the progressive creatures that struggled for existence.

None of the more advanced ones, bipeds or quadrupeds, were aware that the climatic changes were even taking place. They simply reacted to whatever circumstances were thrust upon them. When one source of food was no longer available, they looked for something new. When it became too cold, they moved towards the warmth of the sun. If stronger forces attacked them, they either ran away or they were eliminated.

A large part of the land surface was covered with primeval forest, and this gave cover in which the smaller groups of creatures were often able to grow in both numbers and physical strength. Their survival seemed to depend mainly on chance. The hominids had made noticeable progress. They depended much less upon the trees for providing a path from one part of the forest to another. Their ability to remain upright all the day, and to walk or run on their two legs, had grown at the same time that their brains had developed steadily. Some negativity had crept into their lives with the growth of their imaginations. They were usually frightened of the time of darkness.

The dark night was when the little people came near to them and created trouble, stealing the food, and sometimes the babies. Some of them were disguised as snakes, and some of them as big cats. If any of the members of the tribe happened to be at all psychic, they were terrified if they caught a glimpse of one of the Tall Ones, who were occasional visitors. Such a sighting was kept as a secret, after earlier such declarations had resulted in the immediate slaughter of the innocent clairvoyant. Any hint of awareness of spiritual matters was condemned as 'Bad!'

There was a noticeable difference amongst the most advanced group in the north of Africa. The Gyps had a knowledge that there was more to their lives than the simple process of trying to survive. For many centuries there had been a number of differences between them and the other groups that had lived near them.

Firstly, they had retained the ability to communicate by thought. Although this had the effect of retarding the development of their own language, their thinking skills had not been held back. The instant conversations between minds had accelerated their brain development. Questions had been instantly understood without the need for searching for the best word to complete a sentence. There was literally a meeting of the minds of any number of like-minded beings. A group of warrior hunters might be seen sitting close together, apparently resting, when they were, in fact, discussing vital issues such as weapons, or tactics. In a similar way, the leaders of the group considered the various political possibilities for the control and development of the Gyps. It was very much to the advantage of the entire group.

Another difference was the way in which the Gyps had adapted the accidental introduction of slavery into their routines. It had always been accepted, by those beaten in battle, that submission, with a bowed head, was the only attitude to adopt at the time. This usually led to their being taken back to the main camp of the victors, and then they were given duties which ensured that they received sufficient food in the future.

Many more benefits arose, for both the slave and the master. The slaves were encouraged to breed within their own caste, and the owners were able occupy themselves in whatever way they wished, exploring any part of the growing awareness of the facts of their life. The simple basics of such subjects as geography, physics, mathematics, philosophy, and even the management of food supplies, began to be the subjects of the telepathic debates.

During this period of continual mental progress the leaders of the Gyps decided to increase their knowledge of the world beyond their own normal boundaries. Perhaps, there was a trace in the race memory of a land exploration being made in their far distant past. The desire to learn more about the world became overwhelming. The supreme leader, named Kaas, gave the final order for a party of hunters to go to the south, for at least three moons. Communication would be maintained as usual. Any breakdown in this method would signal that the party was to return towards the north, until contact was renewed. Larg was to be the leader, in charge of his two hands of hunters. Nab, with his similar two hands, was to accompany Larg, and accept his orders whilst controlling his own team. They were all to avoid conflict with any strangers that they might meet. This was intended to reduce the risk of casualties and maintain their numbers until they had achieved their objectives. Each of the two team leaders was permitted to take two willing females with them for the purpose of relieving their men of their lusts and preventing them having any desire to make contact with strange groups. The females would help to carry the spare weapons and prepare the food that the hunters brought in from their efforts.

Nab and Larg both had the same father and different mothers. They had a friendly rivalry and were pleased to have been selected for this novel adventure. Armed with the usual weapons of both cutting and throwing stones, spears and leather shields, they set off, carrying two days supply of meat.

The first few days were spent crossing familiar territory, which they had hunted many times in the past. They waved to each of the families who saw them and who knew exactly what they were doing.

Keeping near the river ensured that they would have enough water for their needs and they were also kept moving towards the south, from where the river flowed.

During the first moon of their journey they adapted to a simple routine. They were walking for the first part of the day. Then they had a rest during the hottest period, followed by walking until near the nightfall. They were able to hunt for fresh meat on every second or third day. The benefit of staying near to the river became obvious from the easy hunting. The animals also stayed near to the source of fresh water. There were numerous varieties of deer, together with their predators, mainly the different shapes and sizes of cats. Other dangers lurked in the waters of the slowly moving river. The Gyps had frequent warnings from the sight of young deer being pulled into and under the water by large scaly monsters, with large mouths full of sharp teeth. The cats seemed to find that the huge herds of lively deer provided so much easy food for them that they rarely made any attempt to attack the Gyps.

During the first moon of their trek, they reported that the land, away from the river, was very dry, with little vegetation that could support the animals. This altered as they continued to move to the south. The land was rising slowly. Sometimes the river waters moved more quickly, as they flowed from higher land. The hunters passed a series of rapids where the river had cut into the ground and where it was not so easily accessible. They were now well into unknown territory. The land continued to rise until they arrived on the edge of a large open plain with its own river system. They could see that other new groups of hominids were hunting the area. Keeping themselves concealed in the vegetation, the Gyps watched these strangers for a day before it was decided that there was little to learn from them. They were shorter and blacker skinned than they were. The few females that they saw had little to attract any attention.

Larg had an easy decision to make. "We move south again, towards the noises of the night." This referred to the occasional rumbling that they had heard during the dark hours of the past few days. They all understood the noises of the thunderstorms that they had experienced through their lives. This was somewhat different. Nab had told his brother that his own team were, at first, puzzled by the strange noises. When these had continued for a few days, they had shown signs of fear of the unknown. Thoughts, including the pictures of demons and giant cats, had been noted by both the team leaders, and, naturally, these had been transmitted back to Kaas at the river estuary.

The new orders issued to Larg were clear. "You are now approaching the end of the three moons of your journey to the south. You have reported little of benefit to the Gyps, but you now have a question to answer. You will continue to move to the south until you have found the reason for the noises that you have reported. Your thoughts will be read each day but it is said that you will find the answer to the question and something of real benefit to us all. Go!"

The two leaders willingly accepted the new orders and the twenty-six creatures continued to walk towards the south for almost another moon. The females were an asset to the males, sharing their favours with all and every one of them, without any problems. They fully understood their subservient position. The rumbling noises gradually became louder each night. They could also be heard throughout most of each day.

On one day, they had to take cover behind some large rocks on the edge of the valley through which they were passing. The loud noise coming from their front was obviously created by a black mass of large meat creatures coming straight at them from the south. The majority of them were carrying two huge curved horns on their heads. Mixed amongst them were quantities of a slightly smaller deer like creature, which also carried two long pointed horns. The noise made it difficult for anyone to speak and the mental messages were all similar. The animals were in panic. They were all racing away from the south as fast as they could run. But, there were so many of them. Larg knew that the entire race of Gyps could not possibly kill and eat so much meat. If they could only keep track of such a large herd they would have an endless source of food and would be able to grow into a bigger group than they had ever contemplated.

The animals had started to pass them when the sun was at its highest. They continued to thunder past them throughout the rest of the day. There were still some of them galloping past when the sun was setting. The Gyps killed two of the stragglers and feasted off the meat.

It was a good night until the noises started again. They began with a heavy rumbling in the south. Then, louder and louder, until they could feel the noises coming from the very ground on which they were lying. At the same time, the red lights flickered in the black sky, getting brighter as the noise increased. All the Gyps were frightened and they sent signals back to Kaas and the others in the north. The reply came from Kaas, himself.

"Hunters of the Gyps, be not afraid. You are on a special mission and will be tested from time to time. We are all with you in this time of testing. The noises that you hear, and which give fear to the meat animals, are from the earth itself. It is in pain and suffering from the wounds received over the years. You must continue to move to the south until you come across the red lights of the earth's pain. There you will find the secret that you have been sent to find. You will know immediately when you find it. Then, I shall also know your thoughts, and this secret. You will all be well rewarded. The knowledge was in our race memory, but it was lost in the passing of time. You are not alone."

Both Larg and Nab felt better for the message from the man whom they respected as their Leader and Master. The attitudes of both their teams were improved to the point of their continuing to walk to the south. They had heard tribal stories of volcanic eruptions before but they had no personal knowledge of them. They would soon be able to tell of their own experiences.

Setting off at dawn, the group made steady progress, seeing very few animals at all. Those that they came across were damaged creatures that had been hurt in the stampede of the previous day. The loud noises under their feet continued, as they started to climb up the mountains that were ahead of them. Larg had sent one of his team well ahead of the main party, in order to know immediately should any problem arise. The scout was the first one to reach the summit and he was stopped in his tracks when he looked across the wide valley ahead of him.

The other side of this valley was filled with the smoke from the burning of trees and undergrowth. It was a fire created from the red-hot tongues of molten lava flowing from the newly forming volcanoes and it spread as far as the eye could see to both the east and the west. The wind, blowing from the north-east, was taking the thickest of the smoke away from the hunters.

Once more, all the Gyps automatically received this sight, and Kaas again gave them instructions. He told them to move forward and search the area at the edge of the fires.

The forward scout waited on the top of the ridge until the rest of the hunters joined him. They all then spread out and advanced, down the slopes of the mountain, until they reached the level of the plain. In some parts they found that the fires had worked their way along the higher places where the dried shrubs and trees had ignited and had been reduced to ash. Larg was leading his team when he trod on some still-hot ashes.

The heat penetrated the thick, leathery soles of his feet and he shouted with pain, whilst limping back to join the others. They all felt his pain. Brother Nab had the answer to the problem. "Cut up your aprons and wrap the thickest part of the skins around your feet", he ordered. This was soon done and the group continued to move forward, more warily than before. They avoided treading on any more of the hot ashes and were able to get close to some of the burning trees without damaging themselves.

"The animals have all gone to the north", commented Nab, realising that it was the day when they should have been replenishing their stocks of food. "There is one over there," said Larg, pointing ahead of them. "It has been killed by the fire. Let's eat that before we go any further."

The other hunters, who had been feeling the need for nourishment, welcomed this. They were all aware of the fact that they had not eaten all that day. They were about to have a surprise.

As they approached the still burning tree, against which they could see the body of a 'big horn' beast, with its skin burned off the flesh, they were all aware of the smell. It was not the smell, which they all recognised, of newly killed meat, but something entirely new to them. They were the first hominids in Africa to smell roast beef. Their mouths watered as they rushed up to the carcass and attacked it with their cutting stones. The blackened skin was easily pulled off the flesh and the hot, juicy flesh simply fell apart in their eager hands. They gorged themselves. No interference came from the listeners, who were also enjoying the novel experience. Kaas and the others, who could not smell the aroma, were puzzled, but curious.

Nab had noticed that there were parts of the beast that had not been heated or burnt by the recent fire, and he had already cut out the liver and heart in order to carry them away from the next day. "Let's see what the fire will do to this meat if we put them together."

He laid pieces of the raw meat on the hot embers from the tree and waited. They all crowded around the experiment, listening to the sizzle and smelling the newly cooking meat, whilst chattering mentally, silently. After a short time, Nab and Larg picked up odd pieces of the scorching meat and tasted them, before returning them to the heat, raw sides down on the glowing embers. It was a great success. They all tasted the new form of meat and then packed some of it away for later use.

The new orders from Kaas came through clearly. "Look for more hot meat and bring it back the this land. The flame is the secret. Capture it and bring it also. Come back here as soon as you have done that".

The hunters spent another moon in the area. They did find a few more cooked animals during the first few days, but they had to eat the flesh in order to survive in a land devoid of live creatures. Water was still available in the streams running down from the mountains. They would not starve, but holding a flame was a more difficult task.

Their first attempts to hold some of the fire resulted in burned hands and a reduced number of volunteers. Those of them that picked up a burning branch were more successful, but only for a short time. Eventually, they realised that there was a need to have a pile of some dry grasses, or sticks, ready to have a burning branch thrust into it. This helped the flame to live, and it was under their control, ready to grow again, when more material was put on it. More branches could be put into the fire to be ignited and then they could walk a short distance before reassembling the fire, and feeding the flames. It was a tedious system, but it worked. Kaas was pleased enough to see that his orders were being obeyed and that fire was being brought back to him. Some of the cooked meat was already becoming foul smelling and inedible. He was not worried about that not being brought back by the hunters. He knew that he could cook raw meat at any time, now that he was going to have the fire to do so.

It was his turn to have a surprise. One moon after the start of the return journey, on the darkest night of their experience, heavy black clouds gathered over the hunters and the thunderstorms started. The heavy rainfall poured down on them all and their carefully nurtured fires were washed away. They had been enjoying cooked meat until then, and now they had to return to the old ways of eating their meat raw, but, if possible, hot from a fresh kill.

During the past four moons, Nab had been having vivid dreams, which he kept to himself. Some of them had been very pleasant, including physical contact with the mates that he had left behind, before he and Larg had set out on the present adventure. Later, they became more serious.

On the night of the heavy rain and the disaster of losing their fire, a tall severe looking man was standing at his feet, looking straight into his eyes. "Nab", he said, "you have been chosen to be given some news of your future. You will not tell any of the others in your group but you will see it all come true. You will then know that you have been told the truth and you will believe the things that you will be told later. You will be the leader of the returning hunters, and you will be the one to tell the facts about the fire to Kaas. Your brother, Larg, will not return with you because he will remain near this place. Your knowledge of the fire will place you in an important position with your people and you will gain their respect. You must now think about how the fire was created, and how you can create more heat in order to recreate the flames as and when you require them. There is a way of doing that and you will find it." The Tall One faded from his dream.

Nab awoke from the night's sleep with a feeling of joy and confidence in the future, tinged with anxiety about Larg. He knew that his brother had been limping on the march for the past few days and he now asked him to show him his feet. They were badly scarred, cracked and bleeding. Damaged by the burns experienced on the hot ashes in the burning forest, Larg was in no condition to continue walking. Nab ordered the men to take turns in carrying their leader, until the wounds were healed.

The returning hunters trudged another day towards the north, carrying the damaged Larg, as well as the usual supply of stones, spears and surplus meat. The patient complained all day about the pain in his legs and the fact that he could not walk. During the night, his feet had swollen to the point of agony and he asked his men to kill him and give him peace. They refused. The next day took them higher up a mountain in single file. The continual screaming from the damaged Larg was suddenly stopped, whilst they were moving along a narrow track, and the entire group looked to where he had been. His carriers were standing on the path, looking over the side. One of them turned towards Nab and thought, "He cursed me and I stumbled." The other one agreed, and explained, "I could not hold him alone". Nab believed them both. "It was what he wanted, and he could not have lived more than another day". They were all fatalistic

125

about sudden death.

One moon after the death of Larg, Nab halted the group at the edge of a dry plain and pointed out a number of dead trees. Some were standing, but many had fallen to the ground and had started to decay. He prodded the trunk of one of them with the hardwood butt of his spear. The log had almost turned to dust. "These dead trees are in the same condition as those that we saw in the south, after they had been heated by the fire", he pointed out. "We saw some of them light up from the heat of the other fires. Let us see if we can make this tree hot enough to give us a fire".

He started to rub the rounded spear butt along a groove in the bark of the tree, pressing downwards at the same time. After a short time of this exercise, he put his hand on to the spear and immediately burnt himself. "It's hot, it's hot", he shouted, and immediately continued the movements. Within a short time he could see that the dry powdery wood was starting to glow and the warm wind helped it to give a flicker of flame. "Feed the fire", he shouted, and the watchers knew exactly what to do. The time that they had spent near the volcanoes had not been wasted.

Dried grasses were fed gently to the flame and they quickly had a fire burning on the top of the log. More grass and some small twigs helped it all to grow into a large cooking fire, in which the log itself became a major part. They were all shouting with the excitement of their surprise success. Two of the hunters put some of their raw meat into the flames and they were soon enjoying the delicious aroma. Others put pieces of their meat on to the tips of their spears and then they held them in the flames. They all suffered burn damage to their skins in some way. Mouths were burned during the eager tasting of the roast taken straight from the fire. Many lessons were learned that day. The feasting developed into a night of celebration, and the females did not have any rest until the dawn. By that time the fire had burnt itself out, into a pile of hot ash.

Nab tested the heat of the ash by putting some more dry grass on to it and he was delighted to find that he had the makings for another new fire. The flames flickered and responded to the addition of more twigs. He had mastered the flames. He knew that he could reproduce the right conditions and make another fire at will. The listeners, back in their base area, had received their message of joy. Orders arrived very quickly from Kaas. "Return here now, well done".

After the return of the hunters, Kaas and all the elders of the Gyps feted Nab and his team. He was appointed to the new position of First Guardian of the Flame after he had demonstrated to them that he could produce a fire, almost on demand.

It was the beginning of an era. The other 'fire hunters', and the four females with their offspring, were shown the greatest respect by the remainder of the Gyps. Their numbers were maintained by the annual births of four or five babies, and the secret of the creation of heat from friction was kept for a few generations. Nab continued to have frequent contact with the Tall Ones, mostly by dreams at night but there was one occasion when he saw a vision during the daytime. He saw some armed members of a foreign race approaching the Gyp land boundaries. He told Kaas of the risks of 'others who would want to take their fire from them' and gave him the thought that their hunters should all be brought to a state of readiness. This helped Kaas to prove his leadership abilities yet again, and the invaders were deflected away.

Much later, one 'Great Leader' decided that all of the smaller group leaders should be educated in the mystique of making fire and the knowledge spread throughout the area around the Sea of the Middle of the Earth. The benefits of being able to cook the raw meats of the hunters were enjoyed by nearly all the hominids within a few centuries of Nab's success.

CHAPTER SIXTEEN
THE REVIEW

The Committee members were all smiling when they assembled for the review of 2mBC up to date. Each one of them had been fully aware of the real benefits that the creatures would receive from being able to enjoy cooked food, even if it were only once a day, or, even, once in two days. They had expressed their wishes for this to the Chairman, on a number of occasions, but Ywancontin had invariably refused them.

"I agree that the hominids would be placed in a stronger position, if they were to be given the secret of fire, but you are all fully aware of the need for them to make their own progress, as and when their brains can absorb the necessary knowledge. If they are not able to think through the required steps in order to make, and control, fire, then they will need to continue to try to survive without that advancement". That had been the usual reaction from him whenever the subject had been raised.

Now, his discipline had enabled him to highlight the point.

"You are entitled to show your pleasure in the fact that the Gyps have mastered the art of fire-making. You will see that the knowledge will spread throughout the planet, over a period of time, and all the hominids will receive much benefit from the skill. Other new skills will be discovered and passed on to the others, whether there is an attempt to keep the secrets or not. That is the nature of these creatures, which are rapidly moving forward to the point where we can refer to them as 'mankind'.

We are aware, from our observations, that the increasing number of Gyps indicates a measure of their success in surviving. They are not only recording success in their physical lives but also in their spiritual progress. The gifted ones are showing wisdom in the way in which they retain such knowledge, without releasing it through their mental means of communication. This will tend to encourage the development of their vocal skills, and language will become the main means of sharing their thoughts about the daily routine. Telepathy will be retained by the ruling class, mainly for the purpose of the defence of their land, but, also, for the development of procedures that will grow into religious control of the masses of the unknowing. Some of those who are spiritually aware will be included in that control and some of them will be excluded from it. In this way, the ruling group will not become complacent and will apply all their mental energy to whatever is required in order to retain their control. This sense of urgency will help all the brains to grow and make progress.

There seems to be no doubt in our minds that the Gyps are likely to continue to make the most progress in Africa and all the area around the Middle Earth Sea, but we must consider the possibility of their being eliminated. This could be the result of the invasion of stronger groups from the north, or the development of some micro-organism that might weaken their health to the point of obliteration.

We know that there are many surviving groups of the Utee, spread across the plains of Asia and up to the edges of the frozen forests to the north and east of this landmass. They all can be traced back to having some of the same forebears as the groups that you have been monitoring over the aeons. You will now prepare a plan to spend some time with these various groups, or tribes, if you prefer that word, and report back to this Committee with your recommendations for ensuring that some of them survive through the next million years.

You are all well aware that there is a new continent awaiting the introduction of these more advanced creatures. Its ecology has developed independently since it broke away from the original landmass, although a few species have been able to cross the ice linking it with Asia. The successful ones have mostly been birds, able to fly over in sufficient numbers to establish a viable group before spreading towards the warmer southern parts. I require your recommendations for introducing a number of groups that will be most suited for seeding this New World. I will be looking for spiritual, as well as physical abilities, which can be encouraged to prosper in a new environment.

Marcus, I want you to take Solem and Lucus to the north eastern area of the Utee and select the groups most qualified for both the hazardous journey and the transfer into the new lands. At the same time, Mellak, you will take both Bevak and Surtyn into the north western area. You will make a similar assessment of those more successful groups, and make whatever recommendations you feel are necessary for their progress.

In this way, we will be able to assess the rate of progress, both spiritually and physically, in three totally different areas of the planet. Those under observation will not be aware that they are competing in any way with the others. In fact, they are unlikely even to know of the existence of people who are at such a distance from where they operate.

Marcus and Melak, do you understand what is required of you both?" The two leaders inclined their heads. "Then you can start immediately".

CHAPTER SEVENTEEN
SELECTION

Marcus was delighted to have been made responsible for the assessment of the Utee in the eastern parts of Asia. He and his colleagues had studied them at times, throughout the aeons, and he had developed an admiration for many of their traits. Their determination to survive had been passed down through the years to the steadily growing numbers of these strong dark skinned people. They had used any knowledge gained, in various ways, to build up an awareness of the nature of the Earth plane. This had helped them to make progress.

The ability to tan leather had enabled them to adapt the skins of the animals that they killed for food, and ensure that there were always sufficient garments for all the tribe to wear and keep warm. This prevented the normal high losses of young members during the colder spells. They had also learned how to arrange some of the skins, from the largest animals, around a tripod of wooden stakes and give them protection when the weather was being difficult. These shelters could then be dismantled, dragged by the females, who rarely went on the hunt, and moved to the next hunting ground.

As they made the first few contacts with the scattered tribes, Marcus noticed that there were some basic differences in the features of the groups that were the furthest apart. Those that hunted along the northern edges of the cold forests had begun to show characteristics that were not to be seen in the southern tribes. The skin colour of those in the south tended to be more light brown, or even yellow, than the darker brown of the north. He accepted that this was the result of isolation from each other. The lack of regular meetings of all the tribes resulted in a more localised concentration of some of the genes. Strong genes continued to show their presence whilst the less powerful ones were reduced, to the point of being ineffective and eventually unnoticed.

The tribe of Great Bear had been able to dominate a large part of the coastal area on the shores facing the morning sun. They had grown slowly but surely in numbers and they were now too strong to be vanquished easily. Over many years, they had learned from the occasional contact with other tribes. They had also gained much knowledge from their own experiences.

Their hunters were equipped with straight, hardwood, spears, headed with sharp, pointed, flint stones that were firmly lodged in the end of the shaft. They were able to throw them heavily and accurately. They used them to isolate and kill fully mature mammoths, when they needed that amount of meat for the tribe. Other aggressive Utee tribes had learned from this knowledge that they should not to try to attack the Great Bears.

During their visits to different parts of the coastline, their craftsmen, and the females, would collect a variety of useful items. Large flint stones were carried away, for napping into the required shapes, at a later date. Soft clay would be taken, wrapped in skins, to be moulded into shapes that could hold water, such as a type of bowl with a handle attached. These were hardened in the hot sun and were really used as an experiment for carrying water to the lips of small children and any sick adults. They were not considered to be a success, until one of the bowls was accidentally 'fired' in a very hot fire. When it was discovered that the pot was then hard and reliable for carrying water, the fortunate one who created it was appointed the tribal potter, and excused all other duties, whilst he tried to discover the most suitable shapes to make. This craft was claimed to be a Great Bear tribal invention and retained as a secret for a few generations.

The Great Bear himself was lying in his skin shelter waiting for the morning sun to warm his flesh. His women were squatting and standing around him, knowing that this was his last day before he joined all those other hunters and chieftains who had gone before him. They were fatalists. Life had always been hard for them, despite the confidence that Great Bear had always shown. Certainly, there had been no invasion of their hunting grounds during his leadership. Their enemies had kept well away from them.

They had not starved; in fact, they had prospered in many ways. Their hunters had usually been able to find and kill plenty of good meat animals. Their fire maker had never failed to create a flame when it was required. They all knew the secret of having a supply of dry tinder ready for the spark, when he made it, and they ensured that it was always available.

Under this leader, one of their males had concentrated on searching in the ground for new foods. He had been named Dig, and had used a flat piece of flint stone to make a hole in the ground next to some of the succulent plants that they found growing at the edges of the forest. He discovered that some of the roots had been fat and juicy and they were eaten, after being cursorily washed in the water of a nearby stream. Dig also found that some of the roots and, also, some of the leaves growing on other plants, could be more enjoyable, if they were put into boiling water for a time. This brought together the three new interests of fire, pottery and botany.

The watchers waited with mixed feelings. Great Bear should have lived for a few more years, at least. Life had decided that he would meet the big cat two days earlier, and life had also decided that the cat would be able to get its claw under the spear and to tear open the belly of the leader. The skin had been replaced inside his skirt, but that had not stopped the loss of blood. As the sun rose over the big salt water, the eyes of Great Bear faded and he stopped breathing.

The wailing of the females alerted all the nearby hunters and they gathered around the shelter, showing their respect with downcast eyes. "Great Bear has earned a special farewell to help him on his way to his new life", said Flame, the fire-maker. "I will make a funeral fire that will take his knowledge with him to help him in the future". This appeared to be a mark of respect that had been earned by their dead leader. It would be the first intended cremation.

In recent years, after they had learned about the methods of making fire, there had been a few accidents, where an individual had been killed in an uncontrollable fire. In each case, it had been noted that the flames had consumed most of the body in the hottest part of the fire. The thinkers had decided that this was a good result. It was better than having a body decaying in or on the ground. It was much better then letting the big cats come and fight over the remains. Yes. The suggestion was accepted.

Flame sent all the members of the tribe out into the wooded

area to find plenty of brushwood and dry branches. With all this material he built a large pyre and had the body of their leader placed gently on top of it. The tribe gathered around as a new spark was created by Flame rubbing the butt of Great Bear's spear on a tinder dry log. As the twigs caught alight, they were placed under the pyre, until the fire roared through the complete pile of wood, including the spear, and the body was quickly consumed.

Flame studied the crowd. They all showed respect. Some of the females and the younger ones were crying quietly. This was the end of a period of stability in a very unstable world. The fire-maker had a sudden shock. He could see three tall strangers standing together near the fire. They were not wearing the usual leather skirt but had a full-length garb of a beauty and light colour that he had never before imagined.

Flame looked quickly at the other hunters who were standing near to him, expecting that they would be turning to deal with these invaders. None of them seemed to be aware of their existence. He looked back at the three men, but they were no longer to be seen. He felt a cold shiver run down his spine. He could not have imagined them.

By now, the fire was burning down into hot ashes and the crowd was wandering back to attend to the normal chores of the day. That night, Flame had a vivid dream and saw the three tall men again. The most serious looking one of them spoke his name.

"Do not be afraid, Flame, we are here to help you and your tribe and we come in peace. We come from the Great Spirit, who has made you and who wishes you to make progress in this world. You could see us at the funeral of Great Bear, because you were thinking along a spiritual path, asking where was the living Great Bear, now he had been eaten by the fire. It is good for you to think in that way. There is so much to learn and you have now found the way to move forward on your path of life.

Since we have made this contact we will continue to meet with you in your dreams. You will be able to learn so much more, and you will know that you are being given the truth. During the day, you will be able to ask for help in making your decisions about all the daily problems, as they arise. The answers will come to you, in your mind, from one of your helpers who have been with you from the days of your boyhood. You will never feel alone on your path. Go forward, in peace, my friend".

Flame awoke, immediately. He was puzzled and, at the same time, feeling elated. The experience of the dream was so real, and he knew that it was also true. His awareness of wisdom of the three Tall Ones made him realise his own lack of knowledge, but he knew that he could trust them completely. He mentally said 'thank you'.

During the next two days, the tribe talked about the past and the future. The elders decided that their new leader should be Little Wolf, the young brother of Great Bear, because they had hunted with him for a few years, they trusted him, and he was really a younger version of his brother. Flame was given the honour of making the announcement.

"Hunters of the tribe of Great Bear, now that our Leader has gone to hunt in the world ahead of us all, it has been decided that our new Leader is Little Wolf, who knows what is needed from his own life up to now. His name is changed to Great Bear, like the one who walked before him".

The grunts of approval came from all present, hunters, craftsmen and females alike. Great Bear listened, until it became quiet. "When the sun rises tomorrow, we will go to the Big Salt Water and eat fish". The tribe did as they were told.

Fishing in the salt water was always frustrating and, occasionally, rewarding. The success depended on the state of the tide and whether a shoal of fish had been trapped in the shallows on the landside of the sandy beach. The tribe arrived in time to see the tide receding quickly. In the trapped water, under the low cliff, they could a mass of small fish changing direction as they came to each end of the shallow lake. Whooping with joy at the sight of so much tasty food, the hunters invaded the water from one end, standing close to each other, they moved steadily towards the other end, driving the shoal in front of them. The stabbing spears lifted the fish out of the water and they were then thrown to the waiting females.

When they reached the end of the lake, most of the fish had slipped through between the legs of the men and the process was then repeated. The hunter/fishermen turned round and started to walk back, killing as they went. This process went on until there were enough dead fish for every member to have a large meal. Throughout this time, all the observers, females and children alike, maintained a steady, rhythmic chanting that mesmerised the anglers. It was a pulsing, almost musical, sound created by the welling of feelings of joy that came from within each one of them.

Flame had already lit a number of cooking fires on the cliff top and the hot ashes were waiting for the fish to be placed in them, to create a feast for the whole tribe. Laughter and contentment ruled the day.

Marcus prepared his report after having visited a total of four different tribes of the eastern Utee.

"There is little to choose between the tribes that were under observation. Solem, Lucus and I, all agree that these Utee have developed steadily and confidently since they were last studied. Physically, they have advanced to the point where they are sure of their own position in the natural world in which they live.

Their brains are able to cope with new situations and new subjects for understanding. They are able to create and use new crafts, based on the facts that they have discovered for themselves. New sciences, some of them are only in a basic form, are growing and being applied to their everyday lives, to their great advantage. Their interest in finding new foods is leading them towards the testing, and tasting, of every type of plant that they find. They are aware of some of the medical benefits of small quantities of these roots and leaves, imbibed as a form of a tea.

They have noticed that the majority of new ideas are discovered by accident. They are not yet aware that they have a source of inspiration from within their own mentalities. All credit for some novel benefit is given to the person who had pointed it out to them.

Although a limited number of them are aware of the existence of Spirit, they do not yet give credit, for all the good things that they receive, to any other source than their own efforts. They are moving nearer to that discovery. The thought is in the minds of a very few that there is some form of life for them, other than the short, sharp life on Earth. They are beginning to talk about a future after death. The seeds have been sown and will continue to grow. Spiritually, they are as advanced as any other groups on the planet, perhaps a little more so.

Physically, they are a strong, resilient group that will continue to ask questions amongst themselves, learning from each other, and from their own experiences. The rudimentary crafts that are developing will occupy their ingenuity and strength, at the same time they will help their brains to continue to develop and move them along their path into the future. We will see them learning more skills, as their knowledge increases, in mental subjects like medicine and philosophy, and in the practical subjects such as pottery, tannery and woodworking. Soon, they will be able to venture on to the surface of water, using floating materials.

We found that they have almost totally lost the skills of telepathic communication. This was a direct result of the development of the spoken word, but we will see the continuing growth of a variety of languages amongst all the tribes. The remaining traces of telepathy are seen in the ability of only a few to read the thoughts of another. The deeper thinkers appear to be amongst the few with that inherited skill. The pattern of use of that skill tends to vary from one to another amongst those with the gift. The lesser-gifted adults have some awareness of caring for the problems of others, in such as the one that finds beneficial plants, or the one skilled in advising the bereaved on how to accept the future. Some of the tribes already name such a character as the 'helper' or the 'medicine-man'. Interdependency is helping to build these tribes into a unity of power and purpose. It will continue to help them to make real progress. We recommend that any of the tribes that we have visited should be considered for moving to the New World, at any time that may be appropriate".

The Chairman accepted the report, with his thanks to the three members concerned.

CHAPTER EIGHTEEN
2mBC SELECTION NW

Mellak, Bevak and Surtyn decided to spend a period of time with each of four tribes, randomly selected from the two main Utee groups in the north-western part of the main landmass. The Hoons and the Gols had each grown in size until they were too large to be controlled by a single leader. Internal strife had arisen sporadically, and this had usually resulted in a challenger for the leadership taking fifty or sixty supporters away to form a new group or tribe.

Some of these new tribes had been established for thousands of years and they had little memory of their own history, only tales of past leaders and their successes in battle. Bad experiences were recalled around the cooking fires in the form of stories about the 'Little People' who caused famine and illness, and about the giants that ate the babies. They quickly forgot about the newly formed tribes that had prospered for only a short time, before disappearing during a cold period, or after a failed attempt to eliminate another tribe, that was more effective in their hunting and killing abilities.

When a new tribe was formed, there was a noticeable simplicity in the structure that could not be seen in the older, larger tribes. The new leader, who was often self-appointed and prepared to fight to the death to keep that position, would stress his authority by insisting on being the first to mate with each young female, when she reached puberty. Once she was pregnant, she would be released from that control and she could then mate with any other willing member of the tribe. This naturally resulted in the majority of the youngsters in the new tribe being the offspring of the leader, who found little difficulty in controlling them all.

With growing numbers and successes over a long period, the problems, already seen in the larger tribes, would tend to appear; criticism of leadership and the fracturing of the society led to more new tribes seeking more new hunting grounds. The desired increases in the population numbers were very apparent, but the resulting increase in strife had its negative affect.

The new tribe of the Powl, formed ten years earlier by Powl, himself, was a breakaway group of the Gols. They were mostly fair-skinned, with long brown hair hanging down to their shoulders. Half the adult males were the natural sons of the leader, and all the tribe, females as well as males, were strong, capable fighters. Their preferred weapons were the spear and the throwing stone, usually a flint that had been sharpened at two ends.

Like all the Gols, the Powls lived a nomadic life, following the huge herds of grazing meat animals as they moved seasonally to the north in the summer or to the south in the cold winter. They had mastered the craft of using animal leathers to make wrappings that kept them warm, and were successful in the making of wrappers that were bound around their feet and ankles. These were very helpful in preventing much of the damage that had previously been experienced, when running, and fighting, barefoot on the stony ground. A cut foot could become a much more serious danger for a nomadic hunter, it could possibly be the cause of his being left behind, when the tribe moved on to their next camp.

Powl had a problem, which his told to his hunters, as they chewed on the hunks of cooked meat that night. "You all know that the Powl tribe must grow each year, if we are going to survive. We can help by making each female have her baby each year, but we are losing too many males when out hunting. It is not just the loss of strong young hunters, who are killed by the mammoth, the bear or the big cat. You know that we have lost two teams of hunters in the past two moons. Two hands of our best males have not returned from their work. The animals that they were hunting did not kill them. We would have found their remains. They must have been taken by the Hoons". The others grunted and continued to eat.

"We must keep our eyes open for the sight of any strangers, and get the news back to me when they are seen," continued Powl. "We know that others have been eating our meat animals and we must stop them".

The warning was effective. Within two days, one hunter ran back to Powl to tell him that a small group of strange hunters was attacking a herd of deer that he had been stalking. The swift result was that two hands of Powls were soon stalking the strangers, identified as dark-haired Hoons. Each one of them was fully a head taller, nearly twice the weight of the Powls, and looking better equipped. Their body wrappings were of leather, with the woollen fur worn on the inside, and their spears appeared to be longer and stronger than those of the watchers. Powl felt fear for the first time when out hunting. He knew that his men outnumbered the Hoons by two to one, but he also knew that he must destroy them, if his tribe were to survive.

He signalled to attack and the Powls ran forward, to surround the interlopers. The reaction was immediate. The Hoons turned into a circle, facing outwards, with their long spears creating a defence that stopped the Powls in their tracks. Their thrown shorter spears were deflected by the small arm-shields, worn inside the circle, and the defenders won the day by thrusting their long spears to their full length, retaining their hold on the butts of their weapons. These were then pulled back, ready for another thrust at the remaining, unwounded attackers. The Powls were no match for the heavier, and more experienced, Hoons.

It was all over, very quickly. The victors made one of the few wounded prisoners lead them back to the remaining members of the tribe, mostly females and babies, who were sheltering around the smoking fires. The slaughter was continued and completed here, after the females had been raped by the Hoons. The Powls had ceased to exist.

It was possible to detect a degree of sadness in the voice of Mellak, when he gave his preliminary report for the north-western tribes.

"We found a similar situation amongst all the Utee tribes that we visited. Whether they were small or large, new or well established, all those under survey encouraged and used their aggressive talents to the full. The numerically weak tribes did so in self-defence. The larger ones had great satisfaction when they came across a smaller group and were able to eliminate it with little difficulty. It did not seem to matter whether they perceived a threat to their own supplies of food, because of a local increase in the number of mouths to be fed. They enjoyed asserting their own strength and

overcoming any weaker beings. Rape and pillage seem to have become an established way of life.

I regret to say that these developing creatures are simply not making any progress on the path that we had envisaged for them. Their offensive traits have been practised over such a long period that they are ingrained and established as an accepted way of life. In fact, it has become the only way of life that the majority of them accept and desire for their future.

We found an almost non-existence of spiritual awareness. There were only the occasional females who asked questions, and then only when in solitude. It was rare, indeed, to perceive a thought such as, 'where do I come from'? or 'what happens when I die'?

Of all the Utee tribes that we contacted, we did not find any one of them that could be re-examined as a possible selection for advancement, in the ways under consideration. Unless the appalling desire to kill and maim is reduced, or eliminated, there can only be a steady decline in the numerical strength of the population. We know that this weakness has already led to the loss of the Yutee, a very slow starter, and also, almost the entire world population of 'little people' have disappeared - people who showed such promise in mental abilities, and the kinder attributes. There is a real danger that these brutal creatures can become so widely spread over the earth that they will remove any possibility of the Earth Project succeeding.

We endorse the possibility of moving the north-eastern tribes, suggested by Marcus, into the New World. We would like to make a strong point about the timing of the operation. It appears vital that these forward-looking people should be saved for a long time into the future, but there is the inherent risk of the Hoons becoming aware of their existence. That alone could be considered a challenge for the aggressors to develop an urge to eliminate them, and our hopes.

May I ask that these views be considered in the constructive way, which I intended. My anxieties may have become apparent through my words, but I do have a positive wish for the success of all our plans".

The message, which they all received from Ywancontin, was to be seen in his blue-grey eyes. They clearly showed his complete

141

understanding of their thoughts, their anxieties, and their wishes, for these changing and determined creatures, that were developing throughout the millions of years being studied. He was fully aware of each one of their individual experiences during the periods of study, especially when they spent time within the hominid bodies. He had hunted with them, eaten the raw meat, been with them in battle and shared both success and failure. He knew why they presented their reports, in the way that they chose. He could agree with all their sentiments. But, he had his own responsibilities as Chairman of the Development Committee.

"My Brothers of the Light, your efforts and your views are greatly appreciated. You have each applied your own experiences and your deep thought to the situation, and you are aware of the potential problems and the results under various criteria. I thank you all.

We know that there is a New World, as it is termed, that is now ready and waiting for occupation by a more intelligent creature. It has experienced the growth of many other animal species. Some of them have succeeded and many of them have faded and disappeared. The turmoil of subterranean activity is far from being completed and it will continue indefinitely.

It is considered that this area should be populated with a seeding of a race of hominids, selected from those that are currently surviving in the old known world. They should already be showing the positive and forward thinking that is sought as a main requisite of the bearers of the divine spark of Light. They will have a controlled ability to survive attack from the other carnivorous animals that exist there already, but it is desirable that they will not use any aggressive instincts in order to start to destroy each other.

Marcus, Solem and Lucus have identified a number of tribes of the north-eastern Utee which are showing many of the required attributes, and their recommendation has been endorsed by Mellak and his team. I agree with you all on the choice that you have made. I do not agree that there is any urgency in the need to move these people to the new lands. You do not have all the relevant facts.

Firstly, we all know that the Americas, as they will become known, are slowly moving away from the Old World. The tectonic plate is very fragile in the middle part, which connects the north with the south by means of a narrow strip of land, or isthmus, and there is always a possibility that the two major parts of the continent will separate. It is desired that any new population will be able to move from the point of entry, in the north, all the way down the land area, as far as the southern tip of land. Until the time that there is an ability to travel over water, this risk must be borne in mind.

You will understand that these points can add a degree of urgency to the plan for moving the tribes in the near future, perhaps in the next half million years, but there are contra points which have a bearing on the final decision. If our main hopes are to be placed within the culture of these people, we need to have a similar amount of time to study and assess them in their present situation. For those reasons, I shall not agree to any immediate migration.

Secondly, there is a point which none of you has raised, or even given any thought. Mellak has seen a risk that the more aggressive tribes, such as the Hoons, might become aware of the presence of a more spiritual race, like the eastern tribes, which we have discussed. They might then go to the extremes of finding them and destroying them.

Have you put your minds into the future? Think for a short period, looking forward into the time after the chosen people have made the journey to the north of Asia, then turned to the east to cross the straits into their New World and spread to the south, until they have covered the complete continent. Allow them to have half a million years in which to grow numerically, make great progress on their spiritual paths, and develop in the ideal way to suit our plan. What do you think will have happened to the other Utee, during that period?

Do you not think that they will have made progress, also, during the same long time? Will they not have grown more eager for the destructive practices that you have reported recently? It is highly likely that they will have mastered the skills of boat building, and navigation. Sooner or later, there will be expeditions setting out from Asia, or the north of Europe, or from the Middle Earth Sea. The Hoons, or other Utee tribes, will have greedy, enquiring minds. The Gyps may well be able to read some of the mental messages from across the water and be stimulated into crossing the seas.

No, gentlemen, it is more important that the selected tribes have much more time in which to develop and become aware of the path that has been chosen for them. They will then be more developed and prepared to face the travails of the times ahead of them.

We will review the situation in 1mBC".

CHAPTER NINETEEN
1mBC

A quiet and serious Solem presented the first notes that had been prepared for the Committee meeting.

"The one inescapable fact that we must consider is that the world population of human beings, at this time, has not increased since our last meeting in the year 2mBC. In fact, it has decreased by nearly 20%. During that period, there have been some sporadic increases, but these have been countered by the conditions of the time. Rapid changes in the climate, and an increase in the aggressive attitudes of many of the tribes, have both had a serious affect on the number of survivors. We will need to apply some consideration to these causes, and to the results.

One substantial positive point is the growing awareness of a higher being, which is responsible for the various factors that are 'good' or 'bad', in the minds of these developing beings. They are beginning to pass judgement. They have someone to blame or thank for the unexpected things that occur and that have a serious affect on them. This indicates another step forward on their path. It will help them to develop their philosophy and make a little more progress.

May I suggest a brief study of the tribes where there is the most spiritual progress? These should include the Utee, that we studied, on the north east coastal area, who were listed as potential emigrants to the 'New World'. I would also recommend the well-established tribe of Gyps on the north African coastal plains.

There are some of the Utee, in the north and western areas, who are becoming increasingly aggressive and who have been the major cause of the reduction in the population in those parts. A study of the Hoons, and some of their sub-tribes, such as the Vands, might help us to understand why they are so destructive, and indicate the direction in which we should move in order to reverse the trend."

Complete silence had been ordered. The pitch-black night was not disturbed by any man-made noise, but the sound of a single owl, hooting amongst the trees, sent shivers through the waiting group of Gyps. They had eaten during that day, not a feast, but sufficient for them to know that life was good. They were waiting for the first sign of the god, who made regular visits to their land, to thank him for all their blessings.

Ula, the wise one, had taught them much in the few years that he had been their medicine giver. Of course, he had discovered new plants and he had shown them how to make hot drinks with the leaves and roots. Those treatments had usually helped to remove the pain from cuts, bruises and body aches, but he had also talked with them about the stranger side of life. He had told them that he was aware of their maker, the bringer of life and all the good things that they enjoyed.

"You have all seen the goodness that you have received each day, a day when the Sun-god shines upon you and your land, when our hunters bring fresh meat for us to eat, when the fresh green leaves and juicy roots are brought in by the gatherers. You enjoy the fruits and nuts when they are in season. You know that he rests each night, ready for the next day of blessings, and that his light is kept warm by the Moon-god each night?

We know that the light is slowly taken from the Moon-god, during each moon period, and that it is then made new again. We know that tonight will show us the biggest light in this period, but what you do not know is that there will be a sign of a disaster that will be coming to us all."

The wailing of the crowd grew into a shrieking, which slowly faded into a sobbing of the females. Within the mind of Ula was the awareness of an omen, an anxiety, but he was puzzled when he heard his own voice saying those words. He had always been fully aware that he had an 'inner voice', a conscience, a guide who would give him a signal that, where he had two opportunities, he could understand which choice was the right one. He had never tried to explain this to any other Gyp, but he was well used to listening and acting on the advice that he received in this way. The helper had never misled him, but this was the first time that he had spoken words that he had not prepared.

The crowd quietened and they all settled down and looked towards the east to await the arrival of the full moon.

After a little time, they could see the darkness fading, exactly in the place where they expected to see the full moon. The murmuring of the questioning voices was very low, at first. As the moon slowly arose out of the dark horizon, it became louder and louder, until they could all see the glorious Moon-god in all its usual detail. Then, the shouts of joy, 'Moon-god, Moon-god', became a chant of celebration. These quickly changed into a chant of criticism of Ula, with the crowd facing him, questioning him about his disaster words. Ula's reply was, "Wait, and watch."

They did not have to wait for very long. When the moon was only its own width above the horizon, the sighs and groans of the watching Gyps confirmed that they were all now aware of the disaster that had been forecast. A darkness was starting to eat into their Moon-god. As the crowd watched and moaned, the top of the moon began to disappear. As the shadow of the earth planet moved across the moon the Gyps knew that their god was being eaten by some horror. They became very quiet. This was the disaster that Ula had told them would happen. They realised that they should not have been so quick to criticise him. He had always been helpful in the past.

Ula was as shocked as the others, when the shadow started to creep over the face of the moon, but he had, at least, the inner knowledge of his faith in his informant. He had no knowledge of astronomy or eclipses, no experience of such a thing happening before now, but he knew that it was only a sign of approaching disaster. They would not be losing their Moon-god for more than a short period of time.

Before the agitation and shouting had stopped, the shadow could already be seen to have moved further down the face of the moon, leaving a part of it still lit up for them to see. Within a short time the full face was again exposed. The shouts of joy were tinged with questions for Ula, who gave a quick reply, in order to gain time for some meditation. "You will be given the answers to your questions, after we have the Sun-god smiling on us again tomorrow!" The puzzled crowd made their way back to their sleeping area, learning nothing from the questions that were on the lips of all the adults.

As the sun rose the next morning, Ula walked to the area of the tribal chief and he was immediately drawn into a private space to be questioned. Ro had heard a report of the eclipse and he wanted to hear the opinion of the medicine giver. Ula spoke as the words came to him.

"As you know, the night of the full face of the moon-god is always treated with respect, when we offer our thanks for the good things that we receive. Last night was expected to be the same as the other similar nights over the past many years. I was given words to say, before he appeared, and I told the people that we would receive a warning from the moon-god that would affect us all. I had no idea what the warning would be, and I was as surprised as all the others when the darkness took a bite from the light.

He was not damaged for more than a short time. He was not bitten again during the night and I am sure that no real harm was done to him. It was only a warning for us, and I believe that I know what the warning was." Ro jumped to his feet, at this comment, "Tell me, Ula, you must always tell me these things, before you tell any other! And tell me with words, not your thoughts. I do not want the others to be replanning their lives until we have looked at every possible way of dealing with this".

Ula spoke slowly and quietly. He was becoming aware of new thoughts and new ideas, even as he spoke to Ro. "The message was intended to be a warning. We must accept it as a truth, but it came to us all with another meaning. I know that we were not being told that the Moon-god was damaged or threatened in any way. We were being told that it is our own food supplies that are in danger". The two men waited for more inspiration to come to Ula, chewing on some nuts that had been placed before them.

"We have always relied on our hunters finding fresh food in good supply, as and when we need it. Added to the meat, we have always been able to find plenty of fruit, nuts and roots, in and near the wooded areas and close to the flowing waters. If the waters are weakened, or stopped, that will affect all those supplies, very quickly. We must now make a plan to bring all those foods nearer our base camps, closer to the waters of the big river. In that way we can keep the plants alive by carrying some of the water to them every day".

Ro interrupted. "That might be possible for the plants, the roots and the fruit and nut trees, but it will not work for the wild meat animals, that the hunters have to find in many scattered places. How can we keep them near to the big river?"

"This has troubled me for some years", said Ula. "All the meat animals run away, when they see or smell our hunters. They do not wish to be friendly with those who will kill and eat them. If we could make a place for them, where they could walk about, eat the grasses and leaves on the trees, but not be able to run away, then we would be able to keep them near us. They would become less frightened, they would be used to our smell. They could mate with each other and have their young. These would grow bigger and help to keep the numbers that we require. Yes, we would find that there are some other good things that would be discovered later. I'm thinking that we might be able to use some of their milk to feed our own young. The animals could be made to help us in our labours, by pulling some of the heavier loads that we put on the heads of our females. All these things will help us to make our own progress and to grow stronger, more powerful".

"You are a deep thinker, Ula", said Ro. "You have some wonderful thoughts, but how can you do this, how can you stop the meat animals from going away from where you have cornered them?"

"We have had the labour of our slaves for a long time, and now is the chance to make the best use of them. They will make a barrier, of wood and thorn, in a large ring. This will have a small opening through which we will drive the animals, before we close the entrance. There must be fresh water and plenty of food inside, so that they do not need to try to get out of the ring. Our elders will need to find a suitable place for the ring that is no more than one day's walk from our base. This will help our butchers to lead the live animals back here, when required for the killing, without needing to feed or water them on the journey. For the rest of the time, the guards will be watching over them and treating the animals with quiet respect. They will then grow more used to being near to us, and they will become less angry and more willing to accept a new way of life for them and for us".

"That is a good plan, Ula," said Ro, "we must have all the elders involved in planning the details. They are still able to use the old means of talking and I see that it will be needed when we start the driving of the animals towards the ring. The collection of the green food plants and roots will not be so difficult and that can be spread over a period of moons, or even one or two years. We will all meet tomorrow and decide where we will have the ring erected and we can then share the responsibilities".

A similar idea had arrived in the mind of one of the northern Hoons. Koi the hunter was usually a very successful producer of meat food, but he had started to use his brain much more than normal. There were so many times when he and his fellow hunters were within a short distance of the herd of animals, and they were outwitted by the food creatures, which simply ran away. Their speed helped them to remain alive, when threatened by the most effective of killers, man.

The Hoons enjoyed a variety of different meats. The mammoth provided a strong, dark flesh, in huge quantities, which usually gave a reason for a feast when one was killed. Cloven-hoofed animals, of differing sizes, had very pleasant meat, but they all seemed to object strongly to being chased and killed for food. They mostly had a variety of horns fixed in the head and these were heavily used in self-defence, by an animal under pressure. When approached from the front, they were likely to do some real damage to the hunter. Another meat animal, of a similar size, was the quagga, which did not grow any kind of horn, and the flesh was welcomed when it was brought back to the tribe. The problem was the speed at which this animal could run. It never hesitated when it was being hunted. One sound of man and it could turn in its tracks and be away from danger.

Koi had been near to this forerunner of the horse many times. When he had made a kill he was pleased with the meat. What he really wanted from the creature was its speed. "If only", he mused, "if only I could get one, and keep it alive, so that I could travel on its back, and catch up with those other quick animals. I could be the fastest in the tribe. I could show the others how to do the same. I could lead the whole tribe, each on his own speed-animal, to attack those other tribes that trouble us, then we would leave them and return to our own camp, before they could hurt us". It was a daydream, a fantasy, but he knew it was possible. He could do it. He would do it!

Koi told his tribal leader, Karl, that he had a good idea for providing meat food when supplies were not to be found easily. This produced an immediate interest in Karl, who was then told a story similar to the one told by Ula of the Gyps to Ro.

Koi made the obvious comment that there was always plenty of food-on-the-hoof, somewhere in the forest or on the plains. Their hunters had to be out searching for the herds every day, in order to know where they could make a kill. He described his imagined stockade, made from stakes, taken from the forest, and how to drive a herd of meat-food into captivity. The leader never hesitated. Karl and Koi spent several days touring the edge of the forest before they found an ideal site. A long, wide valley, supplied with a stream of flowing water, only required a fence at the forest end in order to stop any animals from escaping to the north. The two sides of the valley showed that it had been created by a small rift in the ground level. They were steep enough to prevent any animal, except perhaps man, from climbing up and out of the valley. The only other requirement was to make two portable fences, that would be used near the entrance of the valley as a funnel. After the herd of captives had been driven into the snare, the fences would be carried across the opening to form a rigid gate and thus seal the valley. In theory this would work well. It remained to be tested. Karl told Koi that he was to be the hunter-in-charge of finding and driving the selected herd.

CHAPTER TWENTY
PROMISE

During the review of the reports presented to the Committee, Ywancontin became aware of a hint of anxiety in the voices of Solem and Mellak. He had heard this, on earlier occasions, from some of the others. Those worries had been discussed at the time and resolved. They had usually arisen because there was some imagined possible threat to the individual's favourite interest in the development. On this occasion similar thoughts came from two of the members with the biggest difference in their normal attitudes.

Solem had been pleased with the acceptance of his proposal to study some of the Gyps and the Hoons. The results appeared to have justified his suggestion.

"The time that I spent with the Gyps gave me the opportunity to check that my previous impressions were still on a sound basis. There is no doubt in my mind that this tribe has retained the trait of compassion. There are signs of its presence in both the males and the females. It is very pleasing to know that they have, within them, a strongly placed ability to counter the usually masculine tendency towards aggression.

We also should note, at this point, that there were occasions when I noticed the beginnings of a faint trace of an overlapping of the sexes. By that, I wish to record that there are a few of the females which have indicated a tendency towards having a male trait of assertiveness. At the same time, I can confirm that a few of the males have acquired, or retained, some female habits, such as taking pleasure from the attentions of a male, either enjoying his company, or touching him, to an excess. This might be a good thing to happen in a tribe, which is growing in numbers and interests. May I suggest that it be monitored for future reports?

The Gyps' brains are developing slowly, but surely. The pace of the growth is satisfactory. New crafts are being developed, alongside the earlier crafts of leather tanning, the making of suitable skin garments, and the production of stone implements for making weapons, craft tools and the rest. The most elementary form of pottery is being practised, and it will, no doubt, continue to improve.

They are using their slave labour wisely, for the benefit of all the tribe, freemen and slaves alike. They are about to take a very large step forward by starting the domestication of some of the wild animals and the beginning of their agricultural economy. During the entrapment of the cloven hoofed beasts, they will accidentally capture their first few quagga. This will lead to their thinking of a way in which to subjugate the animal, and they will soon learn to ride upon its back, rather than to eat it.

Spiritually, they appear to be advancing at a satisfactory pace. The majority of them have a healthy awareness of a 'higher being' that can affect their lives in many ways. They have an embryonic religion in their worship of the sun and moon, being the most obvious form of the 'Light'. This is a healthy resolution of their need for a god. Their progress will depend on their using the spiritual awareness and knowledge in order to gain knowledge rather than power over the less intelligent of their subjects. Some of them will be tempted to do the latter. We will be kept informed through the usual channels of their helpers and guides.

I have no doubt that this tribe of Gyps is moving forward on its path, in the right direction, and that it has the ability to continue to grow numerically and spiritually, as we might wish.

My main concern is regarding the form of the advancement of the northern tribes that we have recently studied. Over the whole of the Northern Hemisphere, those whom we used to classify as the Utee have developed and changed over a very long time. We have seen some of the more assertive sub-tribes, such as the Hoons, have grown in numbers and formed even more sub-tribes who are hardly recognised as close relatives. These aggressors, who appear to be intent on destroying any tribe that they might meet, have eliminated most of the smaller peoples.

We have recently completed a visit to the descendants of the promising Bear tribe and they continue to make satisfactory progress on their spiritual paths. They are steadily approaching the position where they will be ready to make that important trek to the north, before crossing the straits between Asia and the Promised New World. There will be some risk of their numbers being depleted during that journey to the north. Aggressive tribes are active in the areas through which they will pass. I recommend that we encourage them to build up their strength, both numerically and in personal physique.

They have a valuable awareness of the glories of Nature, and their knowledge of the medicinal use of the plants and herbs is helping them to enjoy better and slightly longer lives. This enables the older ones to spend time in the company of the youngsters, and pass on to them all the secrets of nature that have been acquired so far. The growing respect for the elders helps to establish a discipline that strengthens the bond between all members of the same tribe. It is to be treasured by them all.

It appears to me that the best time for them to start their journey to the north might well be during the next half million years".

"Thank you", said Ywancontin, "you have raised some valuable points and you opinion is appreciated. I see that Mellak wishes to express his thoughts about the attitudes of some of the northern tribes?"

"That is so," Mellak smiled to the Committee, "I must agree with much of what Solem had said. May I suggest that we apply more time to the study of the situation in the north western part of the land?

We must consider that the Hoons, for example, are descended from the original Utee, whom we were so pleased to encourage in the times of early growth. That was when we were wondering whether any of the hominoid creatures would survive for more than a few thousand years. Simple survival was the tool by which we measured the potential of the creatures. We were well aware of the benefits of both their continual sexual activity and their ability to defend themselves. Now, we are looking at some of the descendants of those early successes, and asking whether it is a good thing for them to have developed so far along these lines. We see some of the results of so much activity.

Mating has become, not just a way of reproducing and growing numerically, but a pastime, an expression of power, a method of proving that one male is stronger or more effective than another. In a more sinister way, it has become a reason for applying the aggression, that we now question, and attacking other tribes. These attacks can start by simply molesting a female who is working in the forest. Such a rape can quickly lead to one tribe attacking another, with the intention of destroying every member of that tribe. It can be a disaster. It has led to a decrease in the numbers of beings, in some areas. That is not in the interests of our plans.

Our latest intelligence informs us that some of these destructive tribes are moving in the direction of becoming capable of domesticating the quagga, as well as some of the other meat animals. When that happens, it will be easier for them to extend their offensive forays, and they will be able to attack other tribes at will. We know that any new step forward, in one tribe, is quickly learned and understood by the other tribes, and it is then copied by them, and used. We call it progress.

I make no suggestion that we even try to delay such progress. It is the natural law, and the developing brains will continue to understand more about every subject, with the passing of time.

I would like to make one positive suggestion that will help to counter the negatives arising from the results of the creative action. If we can help to stimulate the spiritual aspects in the human mind, there could be a natural flow of enquiries as to how and why things happen. This could start the germ of an idea that would grow into an ever-widening philosophy. We are already aware of the rudimentary religion amongst the Gyps. This also appears to be a natural process and it could be encouraged with only a slight stimulation from the guides and helpers, through that inner voice of conscience.

We have not yet had any progress reports on results from the reintroduction of spirits to the earth plane. I understand that this was to be applied on a very small scale, but it could be used as a method of stimulating a greater spiritual awareness. Your comments would be appreciated".

The Chairman inclined his head as a token of appreciation.

"Thank you, Mellak. Reintroduction was considered and the subject is still sub judice. You will be informed when it is considered the correct time for further discussion. Your continuing application of thought to the spiritual side of the existence of these beings is very useful. Your constructive suggestions are, as usual, based on your

wide and lengthy experience. Your comments, together with those of Solemn, are being studied and will be given full consideration.

    None of you appear to doubt that the two traits that we have discussed were essential for survival during the earlier stages of development. Without an ability to mate throughout the year, there could not have been any rapid replacement of losses, which arose for a variety of reasons. Similarly, the lack of a strong urge for self-survival would have easily led to the disappearance of most, if not all, of the tribes of beings that we see here at this time. Many of you have raised the subject in your reports throughout the full time of this Committee. You are also well aware of the rules applied, that a species must survive by its merits and abilities. It is not permitted to make changes in the basic nature, which has evolved over a long period.

    You will recall that we introduced the quality of compassion to just one female alive on the continent of Africa. That was for a trial period, only. At this point in time, we can find traces of the trait in the majority of the tribes in each of the other continents. During the early periods, it was to be found amongst the females only. Much later, it appeared in a few of the males. Now, we can find it amongst both the males and females in almost every tribe throughout the occupied world. It tends to be suppressed amongst the more assertive tribes that have been studied, particularly in the north. We must allow the natural laws to continue to be applied.

    If the mastering of the horse creatures leads to an increase in the range of the marauding tribes, then we will see if compassion is an effective antidote. The developing brains will continue to lead to discussion, debate and, we may wish, to decisions to follow the right path. The alternative could easily lead to the destruction of life for more species than just the one creating the trouble.

    We also need to consider the possibility of such progress, during the next few million years, that the planet becomes too crowded with a successful race. That can be kept in the agenda for our future meetings.

    I agree that the selected tribe of the Bear should continue to be listed as the most suitable one for transferring to the New World. It would seem to be wise to keep them near where they are now, until they have mastered the skills of riding the horse. The animal will be able to pull some of the supplies of food and bedding on the long journey to the north, and later, to the south of their new homeland.

I will call the next meeting for the year 0.5mBC, sooner than is usual, due to the increase that is envisaged in the development of the human brain. We can look for the great trek of the Bear tribe and, soon after that, the experiments that will lead to the invention of the wheel".

CHAPTER TWENTY ONE
0.5mBC THE BEAR

The Bear tribe had built a tradition over many thousands of years. They had developed from a quietly successful group, of nearly three hundred hunters, into their present strength of two thousand. If the females and children were also counted, the numbers would be increased by half as much again.

They had faced up to the obvious problems of organising themselves to ensure their own security by retaining a supreme leader, Great Bear himself, and accepting the fact of having ten sub-tribes, each with its own chief. None of these sub-tribes made any attempt to move far away from the main group. None of the lesser chiefs showed any desire to be leading his own tribe as a separate entity. This had arisen from the continual leadership of respected elders, through many thousands of years, and it had allowed the main tribe to make progress at a steady rate, with very little dissension.

Great Bear called a meeting of all the males, at the time of the midday sun. The other members of the tribe were permitted to be seated on the fringe.

"Members of the tribe of the Great Bear", he began, "you are brought here together to hear words that you have not heard before now." The male faces were unmoved, but serious. The females looked quickly at each other, and, at the same time, arm movements were used to quieten a few of the children. "You are all aware of the fact that we are a chosen people, selected to enjoy the goodness sent from the Great Spirit in the sky. We live in a world that is full of wonder. We can have every thing that we wish to have, fresh meat and other foods are here to be taken by our hunters and gatherers. When there is any sickness, we can relieve the pain by taking the treatments given by our medicine men. We have been given the ability to take the wild horses and train them to work with us. Our hunters can now ride faster than some of the meat animals are able to run away from them. When we move to new hunting grounds, these horses help to pull all our shelters, our families and our spare food. You know all these things.

You also know that we might have a short life on this world.

Accidents, illness and, occasionally, attacks from our enemies, can take away our ability to stay here with our families. We are all born to this. But, we know that the Great Spirit has a prepared place for each one of us in the hunting grounds above the earth on which we now stand. We are all very well blessed.

Some of you, but not all of you, have been told how we know these facts. This is the truth. The elders of this tribe of the Great Bear are all informed of what they need to know by listening to the voices of the Great Spirit. When they hear a voice speaking within themselves, they listen. They are usually the voices of the Tall Ones. The Tall Ones sometimes show themselves to our elders, especially when they have a serious message for us. They are more than a head taller than our tallest hunters, and they wear, not skins taken from animals, but garments made from very fine materials, which have not yet been seen on this earth by any one of us. They are serious but kindly people, who want to help us. Last night they came to visit us, and these are their words.

'People of the Great Bear, you have earned a blessing, that has been prepared for you during the past aeons, and is now ready for you to find and experience. It is a new land, far away from here, that has grown without being damaged by the hands of beings like yourselves. It is full of mountains, streams and big rivers, full of deer and other new meat animals. The forests cover a large part of the land and they are full of trees, plants and herbs that will keep your medicine men occupied, finding all the benefits that will be offered to the users of their brews. This land is for you, and your offspring. You will be able to enter into this New World and then spread yourselves over the whole of its land. This will give you the opportunity to increase numerically, in safety, but, mainly, you will be able to progress spiritually to the point where you will be a long way ahead of all the other tribes on the Earth. That is our wish for you.

You will find your way there by making a journey to the north and keeping near to the eastern coastline after you have crossed the big yellow river. You will not be able to cross this river if you are too near to the salt sea. You will be known as the Wanderers, but you will not be wandering aimlessly. Your purpose will always be there ahead of you. You will arrive in the land of the longest day, before that day begins. You will know that you have arrived because the sun will be with you all the time.

You will all be able to enjoy the long summer period, feasting and storing fresh food in your bodies and dried food on your horse sleds. As the days become shorter and colder, you will begin your last stage of the journey, which will take you all across the frozen sea. We will be with you all the way. Be strong and as determined as you usually are. You will be tested many times on your travels, your hunters will be guarding you against attack and we will be with you to give help and advice when you need it'.

Those are the words of the Tall Ones. Remember them. Recite them to yourselves. Teach them to your children. They will help you to make this great journey to the New World. Tomorrow the chiefs will meet and plan the movement of our people to the north. We will not be stopped from reaching the land that has been promised to us".

A normal part of their lives was spent in packing the few belongings that were essential, and that were not to be found easily, when on the move. They were only surprised by the fact that Great Bear, himself, had made such an important issue of the move. None of them had the smallest idea of the time that was required to travel the distance that would be covered, or of the dangers that could be ahead of them. The complete tribe were confident that the cold winter period, mentioned in the speech as the time of arrival, would be the next winter. It never entered their minds that none of the adults, who had heard Great Bear describe the proposed journey, would still be alive when the tribe arrived in the northernmost point. Only a few of the children would be included in the crossing of the ice in the Bering Strait. They would be amongst the leaders of the tribe.

During the next few years, the Wanderers slowly made their way to the north, until they met their first major barrier. It was the wide yellow river about which they had been warned. Each day of travel started with the armed hunters going ahead on horseback, in order to scout for any sign of an enemy. Their orders were to avoid contact and report back to the Chief. This method helped them to evade trouble, on most occasions. They would then move more quickly for the next two days in the hope of leaving the problems behind them.

The original plan had been for them all to travel for two days, stopping only for a short night's sleep. That would be followed by a halt for two days and nights, for the purpose of hunting for fresh meat, before starting the process over again. The system was efficient for most of the time. There were some changes made to the number of rest days due to occasional delays caused by the interference of strange tribes. They had noticed the Bears travelling through their own protected hunting areas, and they attempted to destroy these invaders. Usually, when the local defenders realised the number of well-armed Bear hunters that were going to oppose them, they faded into the distance and the wanderers continued their journey to the north. There were periods when the tribe was apparently stopped from moving at all. Some of these arose from the early arrival of the winter season. Other times the delays were caused by the sudden onset of a feverish illness, which affected the majority of the adults and some of the children. The medicine men tried all their treatments, and experimented with some new ones. These were often the sad times when the sick ones slipped away to the other world. Many moon periods were lost in this way.

It was long after they had crossed the yellow river, with great difficulty, that the Bear tribe were deliberately attacked by strong forces, determined to eliminate them. They had crossed many ranges of mountains and entered a desert region. The wisdom of the elders then advised that the tribe should turn more towards the rising sun. This would eventually bring them to the eastern coast and thus give them a boundary on their right side.

Scouts from a completely foreign tribe of Vands spotted the leading mounted scouts of the Bears, well in advance of their main party. The Vands followed their natural instincts and attacked.

CHAPTER TWENTY TWO
0.5mBC THE VANDS

Once the Vand tribe had mastered the method of capturing the wild horse, they quickly appreciated the benefit of being able to move about the land so easily. Their hunters were the first to prove the success of being so mobile. Regular supplies of fresh meat kept the whole tribe in comparative luxury, and the more assertive hunters soon turned their efforts towards the great joy of their lives. They organised regular demonstrations of masculine strength, on horseback. The first one of them to jump off a galloping horse, and then jump back on to it in one easy move, was an immediate hero to the others. Many of them broke a limb whilst trying to achieve some new trick. They were all exhibitionists.

The system of steering the wild steed was finally settled by the making of a leather halter, tied around the head, and one rein looped from the halter and held by the rider. Attempts to fix a hard bit, to go in the animal's mouth, were a failure. Wooden bits were quickly chewed into pieces and bone bits easily fractured.

Some of the young hunters practised spearing a target, whilst at the full gallop, and the more proficient of them wanted to ride out, looking for an enemy, in order to try the new killing method. The tribal leader, known as Huk, was very proud of the eagerness being shown by his young men. He liked to ride with them, whenever there was a possibility of attacking another tribe, and he promised them that they would soon be testing their new skills. "It depends on when our scouts can find you a live target, then, I will lead you and show you how to kill the most". Slaughter and brutality were a way of life for them.

Huk had another interest, which occupied a large part of his time. He had started a horse-breeding programme, since the tribe's recent successes in capturing a variety of differently shaped animals. His progress in this field had been restricted when he found that he needed to keep the animals in one fixed place, and that this detracted from his urges to roam around all the nearby valleys, seeking someone or something to attack.

The opportunity came very soon after the first successful

demonstration of lancing on horseback. One of the scouts, who had gone out that morning, returned with the news that a strange tribe was moving into their hunting grounds to the east. Huk quickly ordered a party of twenty hunters to assemble and to follow the scout back to the valley where he had seen the advance party of newcomers. He would lead them personally.

The sight of this tribal leader, taking a group of their hunters into action, raised cries of joy from the watching females. The hunters were dressed in their usual animal skin garments, a sleeveless jacket, with the fur on the inside, short trews of a similar material, and a pair of leather and woollen leg-warmers, which were also wrapped around the feet, all these completed the apparel. They rode bareback, with their matted hair streaming behind them. Their weapons were the usual wooden spears, tipped with a sharp flint point, tied into the head, and a pocket carrying a few mixed stones, for throwing and cutting. They felt unbeatable.

As Huk lead the party at a fast gallop, he was confident that he would show the youngsters the skills that had made him their leader. He also hoped that they would be able to find the main party of the intruders, so that they could continue to eliminate them. 'When they had had their fun with the females' was his afterthought.

The scout, who had returned to them with the news, soon identified the spot where he had left the others. He pointed across the valley, "That is where we saw them, that is where the others have gone". He galloped away to look for his friends and then stopped, suddenly, looking at the three bodies on the ground. They were Vands. They appeared to have been killed with some very short, light spears, which were still sticking out of their chests and bellies. There was no blood on their own spears lying beside them.

Huk was puzzled and he became very serious. "Find their tracks", he said, "they are not far away". It was only a short time before they were able to follow the horse tracks, leading from the place of battle, taking the Vands towards the main group of Bears, who were moving in a cloud of dust towards the east.

The twenty angry Vands galloped towards the dust cloud, and Huk lead them, at the same pace, straight in amongst the horse-drawn sleds of the families. They had been seen before they reached the Bears, and the alarm calls brought a similarly sized group of Bear hunters on horseback. The Vands' spears were already ripping into the bodies of the wanderers, when their hunters loosed their new and secret weapon on to them. They were each hit in the body with a light dart, fired at them by a Bear on horseback. The bow and arrow had been used in defence for the first time.

Great Bear, himself, had been one of the defenders, and he had been hit in the neck by a sharp stone thrown by Huk. The hunters killed all the Vands with their arrows, and the only Bear casualties were their leader and four of the followers. The Bear tribe buried their bodies on a hillside, some distance from the scene of the fighting. The Vands' bodies were left where they fell, after all the arrows had been removed.

There was a brief ceremony where Running Wolf, eldest son of Great Bear, was elected to be the new leader of the tribe. The whole party of wanderers then continued on their way towards the salt sea, in the east, travelling for four days, instead of the usual two, before resting. This was followed by another four days on the move, in the hope that their enemy would not be able to catch up with them. The new leader also sent a small team of hunters to travel half a day behind the main party in order to act as a rearguard. It was two full moons before they realised that a few scouts of the surviving Vands were trailing them. The new Great Bear was informed immediately, and the tribe continued to move steadily towards the saltwater coastline.

Two days later, the rearguard of the Bears could see a large cloud of dust behind them. They knew that their enemy was following them in large numbers and they all rejoined the main party, as instructed. Great Bear ordered the wanderers to form a complete circle, with the females and children in the centre. They carried enough food with them for another two days, and a stream of fresh water ran through the circle. They felt in a strong position. The hunters, numbering nearly one thousand, stood at the outer edge, with their horses and weapons at the ready. They must win the imminent battle. They knew that the Great Spirit was with them, ready to help them beat this threat and to ensure that there would be a tribe of Bears ready to move into the New World.

THE PATH

The tribe of Vands had applied some thought to the strangers and their successful use of darts against them. None of them had seen the weapon that threw the darts, but they had all seen the result, stuck in the bodies of their hunters. If a new and secret weapon had been used against them, then they would find a new answer to the problem.

One of their brightest hunters devised a wood and leather shield, to be held in one hand, that could be used to catch the darts fired at them. They tested it out by throwing short spears at a standing hunter who was defending himself with the sample shield. It seemed to work. At least, the hunter was able to stop some of the spears from hitting him, but his eager colleagues simultaneously threw two spears at him. He caught the one aimed at his head, but the second one hit him in the body and killed him. "Good enough", said the leader, successor to Huk, and he ordered similar shields to be made, one for each hunter.

This work delayed their setting out to follow and destroy the invaders, but it increased their confidence up to their normal state of arrogance. The complete tribe was on the move, travelling to the east, within one moon.

When the Vands knew that they had caught up with the wanderers, they did not rush ahead in order to attack immediately, in their usual way. These invaders were a strong and intelligent tribe. Their new weapons proved that point. No. A large party of Vand hunters galloped to nearly a spear's distance of the defenders. They then continued, at the same pace, and raced round the Bears, making an estimate of their numbers, but avoiding getting near enough to them for the defenders to use any of their weapons. The Vands then returned to their main group.

Both sides had learnt from the exercise. The Vands knew that they had a few more hunters than the Bears, and the Bears had seen the small shield held by each of the Vands. Great Bear understood the purpose and the limitations of these shields. He quickly warned all his hunters that two arrows should be fired at each of the enemy, one at the head, to raise the level of the shield, and the second one at the body or at the horse, to bring the Vand to the ground. His hunters were quickly placed in pairs around the perimeter, each with a clear

165

idea of what was needed. They were all ready for the attack, when the main group of Vand hunters repeated their encircling gallop. This was soon switched into a run, straight at the Bears' defence.

The instant planning of each side was effective, within the limitations of being hurried and untested. The Vands wish to draw the arrows, fired by the Bears, and to catch them on their shields, would have worked well, if only the Bears had fired a single arrow at each man. The second arrow did the damage. Most of the attackers found that they had not only caught an arrow on their shield, but, also, that they had received one in the body or in the leg. A few of them were unhorsed, when their mount was pierced with an arrow. The majority of the Vand assault was dissipated, as their hunters were killed, before they could get to grips with any of the Bears.

One party of about fifty Vands was able to use their speed and aggression to penetrate the defences, using their spears to kill more than one hundred amongst the families sheltering within the circle. The Bear hunters then gave them the same treatment.

The tribe spent one day burying their lost ones, not knowing that a few of the Vands had been able to escape with the story of the disaster. They had also been able to take a few of the arrows and one of the bows with them, proof of the existence of the new weapon. The journey to the north and the east continued.

The new Great Bear decided that his tribe should find a sheltered place, where they would be able to pass a few moons recovering from the recent trauma. His scouts found the ideal valley near to the sea. Hunting was easy during the warm period and all the Bears were becoming more reconciled to the losses caused by the Vands.

Craftsmen were being trained to take on their new responsibilities, and the arrow-makers were very busy producing an even greater stock of the new weapon than had been decided before the recent attack. Many young males were initiated into adulthood, at least one year earlier than they had expected, and they were each issued with a bow and a supply of practice arrows.

The preparations were only just in time for the tribe to be able to withstand another vicious attack from a surviving sub-tribe of the Vands. The first arrows flew into the Bears when they were eating their meat. It was a total surprise but the Bears reacted instantly. All their hunters responded by using their own weapons. Their greater experience helped them to rout the Vands and, again, eliminate almost every one of the enemy.

During the next twenty years, the tribe of the Great Bear suffered sporadic attacks from similar aggressive groups of strangers who appeared to be determined to eliminate them, for the simple satisfaction of exercising their own brute strength. The wanderers managed to survive, despite the continual draining of the numbers. They were blessed with the support from the Spiritual Advisors, who gave them the encouragement to keep on keeping on with the only way of life that they knew. They also were very fertile. Each female bore, at least, one baby each year. And most of them survived to adulthood.

Slowly, the tribe moved to the north, keeping the sea to the east on their right hand side. Eventually, they found themselves at the farthest point that they could go, looking across the sea towards the 'Land over the Water'. The Tall Ones told the elders of the tribe that they were looking at the 'New World' that had been promised to them. Great Bear could not restrain himself. "We have spent many years moving our tribe here, after you promised our fathers that this new land would be ours. Now, we may believe that we can see it over there, but you do not show us the path that will lead us to this land that we shall enjoy?"

The Tall One, who had spoken at first, smiled. "Have no doubts, no fears, my brothers. In a little time, you will be walking across the water, which will be prepared for you and all your tribe. The promises will be kept. At this time, you are enjoying the mild, warmer weather, when you are able to hunt for fresh food in plenty. You know that, after the summer there is always a winter to follow. The winter that will follow this warm period will be hard and cold. It will give you a path that you can follow, so that you will be in your New World before you can know it. We will be with you and show you the way.

You must now use this mild weather in order to hunt for the meat that you most enjoy. Hunt, and make good stocks of that meat, drying it in the way that you know, storing it, so that you can stay near this place until the day that we tell you it is time to cross the water. That will be the day that the water will be gone. It will have become a firm path on which you can move forward, with all your tribe, your wives, your children, your animals and your stocks of dried meats.

You will move away from the attacks of the strange tribes. They will not follow you to your land of plenty, to your New World. You will then move towards the sun, where you will find many new foods. Your stocks of meats and your animals will sustain you until that day. If you need to eat all your animals, in order to survive, then so be it. You are very well blessed by the Great White Spirit".

And so it was.

CHAPTER TWENTY THREE
0.2mBC THE GYPS

Marcus was asked to comment on the progress, being made by the tribe of the Great Bear, since their safe arrival in the New World. He was very enthusiastic about their achievements, since landing safely across the ice, and their prospects of survival in the different parts of the continent that they had explored.

"There is no doubt, in my mind, that these capable people will continue to grow numerically and spiritually. We have seen how they have been following our guidance and forming sub-tribes, which have grown under the same guidelines, and then started to move further to the south, after a period of time. The process has almost covered the complete continent with a large number of new tribes, which have each developed their own characteristics, dialects and even languages. Some words can be found to be common to more than one tribe, but the passage of time will complete the separation and emphasise the differences between the various groups of these descendants of the original Bear tribe

I do not feel that there will be any benefit in making a complete study of the process of the populating of the new continent at this time. The growth and consolidation of the spiritual development of these people is there to be seen by any observer. They are all applying their intelligence to make use of the affluence of the natural landscape, to learn from their close encounters with the animal world, and to appreciate the blessings that they are all receiving. These Wanderers are awaiting the inspiration to experiment with different floating materials, before they will take the first steps towards moving on the surface of the waters. Amongst them, there will be the explorers of the deep oceans, the discoverers of the saltwater islands.

It will be important for us to monitor the situation when there is an influx of any newcomers from either the eastern or the western lands, from what we might call the Old World. Such an occurrence could jeopardise the ongoing growth of spirituality in the New World.

May I suggest that it is more important that we make a study

*of that other tribe, the Gyps, which was also reported as showing
great spiritual promise? They have gained remarkable economical
advancement, at the same time as retaining the skill of mental
communication, and the ability to apply logical thought".*

*Ywancontin gave Marcus a long pensive look before inclining
his head in agreement. "You are right in not wishing to apply too
much time and thought to those who are the most promising of
success. The Gyps have been equally full of hope and promise from
the early studies until now. We should be aware of any tendency on
their part to slip into less positive attitudes. Go ahead, Marcus. You
should take the support of both Mellak and Solem".*

Jell was happy with her daily chores. The simpler ones, of
preparing food for the family, and working her loom, gave her a feeling
of contentment that usually brought a smile to her face. She had
always been a slave and never envisaged any other position in life.
Like her mother, before her, she did not have a father. Slave babies
often arrived after one of the slave owners decided that the woman
should spend some time with him. That was how it happened. There
was no disgrace. Life was mostly good. There was always a secure
home for mother and baby, with the possibility of sufficient education,
to help them to count and to keep a tally of jobs done. Marks on a
tablet of soft clay could be counted, and kept as a record, when the
clay set hard.

Living in the Nile delta, under the auspices of the wise men,
who controlled that part of the world, created a feeling of security
that had been there for many centuries. Food in various forms was
grown and improved within the boundaries of the Land of the Gyps.
Meat was domesticated and farmed in small herds of cattle and
goats. Some flocks of sheep produced another flavour, which was
welcomed. Combined with the produce of the land, root and green
vegetables, fruit and nuts, when in season, the varied diet had helped
the humans to grow their own brains to a high standard. Natural plant
fibres, as well as the combed wool from the sheep, were used to help
in the production of warm and soft materials for clothes. Leather
continued to be used for the heavier garments of the army and the

workers on the land.

A strict caste system had helped in this development. The male leaders applied a discipline that could be harsh, if there should be any attempt to disagree with their edicts. The supreme leader applied similar attitudes to those under his immediate control, supported by his being the commander of the full time army, which was well armed and mobile.

The next level was occupied by the producers of the needs of the community, traders, farmers and craftsmen, all those who could use their skills to make or barter something useful. They fed and equipped the army, willingly, in return for security. On the lowest stratum were the slaves. They, or their antecedents, had been captured in battle and offered the choice of death or slavery. Their skins were of every possible shade from black, through to the whitest known to man, but there was little notice taken of a person's skin colour, whatever their position in that society.

Over the past many centuries, a grouping of religious leaders had developed. The awareness of the power of the Sun-god, and to a lesser degree, the Moon-god, had grown from the dependence on the mild weather conditions in that part of Northern Africa. The routine flooding of the river delta area ensured the spreading of the fertile silt, and this helped in the regular production of food plants for the next year. Everyone appreciated the good treatment that they received from these gods, and, in turn, they respected the Haan, the spokesmen for the gods. They had their own group of slaves and these were able to retain a balance of numbers over a long period.

One of the Haan, named Hai, had been looking at all the young female slaves under his control, hoping to find one suitable for his purpose. So far, they all seemed to be too young, too childish or too heavy in their appearance. Then he noticed Jell, when she was accompanying her mistress to the temple, and made a point of speaking to the lady as she was leaving.

"Madam, it is good that you attend this temple to the Sun-god and give your thanks for all your blessings. Is it ever wished that you could have even more good things in this life?" She was surprised, and then she moved her head in agreement. "Yes, sir. There are other things that I could pray for. The gods know them well".

"Then, if you wish your dreams to come true, why do you not make a sacrifice to the gods? I am told that they will hear, and they will respond. This temple has the need for another helper, like your girl here. Are you willing to spare her, to serve for a period of time"?

The smooth approach had been well planned and it was effective. Jell was taken into the temple and shown how to serve the gods. She lived within the temple boundaries, together with a handful of young male and female acolytes. During a few moons she learned how to keep the place clean, and the water containers filled, ready for the guardians as well as for the visitors. The work was pleasant enough, until Hai showed her the special requirements that she would give to selected people.

He explained that it was his responsibility to teach her to be willing and receptive, when she was told to give favours to the important men in the tribe. She must not share any such pleasures with the other boys in the temple. She was sacred for the gods. Jell had learned from her colleagues that Hai much preferred the company of the boys, during his times of relaxation. The girls were kept pure, for whatever the future may bring. She accepted her fate.

Hai gave her a gentle, academic, introduction to the mechanical activity of sexual contact, whilst Jell listened to his droning voice and accepted the lesson, without any experience of pleasure. "You will be required to do this on only a few rare occasions, when it is essential to please an important leader, for the benefit of the gods. You will only take your intructions from me. Do you understand? Do you accept?" The young girl nodded, "Yes".

Jell soon realised that her normal duties in the temple were simple house-keeping, cooking the simple meals for the staff and training young recruits. She was rarely required to comfort a man, in the way the Hai had shown her. Before and after that happened, she was given a potion of herbs that would 'prevent her from receiving any harm'. She never became pregnant from the sporadic contacts.

Things changed, ten years later, when Hai was taken ill with convulsions. He spent one night in agony and died the next morning. His successor was a different type of man. Hut was transferred from

172

another temple, on the other side of the land of the Gyp, and his appetites were for the girls, not for the boys, who were ignored in that area of interest.

The local inhabitants saw very little difference in the temple procedures, which continued as before. The daily receipt of offerings of fresh food was controlled by Jell, who was now the senior of the temple maidens. Her open authority was encouraged by Hut. He had quickly realised that she was an asset in the organisation, and he delegated even more duties to her. She started to control some of the lesser demonstrations of service to their gods, intoning words that had always been given by Hai in the past. This led to her giving 'inspired thoughts', which surprised Jell, herself, when she heard them. They, sometimes, astounded Hut. It was not what he had planned, when he started to give her more demanding duties. His real aim had been to give Jell a little more responsibility, in order to make her feel more important, to generate more warmth towards him as a man, rather than as the temple guardian and priest.

It was during one of the usual evening services of greeting to the full moon that Hut told Jell to announce her 'thoughts' on the imminent waning of the Light. She spoke.

"People of the land of the Gyp. You are blessed in many ways. Tonight, you witness the joy that you receive each period of the moon. You see the full Light of your god, in the sky above you. You know that this is the Light of the real god, the Sun, which you see each day, in all his glory. The Moon-god holds that Light for you, through the darkness, so that you will remain in the full glory of the Sun-god. Without that Light, you would be in the darkness forever. With that Light, you enjoy all that the world can offer to you, food, water, animals and plants, your females and children.

You know that this 'light in the night' will grow smaller, before it disappears in one night, then it will grow again until it reaches the full size that you see now. That is for the length of one moon-period. It is always for the same length of time, fixed by the moon-god. During each moon-period you will bring a share of your produce to this temple, to be given as a sacrifice to your god. This will ensure that the moon-periods continue to bring you the blessings that you require. Is this understood?"

The response from the congregation present brought a smile to the eyes of Hut. "This is understood. Our thanks go to the Moon-god".

Afterwards, Hut told Jell that she had done what was required during the service. She was showing the correct attitudes, and she was looking after the economic interests of the temple. Her future development depended on her total compliance with the orders she would receive from the gods, through the mouth of their servant, Hut. Jell accepted this statement and asked, "Please show me what I can do to be of greater service to our gods". That was the beginning of a planned initiation into the downward path for the young woman.

During the next twelve moon periods, Hut showed her some of the many ways in which an attractive young woman could entice a man, any man, into agreeing to go against all his training and principles, just for the sexual pleasures that she could offer. She was more than a little puzzled when she found that even Hut, himself, pleaded with her to continue some of the methods that he had recently taught her. At another, calmer, time she asked him to tell her the purpose of it all.

"It is all a matter of power", he said, "power over other beings, who are in positions of authority in this land. Those who are in the highest positions in the land of Gyp have retained a skill from the old days. It is a skill of which you do not have any knowledge, because you are a slave, child of a slave who was captured long ago. It is the ability to know what is in another's mind. They can read the thoughts that you have just received, and they can see what your reactions are to the ideas created by those thoughts. The gods gave the skill to them in the early days of the world. They used it to help the tribes to grow, to be able to defend themselves, when attacked. They were able to lead the people out of the path of the Great Flood, before the waters came near them. A great debt is owed to the gods for helping them with this skill. Sadly, these leaders have not used the skill wisely all the time. They have gained power over many other tribes, which were not able to understand the special means of communicating.

You are now aware of the skill, but you do not have it within your mind to practise it. It can be taught, and I will teach you how to use it. You will then be able to talk mentally with those leaders who come to the temple for spiritual help. When the time is right, and I will tell you when that is, you will be able to use your other talents, in order to distract their minds from their original intentions. You will learn to enjoy using your new power over them.

Working with me, and for me, we shall both build up a very strong power within the temple. It will become a power that all the other strong ones will be seeking, and when they have found that it is within the temple, they will wish to become part of it. They will subordinate their own desires in order to please those who are in charge of the temple, that is you and me".

Jell was unable to speak. Her legs were trembling as her brain attempted to understand all that she had been told. She allowed Hut to lead her away to his room, when he said that the time was ripe for them to practise some of the exercises that he had already taught her. She was an apt pupil and never doubted her instructor.

CHAPTER TWENTY FOUR
DARK FORCES

Marcus had a very serious expression on his face when he approached the Committee Room accompanied by both Mellak and Solem. His opening words confirmed his feelings.

"The three of us are very concerned at our recent experience in the land of the Gyps. This is the first time that we have personally been involved in a place near to site of the deliberate introduction of the Black Arts. We found it extremely difficult not to apply some of the powers that we have carried throughout this lengthy study. We could have stopped it, and we feel that we should have stopped it. Those were our feelings at the time, but we were also well aware of the need to have the approval of this Committee, before there should be any control placed on the human race, in order to change their future actions. We now bring this problem before you.

We are now aware of the tendency for some of those who control the functioning of the temple to use their positions of authority for the purpose of evil. It appeared to start with one of the Haan taking a young girl into the temple in order to train her as a temple servant. That was an innocent move, and it could have led to her development on a spiritual path. The Haan was later replaced, following his passing, and it was his successor who decided that he would train the girl into the more degrading activities of physical lusts. Her innocence was soon forgotten, and she realised that she had the capability to divert men from their own elected ways of living, to the point of making them behave in ways that they hated.

She knew the strength of her own powers when she found that she could control the life of her own teacher, Hut, the Haan who had intended to control her. They are both locked into their own plans to use the attractions of this young woman in order to take over the power of the ruling authorities. The three of us feel that we should place these thoughts with this Committee and ask for approval, or otherwise.

We have seen the tribe of Gyps make very pleasing progress, over countless thousands of years, leading the other tribes on their continent in advancing on their paths of enlightenment. They have retained a vestige of their original ability to use mental communication. They have been the first to make the best use of the slaves that have been captured in battle. Spiritual knowledge and awareness have given the hope that they would be amongst the leaders in those fields. Everything seemed to point to them as the most progressive of the human race.

Now, we find the flaw of 'power-seeking' that is becoming established in the influential classes of their society. These urges are quite deliberately applied. The original traces of a desire to help others is being suppressed and ignored. We find that there is an overwhelming wish to control others in order to gain permanent power of authority. The contrariness of some attitudes is there for all to see. Truth is being replaced with untruth. Talk of the 'light' is used to cover the frequent use of dark forces, for evil purpose. Any sign of reaction, to these changes in attitudes, is met with, firstly, persuasive verbal pressure. If that does not resolve the matter, then force is threatened and then applied. In their early days, the Gyps placed great value on the life of a single person in their tribe. Now, life is very cheap.

This is more than a simple set-back on their path forwards. We feel that it can become a disaster after making so much progress in the past. Sadly, it comes at a time when all humanity is about to take another big step forward in their practical knowledge.

They have already mastered the skill of making bricks from the plentiful supply of clay in the river delta. Their mathematicians are able to design a wide variety of buildings that are being erected with some prospect of permanence.

They will soon understand the significance of rolling a log downhill. From this they will produce a workable wheel, which will lead to a steady advancement in the skills of their inventors. When they add the ability to smelt metals, then there will be no possibility of retarding them in any field. We know that the so-called 'progress' will continue to escalate up to, and beyond the time of anno Domini.

May we ask this Committee to consider our report, and our suggestion that this might be the right time (and, perhaps, the only time) when we can take some decisive action to prevent any further growth in the evil that has been identified. We think that it is possible, not only to stop further developments in evil, but also to start on the eradication of the problem".

Some members of the Committee were surprised to hear this apparent ultimatum. All eyes were turned towards the chairman, who had already made his decision.

"I am saddened," started Ywancontin, as he looked around the room. "I must admit that there are times when I can still be surprised by what I hear. You have all been kept fully informed about all items on our agenda, and you know that I have often referred to the fact that, once a freedom of action has been given to any creature, that freedom cannot be withdrawn. It would appear to be a contradiction, an anomaly, and no satisfactory result would be possible. You know that we started to examine some of the ways in which we could give encouragement and motivation to these developing beings. We introduced the trait of compassion, so long ago, and we can still see the effects, which are widely spread throughout the planet. That is our hope. That is the way forward.

If, as you seem to suggest, we try to stop any of their actions that appear to be merely unwise, we will completely defeat the objective. Humanity must be allowed to make its own progress, its own mistakes, and its own successes. It will learn from its experience, or, it will destroy itself in the process. Consider for a moment, the fact that all these peoples are at the start of a period of one quarter of a million years of invention, by geometric progression, of ever-increasing speed of movement across the planet, on the land, on water, and in the air, to be followed in the space between the planets and stars.

The use of metals, and, later, of plastic materials, will give the majority of them the means to advance at ever-increasing rates of production. Their investigative skills will increase in direct proportion to the rate of growth and development of their brains. They will learn all the secrets of Nature. Diseases of the body will be conquered, to be followed, eventually, by those of the mind.

No, my friends, if we decided, at this point, to prevent any human movement towards evil, we would be deciding that our original planning had been faulty. It was not. There are plenty of other hardy survivors amongst the creatures on this planet. If it should become necessary to study another type of creature then I'm sure you would

178

all feel the benefit from your experiences gained whilst studying the development of the hominids".

The ruler of the tribe of the Gyps was a contented man. On the rare occasions when Twt reviewed his own situation he decided that life was good. His tribe had had very few recent difficulties with the nearest neighbours, and this resulted in the army not suffering many casualties. The tribe had experienced many years of progress, with pleasant weather and a reliable flow of water in the river and its tributaries. He had plenty of wives, who produced a steady flow of lively children and they all amused him in his time of relaxation. His eldest son, Pen, was nearing his tenth anniversary and he intended to help the young man to celebrate his entry into manhood.

At the next full moon, Twt made his usual visit to the temple and he asked Hut for his suggestions as to the best procedure to initiate Pen into the mysteries of his own development. This brought a smile to the face of Hut. He had been hoping for such an opening.

"Lord Twt", he began. "You could not have made a better choice, nor could you have made it at a better time. Amongst my priestesses, there are a few young acolytes, who are learning how to serve their gods, in the way in which they are most blessed. I also have, within the temple, at least one who has been trained, in the most delicate way, to be of service only to the highest in the land. Might I say that she has been saved for just such an occasion as the one that you indicate. Her name is Jell. She has served the gods and retained her purity of thought to this day. May I suggest that we arrange for your son to be brought to the temple on the night of the next New Moon?" This was agreed. Pen was to be left in the hands of Hut, and the priestesses, for a full day and night.

Hut spent some time instructing Jell on how to perform. They were both fully aware of the possibilities that were opening up for them. The temple must be in control of the leadership. This was their opportunity to advance their own interests.

Pen arrived at the temple during the day before the time of his initiation and he was taken into the private rooms, at the rear of the main building. He was given guidance, by Hut, into the adult thinking that he would be required to adopt in the future. "You will already be aware of some of the responsibilities that will fall on to your shoulders, now that you are entering manhood. Your father has informed me of the details. It is his wish that you will be guided into your path of accepting the tasks that will come before you. Some of them are hard and they require long periods of study and practical knowledge". The young man nodded glumly and he remained silent.

"Tonight", said Hut, more cheerfully, "you will be introduced to some of the more pleasing aspects of your new life. You will learn the intimate details of creating a new life, and you will experience all the pleasures of the priestesses of the Moon-god. This will enable you to understand more about the spirit world, the world which can be contacted only through the senior official of this temple.

Your first experience with the priestess will be wonderful. You will never forget it. You will know that you have been selected for serving your god, your father and your country. Each day, until the next new moon, you will come to the temple for further teachings, until I can tell your father that you are a worthy successor to him as the leader in the land of the Gyps. Now, it is time for you to be prepared for the ceremony". He signalled to two of the young maidens to enter the room. "Take our visitor to the cleansing rooms and prepare him for his initiation".

The two girls chosen for the task were identical twins, both with pale skins and fair, long hair, hanging down their backs. They were only a few years older than the visitor. With a pleasant laugh and smiling faces, they led him into an adjoining room which contained a large bath, let into the floor. Within a few moments, they had all stripped off their clothes and were washing each other in the tepid water. Pen quickly lost his inhibitions and enjoyed the cleansing process. They all dried and dressed themselves, before going back into the initiation room and rejoining Jell.

She appeared to be alone, waiting at the foot of a low sleeping-couch, which was covered with the skin of a large cat. The fur was light brown and very soft. Jell pointed to the couch, indicating that Pen should lie down, with his feet towards her. The twins sat at either side, near his shoulders, and each of them placed a hand on his chest and his wrist. They then started to anoint his chest with aromatic oil, taken from a bowl at their side. This procedure caused the half-naked girls' breasts to touch Pen on his arms and chest with the result that his eyes opened wider with excitement.

When Jell saw that both his kilt, and his hips, were stirring with the aroused passion, she swiftly removed the kilt and completed the anointment herself. Pen made a sound, which was a mixture of a groan and a squeal of joy, when she put one foot on either side of the boy, and then raised her own skirt, before squatting down on her heels to take him into her body. She then used only her internal muscles to complete the initiation procedure. Pen lay back on the couch, flushed and perspiring with the elation of the past few moments. 'So, this is manhood?'

After a little time, when all the participants had washed and composed themselves, Hut called them together in the room that they had just used.

"Lord Pen, son of Lord Twt, ruler of the land of the Gyps, you have now received the blessings of the Moon-god, in her temple, and you have entered the state of manhood. Those of the temple guardians, who have helped you to make that progress, are all blessed by your presence and your willingness to link so much closer to your god. You are advised to remember this day, and to recall the blessing, by making a visit here on the same day of the New Moon, each time it occurs. You will be able to renew your experience of initiation with the priestesses on each visit, if you so wish. You are always welcome here, whenever you would like to discuss any problem, or any other matter that you might wish. We are your servants. We only wish to serve you and your father".

Pen was very impressed. He felt like a god, himself. He had expected a rather dismal night of serious announcements, not the erotic introduction that had happened. Now, he was being treated in a similar way to that in which his father was approached by the less important beings in the land. And, he was being offered the chance to repeat the experience as often as he wished! It was good to be his father's son.

"My good friend, Hain Hut, I will be forever indebted, to you and your priestesses, for your kindness and the way in which you have shown me the way to manhood. It was my first time, and an experience that I can never forget. I shall certainly come here for your further blessing, on the night of each New Moon".

After he had returned to his family, with his escort of slaves, Hut took Jell to one side and told her that she had been very successful, to have the son of the Leader so completely under her spell.

"That was the intention and the whole purpose of the ceremony," she answered. "He is now firmly tuned to do whatever we demand, as long as he continues to visit here each full moon. It is most important that he believes that we are his servants, doing whatever is his wish. We must never try to tell him what he must do. Any planning must come from him, as his suggestion. We must find the way to plant ideas in his mind, and I think that the monthly, new moon visit, will be the most likely time to feed him with our wishes. We must work together on this approach and decide jointly how we deal with any new idea". Hut agreed with her and suggested that they go into the smaller room, in order to confirm the partnership, and their joint project, with another initiation ceremony. He had observed her activities with Pen, that night, from behind some draped cloth, over the entrance to an alcove. That observation had included his full telepathic unity with the mind of the young man throughout the ceremony. Jell had advanced further, in the ways of the flesh, than he had imagined.

CHAPTER TWENTY FIVE
TRANSITION

For ten more years, the Hain, Hut, and his high priestess, Jell, used their power and influence with both the leader of the land, and his son. When Twt died, of natural causes, his son Pen became the new leader, and the temple began to have an immediate impact on all the decisions that were made by their protégé. Within one year, the temple two were disagreeing with each other on almost everything that they discussed. Hut realised that Jell had far too much influence over the new leader and that he had no alternative but to be rid of her.

The elimination of Jell was a simple process. On one of the occasions when Hut and she were walking in the temple grounds, the Hain led her along a path which used a small bridge to cross over a stream. For most of the year, there was no water in this stream, but, on this evening, the high river level had left some water when it receded. It had also left a crok, one of the river creatures that had a large mouth, full of teeth, and a taste for any flesh that it could find. Hut had noticed the animal during the day. As they walked over the bridge, he simply pushed Jell over the side and she landed on top of the crok.

There was a short scream from the priestess, and then it was all over. There was some disturbance, whilst the animal basted its meal, until it was ready to be consumed, and within a few moments it was rapidly eaten.

Jell was aware of a feeling of sudden shock, and then she became very calm, and at peace.

She was walking in a darkness that gave the impression of being a tunnel ahead of her. There was a small glimmer of light and she moved towards that. In her mind, she recorded that she felt no pain, or discomfort, after the recent experience. If anything, she felt relieved that an ordeal was over. There appeared to be no others with her, and yet she had an awareness that she was not alone, and with friends. She knew that she should move towards the light and she did so, but she could not feel the ground beneath her feet. She simply moved forward. The light grew larger and she soon emerged into a grassy plain.

The welcoming party were all known to her, although she could not immediately give them all a name. Her mother was there, together with a number of happy-looking adults from her past. They were all smiling and wanting to give her their loving greetings, together with answers to any questions that she might have. She felt that she had come home.

Her mother took hold of her hand and said, "Come with me, my little one, I will show you where you may rest, after your journey, and then we can talk about everything that is on your mind".

Time passed. But, it was a very different sort of time from what Jell had known before. It was not broken into periods. It was not interrupted with stoppages for the preparation, or consumption, of meals. Although she rested quite a lot, during the first stage in her new life, she was not aware that she ever slept. She began to feel much better in health, but she could not find an explanation for the changes in her awareness of the surroundings. She knew that she had died, but she felt in much better condition than she had ever noticed during her life on the earth plane. There must be a snag in it somewhere? Then she realised what it was. She began to think back to her thirty nine years of earth-life.

As it unfolded, in her own internal vision, she could see episodes that had completely disappeared from her memory. Childhood actions, that made her wonder how she was not punished by the adults involved. There were youthful escapades, where she was at great risk, when stealing food or precious objects. The ones that gave her the biggest reasons for anxiety had occurred during her last ten years, when she had been using the powers she held over the young man Pen.

She revisited the temple rooms, where she had held power over many strong, virile men, who believed that they were using her body for their own satisfaction, whilst they were unaware of the demands that would be made upon them, at a later date. Hut and Jell had each believed that they were in control of the other. They had used each other to further their own wishes and lust for power. They had both used murder to stop the progress of some of their opponents. Poisonous snakes, and substances, had been given to many of their victims. But, for what purpose?

When the flashback views of her more questionable actions had been completed, Jell was in a very receptive frame of mind. She was not only willing to listen to any advice from some experienced soul, she actively asked for help from her mother and the others around her.

She found herself in the company of an older man who introduced himself to her as Marcus. Jell smiled to him, but her normal charm simply had no effect. She was aware of an air of serious knowledge, tinged with a wish to be accepted as a friend of long standing. "You must have noticed, Marcus, that I am a newcomer to this world? Can you tell me how and when I will be able to learn how to make progress?"

"You have asked the right questions, my dear, and you are already looking in the right direction. Your first task is to understand where and what you are. You know that you were living on what we call the earth plane, or planet. You left there very suddenly, just when you thought that you had made excellent progress in you chosen path. You thought that you were in full control of your life, and, also, in control of those who worked with you in the temple. It seems that you did not know that your allotted time on earth had reached its end. You do so now, and you are already wiser in many ways. But, there is so much more for you to learn. I can explain a little more of the facts to you.

You are now in a different plane of life. It is the original plane, or vibration, where you started to live, and where you spent a great number of those earth-years in time. You started life as a god-given spark, which you called your soul during your last period as a physical being. You were given the power of being an entity in your own right, with the inherent freedom to make your own decisions. That is what you are at this moment. Only that spark, or spirit, that 'you', has had some experience of living, which has helped you to develop, as you make progress. It has also allowed you to make some decisions which you might have regretted, after they have happened.

I have been privileged to make a study of the people of the land of the Gyps, over a very long period of time. They had many advantages from the start, climate, geography, mental skills, to name but a few. They showed great promise, and they had been considered well worthy of being given extra help, to ensure their continuing development.

During the last few aeons there have been some warning signs of a tendency to use, what we might call, the black arts for the purpose of gaining power". At this point, Jell began to look slightly disturbed. "Yes," continued Marcus, "you can recognise some of the thoughts that are passing through both of our minds? Hut certainly helped you to develop some of your mental skills, even though he intended that you should use them for the wrong reasons".

"When am I to be judged for all the bad things that I did", asked Jell, who had no doubts that he was an important official. Marcus held up one hand. "That depends entirely upon the judge, and I believe that the judgement has already started. You, Jell, are your own judge!" he said quite severely. "You are already becoming more aware of the pain and hurt that you have given to others. Once that you can fully understand the damage that you have caused, you will be able to make plans for a journey, where you can make a start to correcting those wrong decisions".

"Will I be permitted to visit the temple and communicate with Hut, again?" "Of course, you will," answered Marcus, "you will have every opportunity to make your peace with him and to ask for forgiveness for all the things that you regret. If your intention is to take your revenge for being given to the crok, then you might not find your way there so easily. Perhaps you will require a little more time in which to rest and recuperate from your experiences. We have some well-organised Halls of Learning, and I will arrange for you to be enrolled for a little more education into our way of thinking. You will enjoy the experience. Go, with my blessing".

"Now that I have made an in-depth study of the priestess, Jell, who is steadily learning the error of her ways, I would like to submit a proposal to this Committee". Marcus had caught the attention of the Chairman at the end of a meeting. "I am still very concerned that the Gyps, one of the most promising of the early tribes, should

be showing some real signs of retrograde activity.

If we can ensure that Hut receives a program of indoctrination into the recommended positive attitudes that we might wish, then, perhaps, he will be able to follow his late companion, and return to the preferred path. May I ask that Jell be allowed to return, to visit him in his dreams, so that she can let him become aware of the errors in his ways? She could start a dialogue with him, using her personal memories of their closeness during her life there, and help to lead him away from his present destructive path. We will still be permitting him to make whatever mistakes he wishes, and we will merely be giving him the opportunity to recognise the possible attractions of the Way of the Light?"

"You can be very fluent and persuasive, Marcus!" said Ywancontin. "I must ask if you have given sufficient thought to the possible reactions? Firstly, from Jell herself, you might have a blank refusal. She could require more than a few years of rest and rehabilitation before she will be ready for such serious work, and, by that time, Hut could easily have joined us all at this side of the divide. Secondly, if she were to do this immediately, she could stimulate Hut into making a closer union with the dark forces around him. Remember, he has already been training his other maidens into the black arts for a long time. I can recognise the fact that there is still a tendency, within you, to try to control these individual souls. We must not do that".

Turning his head, to look at all the members of the Committee, he continued. "You have all been able to see a little way into the future. You know that the general trend amongst the people of the Land of the Gyps is to develop their mathematical skills and to apply them to the designing and erecting of a wide range of permanent buildings. This will lead to their advancing well ahead of all the other races that are making their own progress, in their own different ways. Other races, from far away, will have so much respect and admiration for them that they will send some of the most promising young men to study there, in Egypt, as it will be termed.

The obsession for building will eventually lead to the erection of some huge memorials for their leaders, memorials that will remain long after their purpose is forgotten. The Egyptians will lose their sense of direction, then their prominence in world affairs and, eventually, their ability to have any serious influence on other races. That is the nature of humankind. They either move forwards, or they slip backwards, when others overtake them on the Path of Life.

Those of you, who are involved in this long term study, will have the opportunity to observe this phenomenon, of the rise and fall of dominant races, over the centuries ahead of you. You should be alert for any signs that can be read, because the trends might have an effect on the races that are under your study at the time. You might look for the reason why this tendency usually moves from the east towards the west, rather than in the opposite direction.

Now that we are aware of the trends in Egypt, let us move forward to a period immediately before Anno Domini".

CHAPTER TWENTY SIX
ANNO DOMINI

It was two years BC when the serious-looking Ywancontin opened the meeting. "You will be pleased to know that all your previous reports, observations and recommendations, have been given the fullest consideration. It is known that you gave your most serious opinions, and that the motivation behind you presentations was unquestionably honest. You are thanked for that.

I am now privileged to inform you that some of your ideas are to be promulgated. They have been considered in the highest echelons, by those who move in levels that are higher than those which I have attained. We have all been congratulated on what is considered to be the best application of our thought, throughout the past five millions years of our study. You have all given of your best. There have been times when you believed that the only way of fully assessing a situation was to amalgamate your mentalities with those under your study. Despite the possible dangers of that exercise, you never hesitated. You spent some long periods, suffering the harshness and shocks of living as a form of life which was lower than the one that you usually take as normal. From that experience, you gained the valuable knowledge which gave you the insight required to find the possible solution to the problems. You are all blessed for your efforts.

There have been a number of occasions during our meetings, when some of you have suggested that direct action should be taken, in order to alter a questionable trend in certain activities on the planet. At those times, I received the impression that you wished for spiritual intervention, to prevent some disaster, such as the elimination of a tribe, or the earlier introduction of a new invention, that might help to accelerate the progress of a promising group. On each occasion, I stopped any move in that direction. That was the proper thing to do. It enabled the continuation of the Spiritual Law, that there should be no interference with the Freedom of Will for each individual, once it had been given". The Chairman became aware of the ripple of excitement that was running through the minds of the members. There were thoughts, such as, "So we were right, after all!" He gave his first smile at that meeting.

"There were times when your earnest desires, to help some of the disadvantaged peoples, confirmed your dedication to the success of the creatures of this planet. I can now inform you that action will soon be taken to give all mankind another opportunity to learn from their mistakes. I am assured that it will not interfere with any Spiritual Law. It will actually enhance it and give every single soul the opportunity to realize the dangers of breaking such Law.

Gentlemen, you are the first to hear of the blessings that are to be granted to all souls, whatever their status or situation. You have often talked of God as your Father. That thought gives you the obvious corollary that you are His sons. That is quite obvious, and proper, even though you are continually aware of your own short-comings, your lack of perfection? We are all carrying that spark of God within us, whilst we strive to eliminate the imperfections, and move, ever onwards, towards the Light of the Spirit.

The exciting news is that God is going to send His own, perfect Son, to be born as a human being, and to live His life on Earth. He will have a very humble start to His humanity, and He will bring the message to the entire world, that everyone should face the facts of their problems, that are mostly of their own making.

There have been times when you believed that the people of Egypt were about to develop, both mentally and spiritually, to the point where they would be the leaders throughout the developing world. They had powers and skills that were impressive. They had developed a system of noting their thoughts as a permanent record, firstly in soft clay, which can be baked hard. Then they chipped the glyphs into a stone surface, and they became even more enduring, and they also invented a kind of paper, from the papyrus plant, so that their thoughts could be transported and stored more easily. Their mathematical applications towards building had, eventually, helped them to erect those huge memorials, the pyramids, and many large temples. It will be a long time before the other races are able even to understand the methods of the builders.

The sons of the leaders of many other successful tribes and races have been sent to Egypt to be educated into the mental skills for which they are famed. With time and practice, these young people have started to educate members of their own races. Throughout the world, such stimulation of the mental processes has accelerated the advancement of humanity. Processes, which would have required a million years before producing useful results in the past, can now become effective within a mere century, or less. This trend continues.

As you know, from your own recent observations, the main effective power, at this time, is that of Rome. Their ever-growing armies expand and consolidate that power, giving the benefit of enabling the movement of people, and ideas, throughout the lands around the Mediterranean Sea, including most of Europe and Asia Minor.

Despite many attempts to put a stop to the spreading of such spiritual ideas, the Christ, as He will be known and respected, will live His allotted span before experiencing a cruel departure. He will make such a dramatic mark on the world that the years will be dated as, BC, Before Christ, and AD, Anno Domini, the year of our Lord. The test will be whether the human race will really listen to His words, and change their thinking and believing, or, whether they will largely ignore the message, and continue their own ways along the path to disaster and final extermination.

This is where we are involved most deeply. This Committee is required to monitor the arrival and the development of the Christ, the reactions as the news spreads throughout most of the planet, the success and failure of man-made plans to encourage action in the right direction, and, finally, be prepared for the outcome, whatever that may be. It is our most serious responsibility.

Our first involvement is to spread the joyful news! He will be born in a stable, to a young maiden, named Mary, and she will name Him, Jesus. You will go now and tell the shepherds who are working in the fields, near to that stable in Bethlehem. Your activities will be noted, and the tale will be told to the many, over thousands of years. The world now has the facility of spreading the news by word of mouth, which is not totally reliable, and by the writings of the many people who become involved in the progress of the new philosophy known as Christianity.

Our work will not involve duplicating these records. Our concern will be to quantify the trends of acceptance and rejection throughout the world. At no time may we attempt to interfere, in any way, with the path that has been decided for the Christ. The Jewish race has already noted the coming of a Messiah, in the prophesies of their wise men, and it will be interesting to note whether they will be prepared to accept His arrival. We will all learn to understand the complex intricacies of human nature. We need to know how and why they have so many different appreciations of truth and falsehood".

CHAPTER TWENTY SEVEN
BARBARIANS

In those days, news from other lands travelled slowly. Official orders and information were sent by messenger, on horseback, and were the quickest and most reliable. Gossip and rumours moved at the speed of the trader, who used his knowledge, of happenings from afar, to gain the interest of his potential customers. Other travellers, such as the wandering minstrel, would help in the spreading of news, but there was a risk of the facts being altered, each time they were heard.

Despite all these difficulties, the news of the life and death of Jesus spread, slowly but surely, throughout most of what was to become recognised as the 'civilised world'. It was started by the Apostles, some of whom set off to preach the Gospel to the Aryans and other non-believers.

A belief in a single, all-powerful, God had been evolving for a few centuries. The Jewish religion had been growing, in depth, maturity, and written records, for even longer than that, and it helped to satisfy a long-felt want in the human soul. It encouraged a belief in the responsibility of family life and respect for the elders, especially for the memory of those who had returned to their God. Some of those who had not been born as a child of Israel had found comfort, and some logic, in the belief of a single God, invisible and omnipotent. They had seen how ineffectual were some of the other objects of worship, often offered by human priests, who would demand a variety of valuable items in return for 'help'. The human brain had developed to the point of being able to recognize the charlatan and reject him.

Lupus was a young singer and entertainer, who had attached himself to the nearest Roman legion that was resting near his village, within one day's march from Rome. He was hungry, as usual, and he found that he could attract the attention of these strong men in uniform by singing bawdy songs to them during their meal time. They particularly liked one that told the tale of a young wolf that was attracted to a village where it could find scraps of food in the rubbish. Its downfall came when it tried to mate with all the other dogs in the locality. It succeeded, and the humour came from the details, inserted by Lupus with much innuendo, of its steady loss of strength as the number of its conquests increased. Each day, the shout from the men would be, "The Wolf, Lupus, give us the Wolf!"

Between songs, they spoke to him as an equal, and that had never happened before now. They shared their simple food with him, and as a sign of his appreciation, he showed them a few conjuring tricks. He even made some of their coins, their denarii, disappear. These were quickly found again, when the soldiers started to feel for their weapons with worried looks on their faces.

The songs and laughter, on that first time, brought the centurion into the circle. "What is your name, boy?" he asked, warming to the youngster. "Lupus, sir, would you like another song?"

"Not now, lad, but stay with us and help to keep our spirits up, tomorrow, we will be getting our new orders then". Lupus took the words literally. He had no strong ties with his neighbours, and his parents had died. Here was an offer of the security that he needed. He walked over to some of the camp followers that could be found near every army, suppliers of food, leatherwork, metal tools, wives, children, and a few girls who would like to find a permanent man. The butcher had heard his songs, and also the invitation from the centurion. "You can help me, son, and help yourself to that meat," was the reaction from the butcher. It was all so easy. He quickly settled in as an assistant butcher, during the day, and as an entertainer, during the evenings.

The butcher, named Bonus, has recently returned to Rome with the legion, after three years based near Jerusalem, in Judaea. He had just started to tell Lupus a little about his experiences in that far land, when they heard the news of the imminent departure of the legion. They had been ordered to march north, to the land of the Gauls, on the north western boundary of the Roman Empire. The followers were to go with them. Bonus told Lupus not to talk about the subject of the political situation in Judaea. "I will tell you more about Jesus and the Christians, when we are alone together. It is dangerous to mention them near these Roman soldiers".

The journey north was hard and testing for all concerned. The road was well made, using blocks of stone, and it presented a

194

fairly smooth surface for those marching. For those travelling with heavy carts, it was noisy, and the passengers often preferred to walk, rather than to being shaken in the unsprung vehicle. The legionaries made their disciplined march each day, resting at regular intervals, and looking forward to their evening meal and entertainment, so the butcher was fully occupied during each night's halt. After ten days forced march, they all arrived at the foot of the mountains that divided them from the land of the Gauls, and here they had a full day resting, before they continued their march through the pass. Fresh food supplies, on the hoof, were handed to the followers from the military camp, which had been established for that purpose.

During that night, Lupus had a dream in colour. A very tall man came to him and led him by the hand, away from the camp, and walked with him up the hillside. He was dressed in a pure white garment, like a toga that could be seen in Rome, and he looked at Lupus with a serene smile on his face. "Lupus, my son, I have come to you tonight to tell you of your good fortune. You have been chosen to tell the story of Jesus to the Gentiles that you will soon be meeting. You will journey over the waters, to a land of barbarians, who are ready to receive the good tidings that you will take to them. You will overcome the problems of not knowing their language. You will learn how to gain their attention with your humour, how to tell them the truths of God's love for them, how they can learn to pass the news on to all who wish to listen. The stories that you have heard from Bonus will be fixed in your memory for all time. You will become another one of the Blessed. The Peace of God will always be with you". Lupus could only say, "Thank you, Sir". He was very subdued when he told Bonus of the dream.

Once through the mountains, the legion continued for another ten days, in a similar way, heading north, until they were halfway across Gaul. By this time, Lupus had heard most of the fascinating stories from the life of Jesus, told by Bonus, who had, in turn, heard them from a number of different observers, some of whom had, in fact, seen and heard Jesus talking to the crowds. He particularly liked the stories of the Birth in the stable, the feeding of the five thousand, and the temptation by the devil in the wilderness. He quickly learned to memorise them all by repeating them to himself, ready for the time when he would have an attentive audience of his own.

On the one day of rest, in the Roman camp in central Gaul, the ever-lively soldiers shouted for Lupus to come and sing to them whilst they were eating their hot meal in the evening. "Come on, Lupus, tell us the one about the Wolf!" They shouted, pushing a pot of raw wine into his hand. He had certainly become very popular with the hard, rough men of the Roman army.

The legion officers announced that they would be making another ten day march to the north, starting the next day. This would take them to the northern coast of Gaul, facing a narrow strip of water between them and the Britannia islands, where they would be based for a long period. They would be replacing another, time-expired legion, which was about to return to Rome. The camp followers were required to cross the water immediately after the advance legions had landed, and they were expected to carry out their usual duties immediately. Bonus accepted the arrangements without any argument. It was just another military posting.

Lupus was more excited and he pressed his employer to give him some idea of what he could expect in this strange new land. "Colonies is colonies, the whole world over", was the cryptic comment from Bonus. "You takes 'em as you finds 'em. Some times you finds a good one, - then, there's others!" Lupus decided not to pre-judge the new colonists, and he landed feeling confident that life held a good future for him.

The followers soon found that they were in a primitive country, inhabited by barbarians. The first Roman invaders had been greeted with sporadic attacks from wild, aggressive natives, who hurled themselves at the strongly defended camps, with little regard for their own safety. That had been nearly one hundred years earlier.

Since then, the civilising influence of the Romans had taken effect. Their various camps had been built and reinforced, becoming small towns and populated by many of the local inhabitants. Many of the Latin expressions, used by the soldiers, were absorbed into the different tongues and dialects currently spoken by the tribes under their control.

Lupus soon found that he could communicate quite easily with the Britons, that he met in the camps. He became the welcome guest of many of them, entertaining them with his repertoire of songs and jokes. This soon led to his identifying those who wanted to fill the void in their spiritual awareness. They welcomed his oft-repeated stories of the life of Jesus, told in the privacy of their own homes.

"This was the most usual method used for introducing the Word to those who sought the truth. There were very few changes in the gist of the stories, and their accuracy remained, until the written accounts of those happenings became available. The spiritual observers were able to ensure that the real meaning of God's love was spread amongst the nations of the world. The simple words, used by the ordinary men selected for the purpose, carried the honesty that convinced the listener.

After 300 years of Roman domination, the empire began to disintegrate, slowly at first, then rapidly, as the strength of the barbarian hordes increased. This coincided with the change in the Roman attitudes towards Christianity. They had tried to eliminate any progress that was being made in spreading the beliefs, but they had failed miserably. Eventually, the Roman leaders started to accept the new religion, but the change of heart came too late to help them to retain their power.

The Dark Ages came to most of the European continent. Civilised, peaceful towns were overrun by hordes of vandals, from the east, who spread fear throughout a large area. Pillage and rape were the order of the day, helped by the availability of metal weapons and the use of speedy horses to increase mobility.

During those dark times, some light was being noticed in other parts of the world. New philosophies were being discovered and extended, in parts of Asia. New forms of paper were made and used to record those thoughts.

The spiritual tribes of the Americas were making their own progress in the awareness of their closeness with nature, and extending their presence all over the whole of their continent. The people of both the New and the Old Worlds had discovered their own ways of making craft that would take them on to the waters of the seas and the inland lakes. Mobility improved all their communications and the time was approaching for the people of both worlds to meet. Sadly, the Europeans were motivated by simple greed. Love of adventure was a poor substitute for the love of a fellow man.

The building of larger boats made it possible for small groups to sail off into the west in order to find whatever was there. They went with the blessing of their church, in the hope of success, which was to be measured by the amount of precious metals, that they brought back with them, and the number of heathen souls that they were able to convert to their own belief. Failure to convert them automatically authorised the killing of the unfortunate natives. This led to the increasing arrogance of the European invaders.

In the early days of the Romans, disciplines had been simple and direct, even though they were harsh at times. Nobody had any doubt about the authority and correctness of orders received from the government. It was only later, after the communicators began to use the sophistications of scholarly Latin and Greek, that problems seemed to arise. The original Christian Church, under the leadership of St Peter, had started to spread the good news even further afield. Christian communities sprang up and children were born into the religion, consolidating the path of progress. Over the centuries, officials of the church assumed that they were receiving all their inspiration from God. They became infallible, in their own estimation. This led to the appointment of some strange and dangerous people into the most senior positions".

CHAPTER TWENTY EIGHT
INQUISITION

"The first thousand years, after the coming of Christ, produced a surge of mental and physical development in the human race. Music and art became more widespread, at the same time as progress was made in the aggressive practices of many of the more mobile tribes. Warfare was studied as a science. New weapons, including the use of explosives, had been tested and used, with even more sophistication, as the years passed. There appeared to be no limits to the ingenuity of man, which was being applied to the means of destruction and terror. The magnitude of man's inventiveness was only matched by his desire and ability to use the results for his own benefit, at the expense of anyone who stood in his way.

Very little effort seemed to be available for the more peaceful pursuits, when compared with warfare, but there were a few signs of hope for progress. Some prophets, and initiators of positively good philosophies, appeared at different times. A few of them made progress, with the spreading of attitudes that had hope for the people who heard them. There were times when the best of intentions were marred by the use of the very cruel methods, condemned in their own beliefs, in order to destroy those who did not readily accept the rules being applied. The seeds of despair were sown within the organisations that had been the first to offer hope for mankind"

The inquisitor, named Vidivici, had been sent from Rome to Granada with the instructions to scrutinise the inhabitants of the city and obtain their sworn acceptance of the rule of the Holy Church. He was to accept no doubters. Any such heretics were to be put under duress so that they would accept the rule without any reservations. There were enough trained and experienced helpers, supplied by the local church community, so that Vidivici could ensure that proper records were kept of the names and the disposals of all those who were examined, especially those who showed any doubts in their beliefs.

Using all the authority of Rome, he sent his spies out into the city and, at the same time, he acquired the use of a large part of El Ambra buildings. Here he organised the areas for reception, examination, persuasion and the ultimate disposal of the heretics that he knew he would find.

This was a position of power that he had wished for throughout his years of serving the Church. He felt completely dedicated to the task of bringing more believers to receive the sacraments, and he knew that there would be great satisfaction for him as he did so. He also knew that he would not hesitate in the cleansing of any who showed doubts in the Holy Scripture. Those who came before him, including the church staff and servants, knew immediately that they were in front of a man of great strength and determination. Tall, dark skinned, with piercing eyes, he intimidated all those that he addressed.

The first man to be brought to the investigation was a local trader, who had attended the church only ten times in the past year. The alms that he gave on those occasions were less than the priest would have liked to receive. His first question made him realise that he had little hope of being released.

"What other god are you serving, man?" The hard, staring eyes, and the impossible question, made the trader tremble at the knees. This was noted, as was his slowness in answering. "You speak so loudly, with your silence", said Vidivici, "you will be made to answer! You have taken a woman from Africa into your home. Is she a Muslim? Do you follow her religion?" The silence that followed aggravated the Inquisitor. Take him down."

The cellar, that had been equipped for 'persuasion', contained the usual paraphernalia of any torture chamber of those times. Man's ingenuity had created a variety of mechanical equipment, including the rack, the thumbscrew and spiked beds, all of which could be very persuasive when applied slowly. If used too quickly, they were usually fatal.

The trader started to talk most fluently, when he began to be stretched on the rack. That was not good enough for Vidivici, who had learned to doubt any confession under duress. He sent for the Muslim woman to be brought to the room and ordered her to have similar treatment on another rack. He felt no sense of shame when both the victims began to scream for mercy. The tension was increased when one of the torturers began to interfere sexually with the woman, in full view of her master. The poor man then started to curse everyone he could name, Vidivici, God, the Pope, the Church.

"Heretics," shouted Vidivici, "kill them, kill them!"

The work continued for that day, and the next, and the next. Very few of those interrogated were considered suitable for survival. The inquisitor began to enjoy his work.

"Human cruelty tends to be increasing in proportion to the rise in the number of souls on the planet. We have recorded many occasions where a few hundred have been killed in one battle, not only the combatants, but also the innocents, who happened to be near the trouble when it started. Wars between two or more nations are growing larger and more deadly, as the years pass.

There were high hopes when contact was about to be made between the Old World, as we call it, and the established, spiritual, peoples of the New World. Surely, they would each learn from the other? The 'American Indians' had spread over the whole continent, growing into different tribes and different cultures, occasionally fighting amongst themselves, setting out over the seas to explore the Pacific Ocean and establish new colonies in the many islands that they found there.

Then, the Europeans found their way across the Atlantic Ocean. Their advanced technology enabled them to start to take the land from the local people as soon as they met. This involved slaughter at every opportunity. The natural defensive reaction caused the native population to try to kill the invaders. These actions created further reaction, ad infinitum. The survivors are now slowly being absorbed into the modern culture of that large continent. It is fortunate that there are so many souls of those 'natural' good folk, who still wish to help to improve the hopes and lives of the sufferers of misfortune on the earth plane, not only their own race, but even those who were the tormentors".

"Similar treatment of native populations continued for a few centuries, under the attempts, to acquire an empire, of a number of

the European countries. Germany, France, Spain, Portugal and even Italy made such efforts. The British were the most successful, for a time. Greed and cruelty played an important part of the strategy. Reactions amongst these imperialists created the most serious world wars on the record. There are many libraries that are full of the records of the awful deeds committed in the name of nationalism.

In World War I, from 1914 to 1918 AD, millions lost their lives in battle. In World War II, from 1939 to 1945, the Japanese joined the Germans and Italians in trying to conquer the world. Although the war lasted longer, and newer, more terrible, weapons were used, the battle casualties were not as many as those of the earlier war. The emphasis on killing was applied to the civilian population of Europe. The Germans had plans to eliminate every Jew living in the countries that they controlled, and they were able to kill a few millions of them in murder camps, before they, in turn, began to suffer from the increasingly heavy bombing of their own cities.

In the Far East, the Japanese armies had been successful in capturing land from many of their neighbours, starting in China, well before World War II. They had offered a 'co-prosperity sphere' to their fellow Asians, but it did not last. Both they and the German governments ordered research into human pain, and a variety of illnesses, mental and physical, using the unfortunates who happened to be either prisoners of war, or members of a subordinate race.

The cries of agony, from these pain-wracked people, were heard throughout both the temporal and spiritual worlds. Those who survived were unable to comprehend why they should have suffered in that way, nor why the perpetrators were often able to escape the judgement and punishment that they deserved. Many of them had previously heard the churches preaching of Hell and Damnation, to follow this life, but they had seen and experienced both of these during their life on the Earth. The religions were not able to supply any satisfactory answers.

It is the opinion of those of us, who are involved in this research, that there is an apparently unstoppable acceleration in all the problems that are growing as we discuss them.

Firstly, the world population continues to grow, and, at the *same time, as a result of advances in medical knowledge, people are living longer than before. This creates the obvious need for increasing resources, particularly for more food and medical care.*

Secondly, the more affluent races, who demand ever-increasing standards, tend to create more pollution, as they consume ever more of the finite resources of the planet. Sea foods, forestry and oil are obvious examples of this greed.

Thirdly, the natural reactions to these two points are that resentment amongst the poorer nations will continue to grow and manifest itself in violence. The greed of the more wealthy nations is obvious, to the whole world, as they continue to expand their own, ever-higher, standards, at the expense of the less efficient, poorer peoples who have large debts, and little hope.

There seems to be some inevitability about this race towards disaster. We are reminded about the story of the lemmings, and their running over the cliff edge. Are the world's political leaders so blinkered, that they are unable to recognise the approaching cataclysm? It appears that they are simply reacting to each signal of potential trouble on an ad hoc basis, never stopping and eliminating the cause of the problem, merely papering over the cracks. They employ many unethical people, who are trained to present any sort of explanation for a problem, other than the truth. They feel that they must retain and consolidate their own position.

May we ask if we are not moving nearer to the time of retribution? Is there not an imminent possibility of a complete breakdown in the society that these people know? The Aids problem is growing on the African continent. Is it not likely that it will spread across the whole world and reduce the population down to a very small percentage of what it is at this time? We are saddened to have the awareness of the problems and to realise that such intelligent creatures choose to ignore the warnings. We will welcome your comments and advice".

CHAPTER TWENTY NINE
RECOMMENDATION

Ywancontin had listened to the comments from the different members of the Development Committee and he now looked carefully into the eyes of each one of them in turn.

"Let me assure you all, that we are not here to decide on the fate of the inhabitants of this world, we are here simply to make our recommendations, based on our own experience of contact with them, over the period of our study. Our opinions are valued by those who will make the final decisions, but there is no possibility of our reports being automatically processed for implementation.

We have all been closely associated with a wide variety of members of the human race, dating from their earliest days of living amongst the trees, and the occasional practice of cannibalism. We have seen them developing their brains by the inclusion of new foods in their diet, adding to the application of their elementary logic and the noting of the effect of many of their new forms of activity. In those early times, their mere survival depended on their speedier thinking, and the rapid action, based on the conclusions of that thought. Now, at the beginning of the third millennium AD, is it not rather surprising that we should even have to ask the question, 'what has happened to the intelligence that was very apparent ten thousand years ago?'

What has changed since those times?

The most obvious changes include the fact that the average lifespan had increased from thirty years to nearer double that figure. Many of them now live for nearly one hundred years. Do we have any real idea of what they do with this extra time? Remember, these extra years are all adult experience, and the first thirty included many which were applied to adapting to human life, as a child, followed by their early education. We need to consider whether there is any development benefit gained during the age-period from 30 to 90 or 100?

During the last ten millennia we have seen examples of the beneficial application of intelligence in the field of medicine, for example, but, when it has been applied to the business of war, it has had very mixed benefits. It has certainly accelerated the development of flying machines, and space invasion. Both these were intended to gain an advantage over the 'enemy', but they had a side effect of speeding civilian transport, of all forms. They had another, adverse, effect of increasing the pollution of the natural world. We need to ask the question, whether there is any benefit in extending the average lifespan of these humans, if they make no useful progress in the bonus years that they receive?

They consider that progress is being made because of the production of 'weapons of mass destruction', which has created a new problem amongst the younger, thinking ones amongst them. After more than fifty years of having the possibility of being eliminated by means of the atomic bomb, many young people now refuse to listen to their elders, or take advice from anyone who could be both older and wiser. They prefer to take what they want, without any thought about who will be hurt in the process. The majority of those in government of the countries appear to be obsessed with the rights of the criminal rather than those of the victim. They attempt to remove the rights, given more than five million years ago, that each creature may defend himself, and his family, from the attack of others.

We have seen their mathematicians and inventors create the electromechanical machines that can mimic, to a very limited degree, the computer systems that are used in the many animal bodies on the Earth. Eventually, they will possibly create more advanced systems that will be interchangeable with the natural ones. At the present point in time, their limitations in logic are only exceeded by their arrogance.

To counter some of these negative thoughts, we can also recognise that there is a growing number of people who ask questions about life as it is now. The increasing interest in spiritual matters proves that some progress has been made, and will continue to be so. Gifted people, with psychic skills, have been able to prove that communication with the spirits, of those who have taken their transition, is not only possible but is welcomed from both sides. They have moved forward from the days when they would eagerly burn to death those who showed any signs of awareness.

An opposite trend is more apparent. The so-called 'permissive society' enables many people to follow any path that they may wish, even if it is one that is evil and drug-inspired. *Those who create pain and misery are often treated as victims of their own making and are given the use of large amounts of the limited resources that are available. Critics of the flawed attitudes are themselves condemned as being negative, even if they present a case for diverting such funds to some more beneficial channel.*

During our time together, in these meetings, some of you have asked about different aspects of spiritual planning and the possibility that such procedures can affect a soul's path throughout its life.

I would like to confirm that each one has been given the gift of freewill. This is not unlimited! One can make a decision to enter the physical world, as on the Earth, and be born into a community, there to start with a clear mind and no memory. All those who have done this understand the joys of learning the various stages of growing into an adult, after the early enlightenment of receiving the benefits of mother-love. They have the opportunity of making their own mistakes, and learning from them. As they become bigger and stronger, they use their new strengths to assert their own will, and that is where the problems start to mar the way forward. The lack of effective parental guidance permits them to continue on a negative, downward path towards the point of 'no-return'. That is where the religions have an opportunity to be really effective. Some of them try to 'save the sinner'. Their successes are few. You will understand why we do not have any religions in Heaven? They have certainly created too many problems on the Earth, some of which may be countered by the good that they have managed to make.

You have asked about the practice, proposed long ago, that there should be some testing of the procedure of reincarnation. This was intended to test the benefits of allowing a soul to experience more than one period of life in the human form. The rule established that each rebirth would have the same complete lack of any awareness of a life before that date, whether in spirit form or in the previous physical life.

I can now tell you that such testing was carried out, under the rules of Spiritual Law. The results are very interesting. Whilst any previous memory was removed, before and throughout the second life, there were signs that the soul concerned was able to make some measurable increase in the progress on his/her path. The very faintest traces of mental and physical skills, from the first life, could be detected during the second. This was only noticeable to the closest spiritual guides, who were actively seeking any possible connections.

These trials were closely monitored, and fully reported, and they were permitted to continue in the same form. The desire to be born a second time had to originate within the soul involved. The records of the results were not disclosed to anyone other than those working on the project. This had the perverse effect that many souls are totally unaware of the possibility of reincarnation, and they naturally continue to deny the existence of such a procedure. They believe that the 'child genius' has a god-given skill, and not that it has been passed to him as a trace memory from a previous life. Perhaps, we should look upon both those two alternatives as the one true fact?

The more pleasing and surprising outcome of the trials was that they have been extended for further testing. Amongst those who made measurable progress in their second incarnation, some were selected for a third, and more reincarnations, if they so wished. A full memory, of each life experienced, is regained on return to this vibration, and substantial steps of progress are noted with great pleasure. The trials continue and give real hope that they will strengthen the belief in the ultimate success and triumph of good over evil.

There is a growing awareness of the existence of a spiritual path for each individual. The desire to help others who are in distress, whether physical or mental, is to be found amongst the widest distribution of members of the human race, and the knowledge that has been gained is being spread in a variety of ways. Spiritual groups and churches are to be found where there is a haven of peace and goodwill. Volunteers are being trained to give genuine help in the form of both contact and distant healing, which is enhanced by the appreciation of the use of selected colours for different aspects of this blessing.

We are now faced with making a decision about the findings of this committee. There appear to be only two possibilities at the present time.

RECOMMENDATION

We can recommend that the population of the World are permitted to continue to make their own choices, regarding the management of their lives and the way in which their governments organise their countries, whether or not they will continue to create increasing chaos. This can lead to the rapid deterioration of living conditions and increasing pollution of the land, the seas, and the atmosphere. Newer diseases than Aids might develop into plague proportions, destroying as they spread. The increasing use of nuclear weapons can create a wave of radio activity that will make it impossible for animal life to survive on the planet.

We can consider an alternative way. We can suggest that there is some divine interference with the established freedom of choice, but we must remember that, once that freedom is removed, it will not be returned. Changes could be brought about by the appearance of spiritual entities in public places, or by the promised Second Coming of Christ.

There are sufficient forms of successfully advanced life, on other planets, and so far ahead of these humans, that they could be brought into contact with them, with enough impact to create a completely new human attitude to life.

These are only a few of the possibilities that face us, and there is no doubt that there will be others. Both these and your views are being considered and we will soon know the result".

EPILOGUE

I have been asked why I wrote this unusual tale, without any research, and without being aware of any plot or continuity.

In the autumn of 2001, a psychic friend, Sheila James, of Wisbech, told me that I would write a new book, without any planning, simply by sitting down with a blank piece of paper in front of me. I would be inspired! I felt rather puzzled by her confidence. Three months later, she reminded me of this and told me that I had not yet even tried. So, I sat at my PC with a blank screen on Windows Word. Within ten minutes I had typed the title of "THE PATH". That was all.

A few months later, Joan Storey, of Peterborough, told me that I should have started my book, and that I would find a new publisher when it was completed. I then opened the small file, headed THE PATH, and waited for some inspiration. Within one minute I started to type frantically, until I was halfway through Chapter One. Then I read it and enjoyed it.

The strange names and other foreign words were all new to me and I had not even hesitated to think of them during the typing. My main feelings were of surprise, and an eagerness to press on in order to learn what happened next. This continued with my typing for one or two hours during the evenings, perhaps four or five times a week. Since then, the few friends who have read a chapter or two have all enthused and encouraged me to try to have the book published.

I hope that the reader will have enjoyed the experience (as I have done) and possibly learned to give some thought to the future, where their path will take them, and what can happen to this amazing planet (depending on whether the government leaders are able and willing to take effective action). I never cease to be amazed by the amount of information that has been accumulated over the centuries, and how little it really is when compared with all that we do not know or understand. Is that an indication of the size and length of eternity?

AFF